MY EYES ARE UP HERE

MY EYES ARE UP HERE

LAURA ZIMMERMANN

DUTTON BOOKS

DUTTON BOOKS

An imprint of Penguin Random House LLC, New York

First published in the United States of America by Dutton Books,
an imprint of Penguin Random House LLC, 2020

First paperback edition published 2021

Visit us online at penguinrandomhouse.com.

LIBRARY OF CONGRESS CATALOGING-IN-PUBLICATION DATA IS AVAILABLE

Printed in the United States of America

ISBN 9781984815262

10 9 8 7 6 5 4 3 2 1

Design by Anna Booth
Text set in Legacy Serif ITC Std

MY EYES ARE UP HERE

PROLOGUE

My mother believes there are two types of people: those who like to be the center of attention, and those who are too shy to want anybody to notice them. She thinks I am the second but should be the first.

What she'd never understand is that some people like to be noticed for some things but not for other things. Like to be noticed for being an excellent piano player, but not for being allergic to peanuts. Or noticed for wearing new shoes, but not for speaking with an accent. Or noticed for being the only Kennedy High student to score a 5 on the AP Human Geography exam, but not for being the only Kennedy High student whose breasts are bigger than her head.

CHAPTER 1

"Come on, Greer. Maybe you'll make a new friend."

I answer in annoyed blinks.

"It's nice to help someone get settled in a new place. It's a chance to give back."

I blink at her harder, because she's pretending like I volunteered for this.

"Half an hour. Forty minutes, tops."

Mom's half hours do not top out at forty minutes. Mom's half hours can last hours. Especially if she has an audience.

We're here for her work. She is a relocation advisor with Relocation Specialists, Inc. Big companies hire her to help settle new employees in the area. She leads neighborhood tours, arranges school visits, and recommends pediatricians, handymen, or Brazilian waxers.

She's very good at it. It satisfies her constant need to share her opinions and justifies the over-the-top luxury SUV she leases, with its interior of baby-seal leather.

Sometimes, like now, if she has a client with a kid my age, she'll drag me along to meet with them, like a junior re-lo advisor. I'm supposed to answer their questions about being a teenager in suburban Illinois. They never have any questions.

It's always the same. It's even the same Starbucks. I sit next to Mom and try to look extra welcoming. The new kid stares at their phone under the table so I know that wherever they came from, they had friends cooler than me. If the client is a mom, she'll ask me the kind of questions she thinks her sulky kid would want to ask if they weren't too sulky to ask them, and once I start to reply, my mom will interrupt with what she thinks I should answer. It's completely uncomfortable for everyone, except Mom. Kathryn Walsh is never uncomfortable.

Believe it or not, there are times being a mild-mannered, high-achieving, generally agreeable teenager does not work for me, and dealing with my mother is one of them. If I fought with her more, like Maggie fights with her mom, or if I was embarrassing, like Tyler, she wouldn't make me do these things. It would be too exhausting. But Kathryn Walsh exhausts me more than I exhaust her, so here I am. She is *just so*. I am just so not.

It is why I go with her to meet the uninterested progeny of people cruel enough/important enough to make their families move during high school.

It is why I help my brother, Tyler, with math homework he could find the answers to online.

It is why I faithfully attend the yearly reunion of the moms and babies from her childbirth class, hosted by this very coffee establishment every May.

This branch of Starbucks is located on the path of least resistance. I follow her inside.

The kid I'm supposed to meet will be a sophomore at Kennedy, like me. That's something. All I have in common with the Natural Birth and Beginnings crowd is being dragged out of the womb by the same midwife. Jackson Oates, whoever he is, is probably going to think this is as awkward as I do, so at least we'll have that in common, too.

Mom greets Mrs. Oates with a hug and they introduce me to Jackson, who does not look like a sulky weirdo. He's actually kind of non-sulky and non-weird. Light-brown hair, dark-brown eyes, and a big smile as soon as we say hello. He puts out his hand to shake mine, which makes me wonder if the place they just moved from was the 1950s. I've been taught to be polite, though, so I shake firmly. He seems pleased.

"Oh, good! Your parents must have drilled the importance of a good handshake into you, too." He says it in a dad voice, with a glance sideways at his mother, who rolls her eyes. "I always feel like I'm closing a German business deal," he adds in a normal voice. His hand is warm. Not sweaty. Just warm like a live body is supposed to be, and like I suspect the usual phone doodlers' hands are not.

"We meet a lot of new people," says his mom, as an excuse.

"Ich will buy zwanzig Apfelkuchens and ein BMW," he says to me, and against all my instincts, I am charmed.

This is not going to be the kind of awkward I thought it would be.

This is a different kind of awkward.

There's a quick negotiation while Mom figures out what

everyone wants, orders for us (she is just so *just so*), and pays. Because she basically views me as her assistant, she says to everyone else, "Let's grab that table. Greer will wait for the drinks." Mom and Mrs. Oates head to Mom's favorite four-topper, the one closest to the outlet. Jackson stays next to me, though, watching the barista steam the milk.

This is the part where the new goon is supposed to slide in next to their mother and act like I personally made them come here. But Jackson is standing next to me, waiting for the drinks, like we're in this together. I must look confused. He says, "You've only got two hands. For four drinks?" Like an idiot, I look down at my hands, as though I'm confirming the number.

"Oh. Right. Yes."

"Hey, thanks for coming here today. I'm sure you've got a lot of things you'd rather be doing."

I thought I did, but this is actually much more interesting than clipping my toenails after all. I sputter, "It's no problem." We stand there in silence for a minute, and I wonder if I'm the non-conversational goon in this arrangement. I add, "You realize you're getting a serious insider's tour right now. This place is kind of an underground favorite with the locals."

He half grins. "Starbucks?"

"Oh, so you've heard of it?"

"Kathryn? Coffee ready for Kathryn?"

We carry the drinks from the counter. I set down Mrs. Oates's café miel and Mom's oh-what's-that-is-it-French-I'll-try-that-too at the table, where they've spread out the Relocation Specialists Resource Binder, where Mom keeps all her pro tips about this "uniquely welcoming and family-oriented community just forty-five minutes from downtown Chicago." I'm pretty sure this Starbucks is in the binder (which is in the Starbucks, which might make it some kind of re-lo wormhole).

Jackson walks right past with my hot chocolate and his chai. "Those cushy chairs are open. Is that good with you?" he says over his shoulder.

Umm, yes?

I leave Mom, Mrs. Oates, and the binder at the table. Jackson and I plop ourselves in a pair of coffee-stained leather chairs next to a fireplace that's not turned on. He looks like he meets strange girls at Starbucks every day. I try to look like I do, too.

It turns out Jackson has questions—good questions. Instead of starting with "What AP classes are there?" because that's on the website, or "Can you letter in making memes?" because he's not one of my brother's seventh-grade friends, he jumps right in with "Is it the kind of school where kids come and go all the time, or where there hasn't been a new kid since second grade?"

"I don't know exactly how many there are each year," I say. He is leaning over the arm of the chair toward me, like I am the keeper of an important piece of navigational advice, which I guess I am. I try to remember how many new kids I had in classes last year, and wonder if I can consider them a representative sample, and extrapolate an overall figure from that, until I realize he doesn't want data; he is asking a different question. A real question. He wants to know what he's walking into, and he's asking me. It's October, halfway through first quarter—maybe not the best time to start at a new school. By now, people have pretty much staked out where they're going to sit and who they're going to talk to.

"Oh. You're trying to figure out if you're going to get lost or be instantly famous." He nods. "I'm not sure. I've never actually been the new kid—"

"Never?!"

"Nope. Even when we moved, we stayed in the same school."

"That's amazing."

I stop for a second, stuck on "amazing." He's not saying *I* am amazing. *Immobility* is amazing. Like bizarre mutations in nature are amazing. But for some reason, that amazing feels kind of nice coming from him. I shake it off.

"Yes," I say, "never leaving the zip code is one of my proudest accomplishments. There's not a lot of brand-new people, but there are three middle schools and only one high school, so there are tons of people I don't even know." He nods, like this is what he was hoping for. "I don't think a new kid would stand out too much. Unless they wanted to."

"What about lunch? If I don't latch on to somebody before then, am I going to have any place to sit?"

I can't imagine that Jackson is not going to find at least forty friends on his first day, because he's adorable and super friendly, but he's obviously had a lot of experience being the new kid and I haven't, so maybe I'm wrong. "It's probably safest to latch on to somebody from fourth period, unless they all seem horrible. Just in case, though, here's what you do: there's this long counter in front of the big window that looks over the track. People sit there if they have to finish homework or charge their phones. If you want to, you can sit there by yourself without looking like a loser. Everyone will just think you're writing wistful poetry or something." What I should have said was "Don't be stupid, you'll sit with me!" but I give myself partial credit for explaining about the counter seats.

"That's perfect. My next question was going to be where I could go to write some wistful poetry."

"Oh, man. I'm sorry to tell you this but they cancelled the Wistful Poetry Club last year. Budget cuts."

"We should probably just go back to Cleveland then."

I know he's joking, but it reminds me that this is all new to him—well, Starbucks isn't new, and according to my mom, moving isn't new—but Kennedy is new, and his house is new, and all the people are going to be new. I'm new.

"What's Cleveland like?"

"It's kind of like everywhere else, I guess." He shrugs. "We were only there a couple of years." He has changed, just the tiniest bit. Still friendly. Still adorable. But the tiniest bit . . . sad, maybe. "My little sister didn't want to move. Like reeeeally didn't want to move."

"She liked Cleveland?"

"Not especially. But she hates to move."

"How about you?"

"I'm used to it," he shrugs. "And there are Starbucks everywhere."

"What?! NO! But at least this is the original one, right?" And we are back to where we were. I thought I spied a tiny sliver of something less than perfectly confident, but then it vanished. It makes me curious about him. More curious. I wish we were some-where different. I wish I was showing him something he hadn't seen a million times before.

We pull up our schedules to compare. We've got a lot of the same classes, but none at the same time. Plus he's in German and I'm in Spanish, and he's one year accelerated in math, but I'm two. I tip my face into my mug so he can't see that I look disappointed.

"You must be pretty good at math," he says.

Mid-sip, I snort. Not because I'm some kind of math god. I'm as good as you can be without being one of those kids who have to take college math because they're too smart for high school math. Last year Mom offered me up as a math tutor to one of her clients when she heard they had a middle schooler who loved math but "needed to be pushed." She'd have loved to list me in the binder under Academic Resources—or at least as a babysitter or some-thing that got me out of the house. The kid turned out to be some kind of genius, though, who took the train to the University of Chicago twice a week to study ergodic theory. I don't even know what that is. I'm just the top of the regular smart kids.

Being good at math—really, at any academics—is pretty much my entire identity. It's funny to talk to someone who doesn't know that.

At school, what people know about me is that I get good grades; I'm Maggie Cleave's quieter, more agreeable friend; and that I wear clothes that are three times too big for a full-grown bear. That's it. I don't play a sport, I'm not in theater, I don't get in trouble, I'm not a girl you'd ever think about going out with. I'm just Smart Girl. Smart Girl who keeps her arms crossed in front of her chest all the time.

But Jackson doesn't know that. All he knows is that my mom tried to order skim milk in my hot chocolate. To Jackson, I could be all kinds of other things, too. Smart Girl *plus*. To the new kid, I'm also new. It's kind of fun to think about for now, even though I know he'll figure it out once he's at school.

"You're not in *any* of my classes? That's weird because as a certified relocation advisor I thought you were going to introduce me at the beginning of each period on Monday. Nicht gut . . ." he adds in his German businessman voice.

He's sitting in a lumpy, scuffed chair that a million customers have sat in before, but he looks like it's shaped exactly for him, like however they stretched or slouched or fell asleep, it was all in order to make this chair fit him perfectly. One knee is half up the armrest, his head is propped against his hand, he looks like every muscle in his body is completely relaxed. Like he belongs there. Like he belongs wherever he goes.

He is smart and funny and just kind of comfortable, which I almost never am. I was wrong when I thought what we'd have in common was thinking this was awkward. That part is just me.

And somehow, this makes me start to unfold. I've had my feet on the chair, knees pulled up tight into to my chest, both hands around my mug. Now I unwrap one leg and then the other and drape them over the armrest. I lean back, just a little, adjusting my sweatshirt so it's still baggy over my body. I hear myself say, "You'll be fine. But your German room is in the same hallway as my math class, first period, so if you start to panic, yell for me. Greer! I'm lost!" His cheeks spread out with a big, real smile. "Greer! Helpen mich por favor!" I'm loud enough that Mom looks over, curious. Not annoyed; surprised. Jackson laughs out loud. "Say it in English, though," I add. "My German is gesundheit."

σ

When it's time to leave, Mom says, "Oh, Jackson! Why don't you take Greer's number? You know, in case you have any more questions about school?" I hate and love her for this.

Mom starts to rattle off my number, and I wonder if Jackson is only pretending to type.

But before she finishes, he stops and hands me his phone. "Do you mind doing it?" and there I am, already added as a new contact: Greer Walsh. He spelled Greer right. No one has ever spelled ~~Grier Garear~~ Gruyere right the first time in my life.

I retype the number twice to make sure it's right, even though I figure a butt dial is the only way he's ever going to use it. I hand it back, he taps a couple of keys, and there is the sweetest little *ping!* in my bag. "Now you've got mine, too." He smiles, and I blush hard in every part of my body. I'm glad he can only see my cheeks turn pink.

On the way out, Mom says, "You should have brought along your daughter, too!"

The whole mood changes. Jackson and his mother look at each other like Mom has just said there would be anchovy and liver subs in the welcome basket.

"We did," starts Mrs. Oates. "She, ah, decided she'd rather stay in the car with the iPad." She looks embarrassed, and Mom cringes in sympathy. "She gets a little nervous around new people."

It's hard, even for my mom, to know what to say to that, knowing that they keep moving the kid around anyway. I don't remember anybody being particularly compassionate as a third grader, so good luck at school on Monday, Oates Girl.

"Actually, it works out perfectly," Jackson finally says. "We like to save Quinlan for after people have already decided to like us. I mean, if they decide to like us." He gives me a shrug and a goofy look.

"*Of course* we like you," says Mom through a little waterfall of a laugh, her eyes on me the whole time.

And we do. We really, really do.

CHAPTER 2

Before the garage door closes on Mom's Land Rover, I'm on my way to my room to do what I always do when I get home: lock my door, take off my shirt and bra, and lie flat on my back on my bed. I've got this old blanket, the kind with satiny trim that's always slippery and cool even when the rest of the blanket is warm. I position myself so that the trim goes just along the indent where the back of my bra was and roll back and forth against it a few times. It's like putting a cold cloth on a hot forehead. I spread out and feel everything I've held tight let go, my spine unfurling into the shape it's supposed to be. Five or six minutes, that's all. Five or six minutes to give my shoulders a break, to give my neck a break, to give myself a break. To breathe.

Usually, I can almost turn off the outside. I don't hear my dad streaming Wilco in the kitchen or my mom asking him for the thousandth time if that's who they saw at Grant Park that time. I don't think about what's due in AP History, or if Tyler is the reason my toothbrush was already wet this morning, or about Maggie calling the vegan club hypocrites because their cats kill birds. I try to not think about anything at all, but just feel like this.

But today, lying here half naked feels different. Because I'm still thinking about Jackson. I feel . . . open. Exposed. Poised. Not like I've unwound; like I'm even more wound up. In a good way. Like maybe I'd rather be in my body than out of it for once.

My breasts slide out to each side, and I can see between them down to my belly button and to the top of my jeans, and all the way down to my feet. There is a whole body here that is not boobs. I forget that sometimes. I arch my back. I lift my legs and flop them down over the edges of my bed. I run a hand over my belly and it's smooth and soft and cool. And then I imagine it's someone else's hand touching that same skin.

And I stop.

This is stupid. It's stupid because I don't even know him. And he doesn't know me. He is nice because he's new and if you are new and not nice, you're going to have a very rough year. And even if he turned out to have some weird quirk or disease that means he likes awkward girls who don't know how to dress, it's stupid because you can only touch someone's stomach for so long before you move your hand up and eureka! you've discovered the mountains. And not the lovely ski peaks they have in the Rockies. You're lost in the Himalayas, which are inhospitable to life and give you altitude sickness. Which are lumpy and painful and sweaty. Okay, that's not the Himalayas, that part is just me. But still, no one vacations at Everest. They scale it, snap a photo, and try to get the hell out alive with a good story to post.

I roll off the bed and dig my clean bra out of the drawer. The other one's too sweaty. I pull on a supersize tee and the rest of me disappears under it, too.

You know who gets to touch my stomach all they want? My breasts. They can hardly help themselves.

CHAPTER 3

Maggie is outraged. As usual.

We were supposed to turn in one page on a poem about dying and not wanting to. It's more complicated than that, but it's basically summed up in the famous lines about raging against the dying of the light.

Maggie turned in five pages about how terminally ill people should have the right to doctor-assisted suicide.

"Maggie, this is AP Lit. The assignment was to analyze the poem, not argue with it."

"How am I supposed to analyze it when I disagree with it?"

"How do you disagree with a poem?!"

The rest of the class has already left, so it's just Maggie, Ms. Mulder, and me. I spend half of my time with Maggie listening to her argue with a teacher. Or a student. Or a parent. Or an eight-year-old trick-or-treater who says Hermione isn't as cool as Harry and Ron because she doesn't play Quidditch.

This is why I didn't tell her about meeting Jackson this

weekend, even though now he's here somewhere in the building—because she is too busy arguing with people. Or maybe it's because she will want me to ask him out, and I will say, "No, I prefer to bury my feelings deep inside this giant sweatshirt so I won't be embarrassed when he rejects me for a regular-shaped girl," and then it will be me that Maggie is arguing with. As a general rule, I avoid arguing with Maggie.

"So if you assigned a poem promoting torture, I should just dissect the rhyme scheme and talk about the descriptive language? You're saying I should not stand up against torture?"

"I didn't assign a poem about torture. I assigned a classic Dylan Thomas poem about a universal human experience."

Maggie is looking at Ms. Mulder like she's asked us to dig a mass grave and fill it with teacup puppies. Ms. Mulder is looking at an insulated lunch bag on her desk. She's never going to get to that sandwich if she doesn't give up.

"All right. You didn't do all the analyses I asked for, but your writing was quite good, and clearly you thought a lot about the poem. I'll give you a B plus, but the next one had better be perfect. Ask Greer if you need help."

This is why I don't want to talk to Maggie. Maggie makes people do what they don't want to do. Like change a C minus to a B plus or admit they have a huge crush on their mom's client's son.

"That seems like a good compromise," I say before Maggie can say anything else. I slip my finger through one of the loose loops in her scarf and tug. I can't argue with her, but I can unravel her knitting if she doesn't get moving. "See you tomorrow," I say to Ms. Mulder as I lead us out.

"Do not go gentle to fourth period!" Maggie says, once we are in the hallway. "Rage, rage against—"

"Everything?"

"At least something, Greer. You've got to rage against *something*."

CHAPTER 4

What would I rage against if I was a raging sort of person? Maude and Mavis.

And who are Maude and Mavis? They are my breasts.

My boobs.

Jugs.

Knockers.

Mammos.

Hooters.

Melons.

Rack.

Simon & Garfunkel.

Lovely lady lumps.

Ta-tas.

Remember what I said about me and math? If breasts were math, I wouldn't just be ahead of all the kids in my grade, I'd be one of those freakishly gifted kids who had to bring her breasts to college because they were too big for high school. They'd give me a year's worth of AP credits just for putting on a tank top.

They are not going to set any world records, but to put it in simple math terms, they are significantly larger than the mean, the median, and the mode.

Not everybody realizes this immediately, because I've been wearing size XXL shirts since ninth grade. *Men's* XXL shirts. Even XXL ladies aren't supposed to have honkers like these.

If I tried to put on the kind of shirt my friends wear, the fabric would burst Hulk-style.

My mom thinks that wearing baggy clothes makes me look fat. Not fat. "Heavy." That's Mom's word for fat. (She would never say "fat," though I'm sure she has an idea of what the optimal ratio of pounds to inches should be.)

She has average-size breasts. C cups, probably. I must have inherited these things from some chesty old lady on my dad's side.

Here's what my friends say about them:

That's right. Nothing. We don't talk about them. Not my mom. Not even Maggie. Maggie knows I'm not thrilled, but if I told her how I really felt, she'd be disappointed in me. She'd either try to get me to show up to first period in a bustier to deliver a lecture to certain individuals about harassment or decide there's no time like age almost-sixteen for permanent body-altering reduction surgery and start interviewing plastic surgeons about how much breast tissue to chop off. I'm not ready to do either of those things right now. I would just like to finish high school.

I'm not the only person who doesn't want to talk about their body. I mean, little things, sure. Someone tall might say, "I can't find any pants long enough," or each of us might point out our own zit. But when something gets worse or weird or whatever, we don't talk about it anymore.

An example. During Eating Disorders Awareness Week every February, a nurse from the district comes to an assembly to tell us to be on alert for eating disorders. She makes it sound like it will be easy to spot them. Like kids are standing in the lunchroom saying, "I am only going to eat eraser dust from now on. And if that becomes too much temptation, I will start using those stubby pencils from Ikea that don't have any erasers at all." And then we will form a trust circle around her and she'll eat a sandwich.

But it's not like that. Most people keep their stuff to themselves.

We had a swimming unit in gym during the fall of freshman year. I was already feeling self-conscious about my shape, but at least they separate boys and girls for anything that involves sex education, swimsuits, or sleeping bags (like the service learning retreat at Camp Hide-Yer-Weed). They made us wear these old Kennedy team suits from 1975, because some of the girls only own triangle bikinis, which do not stay up well when you're trying to learn the fly. The Kennedy suit is a maroon one-piecer cut so high around the neck it's practically a turtleneck and so stretched out that the crotch hangs to your knees. I could still squeeze myself into a 36 then, as long as I didn't try to breathe too deeply.

We got ready, ran through the shower, and lined up against the wall freezing our butts off while Ms. Reinhold lectured us about water safety.

I was trying not to stare at Nella Woster, but it was hard to figure out how she put on the same ugly, old suit as the rest of us and made it look like she was an extra in a rum commercial. Every curve was perfect. It must be hell to shop with her. I bet she has a hard time ruling anything out because it all looks good. "I guess I'll have to take everything." "You can have it all for free if you'll just Instagram yourself in our brand."

It was about at this point that Jessa Timms, super jock and possible bodybuilder, started to walk past me, stopped, looked at my chest, and said, "Whoa, Greer! You're built, girl! I thought you were just a little big."

My face turned the same color as the swimsuit. I was slouching so much I was practically bent in two. No one laughed, just kind of gasped, like they couldn't believe Jessa would say that. *We have rules, Jessa! We don't say things about people's bodies in front of them.* But for the rest of the hour, I noticed girls checking me out, confirming. *Yeah, she's right. Greer Walsh is stacked.* Even though honestly, I was nowhere near the size I am now.

That one day on the pool deck freshman year is as much of a discussion as I've ever had about them. But I bet other people talk about them a lot.

CHAPTER 5

There's this questionnaire online called "Is breast reduction surgery right for your teen?" Half the questions are about "your teen's" pain, growth, genetics, scarring, "onset of menarche and regularity of menstruation," "motivation and psychological readiness," "emotional maturity," and a bunch of other stuff that's none of anybody's business. There's a list of things you're supposed to ask your doctor, too, and even though I'd rather not ask her any of them, I know I have to get over it if I want to know more about the surgery. So when we went for physicals just before school started, I decided that when she said, "Greer, would you like your mother to step out of the room while we do the exam?" I was going to say yes.

I hadn't talked to anybody about my breasts or how I felt about them, and it wasn't like Dr. Garcia would be easy to talk to, but at least I knew she'd have to keep our conversation secret. She'd probably had patients say a lot weirder things to her. I planned to be super professional about it, so she'd know I had the "emotional maturity" you were supposed to have if you were fifteen and walking around with boobs the size of baby manatees. (Apparently if you want any kind of plastic surgery after you are an adult, you don't have to be "emotionally mature" at all. You just have to pay for it.) As soon as my mother left, I was going to say, "I was doing some research about surgical options for breast reduction and I am interested in exploring this for myself." She was going to pull up a chair, answer my questions, and neither of us was going to blush or stutter at all. Maybe she'd even give me a pamphlet titled *Secret, Free, One-Hour Breast Surgeries You Can Have Done During Your Study Period.*

I was sitting there, trying to get that paper they cover the table with to absorb some of the sweat from my palms, when Dr. Garcia pulled out her stethoscope. I almost thought she was going to forget to ask, and then I'd have to ask Mom to leave. But then at the last minute she said, "Greer, would you like your mother to step out of the room while we do the exam?" My heart raced. I was going to have this conversation with a real person, instead of just reading WebMD and watching a couple of YouBoobers describe their experiences. I was half dying to and half dying not to.

Only I must have forgotten who my mother was, because before I answered, she said, "Oh, that's right! I forgot you ask that. Greer, do you have anything private you want to talk to the doctor about this time?" She looked up at me like she was modern and supportive and respected my privacy, but didn't move to put her phone back in her purse or grab her jacket. She said it like she already knew the answer, and the answer was, of course, "Of course not." Dr. Garcia kept looking at me, though, and all that went through my head was that this was why people who are supposed to be on birth control don't end up on birth control: because you'd basically have to say it in front of your mother to get your mother to leave anyway. I shook my head. And really, once you think about it, if I'm too self-conscious to tell my mother to get the hell out so I can ask the doctor if I've stopped growing enough to have my boobs lopped off, how would I get through the next sixteen rounds of questions with nurses, surgeons, insurance providers, hospital staff, my dad, and for the love of god TYLER?

Mom stayed put. I stayed quiet. Dr. Garcia said my heart and lungs sounded healthy, I should remember sunscreen, and I had gained four pounds in the last year. (At least three of them were probably breast tissue.) And then she printed out a copy of the form you need from the clinic if you're going to play a sport. Yeah, right.

CHAPTER 6

"My client is stopping over here. Get your stuff off the table."

Tyler scans the dining room table, which is holding one Scandinavian wood platter, and approximately 450 cubic feet of Tyler's electronics, homework, books, paper footballs, wrappers, socks, and half-empty water bottles. He moves on to the kitchen.

He opens the fridge and pulls out another water bottle, then stands looking inside like he's waiting for a package to appear in the crisper drawer. I'm sitting at the kitchen island watching this whole scene, reminding myself that this is not my responsibility. Tyler being an idiot is Mom's problem, not mine. I tried to tell her that when they brought him home from the hospital thirteen years ago. But I can't stand it.

"Mom said to pick up your stuff."

Tyler glances back over his shoulder at the table.

"It's not all mine."

"Yes, it is."

"No, it's not."

I push back my stool and walk to the table. Tyler wanders over to stand next to me.

"What part's not yours?"

He eyes the spread critically. "Well, that's not mine."

Yes. Agreed. The Kjerstønagsrud turned wood platter that Mom bought for 175 dollars at a museum gift shop is not Tyler's.

"I think that's yours," he tries, waving toward the table with one hand while scrolling through his friends' stories with the other.

"This is mine?" I can't even stand the thought of touching it. I just let my finger hover an inch above it.

"Isn't it?" He's still looking at his phone.

"You honestly think this is mine?"

"Um, I thought so?"

"Tyler, this is a nut cup. A plastic shield that slips into a pair of compression shorts to protect a player's testicles."

He looks up, finally, and crinkles his nose. "Oh yeah. I guess."

"And you still think it's mine? Seeing how I don't wear a cup because I don't have testicles that need protecting? And seeing how even if I did, I don't play any sports anyway? And seeing how I'm not a vile slob who would leave a sweaty plastic thing that's been inside my underwear on the table where people eat?"

My voice gets higher and sharper, and both Tyler and I can hear how much I sound like Mom.

"Or maybe you think I should wear a nut cup when I'm doing homework in case my calc book drops into my lap and crushes my imaginary nads. It's a very heavy book. I'm sure it could do some damage. Are you offering this thing to me? Because that's very sweet of you, Tyler."

And then Jackson Oates is standing in the archway to the dining room, waving awkwardly, greeting me with two syllables, "Hey-ay," to acknowledge that this is a weird, weird conversation to be walking in on. Great. He's going to think Ty and I hang out comparing our testicles all day. That's just the impression I want to give.

"Oh! Hi! My mom said your mom was stopping by—I didn't know you'd be with her."

"We're picking up my dad at the airport. Sorry to barge in." Jackson pushes both hands deep into his pockets in a way that makes his shoulders spread out a little wider, and I wonder if he might be a swimmer or a baseball player or something.

"It's okay. Tyler and I were just deciding where to keep his cup: the middle of the dining room table or right in the refrigerator?"

Tyler bumps me with his elbow. He is not embarrassed to leave his personal penis protector out in the middle of the room, but he does not want me making fun of him in front of other kids. At least he has some sense of decency.

"Maybe you could find a crystal vase?" Jackson pronounces it *vahz*, with a flourish.

"How would that even work?" asks Tyler. He's so literal.

"Jackson, this is my brother, Tyler. Ty, this is Jackson Oates." I hope when I say Jackson Oates it isn't obvious that I've been repeating the phrase Jackson Oates a hundred times a day since I met him.

"You play lacrosse?" Jackson asks, nodding to a neon-pink ball. Jeez, Tyler, it's not even the right *season* to leave a lacrosse ball on the table.

Sulky Tyler brightens up under the attention. "Yeah—do you?"

Jackson shakes his head. "When we lived in Virginia, I wanted to but we moved before the season started. I've played a lot of other things, baseball, soccer, swim team once, but the last couple of years I've mostly played tennis. Kind of depends on where we live. How 'bout you, Greer? What do you play?"

I brighten up under the attention, too. "Oh. I don't play anything."

I don't explain that sports, unlike academics, require that your body cooperate with you, instead of bulging and jiggling and getting in the way. Just last night, Tyler stole my phone and I had to run after him with no bra on under my pajamas, and Mavis bounced up and almost gave me a black eye.

"How'd the first couple of days go?" I'd spotted him a few times, first being led around by one of the deans, then by a couple of well-meaning student council members. By lunch today he was in the middle of a pack of guys who walk down to the taco trucks every day. I'm not surprised he found friends so quickly, but I'm a little disappointed he isn't going to need me to shepherd him through our adolescence.

"Pretty good. I haven't gotten lost. I haven't been beaten up. Nobody stole my lunch money."

"Good thing. The taco trucks don't take the student meal cards." He cocks his head and I blush. I don't want him to know I've been tracking him. "I saw you leaving with Max and those guys. I just wanted to make sure you weren't stuck at the wistful poetry counter."

"You should have come with us. The barbacoa was awesome."

I try to picture the tear in the universe that would happen if I invited myself to the taco trucks with Maggie's brother and the other upperclassmen who have adopted Jackson. "I had some poems to finish up," I say as wistfully as I can.

"Nah-uh. Max said you always sit with his sister."

Jackson talked to Max about me? Now I cock my head, but he doesn't blush. He just smiles. I mean, it was probably "I hope that weirdo with the giant boobs doesn't follow me to the taco trucks, because she's been stalking me all day," "Don't worry, she always sits with my sister, and they never leave school property because Maggie is too lazy to walk anywhere," but at least he was thinking about me.

"Well, if Max or anybody else tries to steal your lunch money, you know where to find me. First period, room one-thirteen," I manage.

There's a sick thump as a blond elf whacks Jackson in the back. He reaches around and grabs her arm before she does it again.

"OWWW!" she growls.

"Knock it off, Q."

"I. Didn't. Do. Anything." My mom told me she was in third grade, but she's tall for her age and wire thin. She could almost pass for a middle schooler if it weren't for her outfit: pink Uggs—in Kathryn Walsh's house! on Kathryn Walsh's carpet!—and too-short leggings with a T-shirt that says YOU DON'T LIKE MY AT-TITUDE? I DON'T LIKE YOUR FACE! in sparkly balloon letters. She jerks her arm out of Jackson's grasp and glares at him.

Jackson doesn't bother to introduce us to Quinlan. "Where's Mom?"

"Being boring."

"We're being boring, too. Go find Mom."

Tyler and I don't like each other; he's disgusting and I'm not. But it's not like we hate each other. Not usually, anyway. I get mad when he leaves things that have touched his nads on the table, and he thinks I shouldn't mention the constipation medicine he sometimes takes in front of his friends, but we can usually tolerate each other.

The tension between Jackson and Quinlan is different. Jackson's usually kind of loose and lanky, like if you happened to bump into him, he'd sway a tiny bit one way then another, then wrap those long arms around you to make sure you didn't fall. Once Quinlan showed up and belted him, it was like he turned to an iron beam. Braced. Tense.

"Did everybody meet everybody?" asks Mom, floating into the room. What she means is, "Greer Eleanor Walsh, I raised you to be a good hostess, even to violent elf girls, and I expect that you will have offered refreshments to the Oates children." Her eyes glide to the contraband on the dining table and she flinches.

"You'll have to excuse the mess." She sighs to Mrs. Oates. "Boys!"

Mrs. Oates, tall and fair like Quinlan but perfectly tailored and comfortable like Jackson, smiles sympathetically, though I bet Jackson files his old homework assignments in folders like I do and puts his sports gear in labeled cubbies as soon as he's done with it.

"Does anybody want something to drink? We have homemade sodas—raspberry or blueberry vanilla, I think," I offer, too late.

"We're out of blueberry," says Tyler, and burps. Ever since we got the SodaStream, he is full of carbon dioxide bubbles all the time. Mom gives him an I-could-kill-you-with-my-bare-hands look, which is how we all feel about Ty much of the time.

"We have to get going," Mrs. Oates says. "We're picking up Ben. He's been in Dubai for two weeks."

"We're not actually picking him up in Dubai," says Jackson, but I am too distracted to be amused. Quinlan is standing in front of a bookcase with her back to us. She's doing something on the shelf, but I can't see what.

"I hope not!" roars Mom, as though it's the funniest idea ever, rather than just a throwaway line. She glances over at me, presumably to see if I've noticed that Jackson is charming.

The Oateses leave, Mom starts in on Tyler about cleaning up his stuff (sounding an awful lot like me), and I head straight for the bookcase.

In front of the books, there sits a row of little glass Snow White and the Seven Dwarfs figurines, Mom's from when she was a girl. They are handblown and very fragile. She gave them to me when I was seven or eight, but I could only play with them at the table, with a flour-sack towel spread underneath, not mixed in with any other toys or Legos, and none of the pieces were allowed to touch each other. So not really play with them so much as move them from the shelf to the table and look at them. Preferably without breathing.

I loved them. I still do. I love that they are tiny and predictable and perfect. This one is always falling asleep. That one is too shy to speak. The fellow on the end is pissed at everything all the time. Life would be less complicated if everything about you could be summed up so easily. If all you ever had to be was Sleepy or Grumpy or Happy. But even Tyler's not Dopey all the time. Sometimes he's Stinky.

My stomach turns. There is Snow White, two bunnies, a nest of tiny bluebirds, and six dwarfs.

Grumpy is gone.

CHAPTER 7

"Uh, hi, Jackson. It was really great to see you and meet your wonderful sister. By the way, I'm pretty sure the darling cherub stole a tiny glass Disney dwarf that is important to me for very mature and rational reasons and I was wondering if I could get him back? Siblings, am I right?"

Yeah. That'll totally work. He'll probably say, "I was wondering where this little guy came from!" and pull out a box with Grumpy safely swaddled in dodo down. "I went ahead and polished up his hat and fixed the chip at the tip of his pickaxe, too. I hope that's all right." And then he'll tell me that he's always wanted to go out with someone who wears bigger T-shirts than he does.

"You didn't tell me you know the new kid." I jump as Maggie bangs her lunch tray on the table.

"You mean Jackson?" I say it like there are tons of new kids she might be referring to, not like I've just been watching him across the cafeteria, making his way out with Max Cleave and another senior.

"He told my brother you were the first person he met here. He said you were really helpful."

"Helpful? I'm not sure I was helpful. My mom made me come with her to meet them. You know how she does that. It's so annoying." False. Meeting Jackson was the least annoying thing she has ever asked me to do. "Why's Max hanging out with a sophomore?"

"Max wants him to play baseball next spring. They need a new second-base inner-fielder or whatever because what's-his-butt graduated and Max doesn't think the kid with the furry beard is any good."

"I think he mostly plays tennis."

Maggie shrugs. All sports are the same to her. Once I said I was going to Tyler's hockey game and she said, "In the winter?"

"What's he like?"

"Jackson?"

"No. Max," she says sarcastically.

"Oh, right. He's nice."

Maggie frowns at me. "'Nice'?"

"I mean he's friendly. And funny." She keeps looking at me. "I don't know. Obviously better at making friends than I am?" She is still looking at me. "I can introduce you to him."

"Why didn't you tell me you met him?"

"I thought I mentioned it to you."

She looks skeptical but lets it go. "Maybe you did and I forgot."

I breathe a sigh of successful avoidance.

Then she adds, "Don't you think he's kind of cute? The new kid?"

"Oh. I never really thought about it," I say. Now she sighs, because she thinks I never think about it.

It's not that I don't think about it. It's that I think about it and then I think of all the reasons not to think about it.

CHAPTER 8

When we were in middle school, Maggie and I kept toothbrushes at each other's houses. It was the only thing we couldn't share if we decided at the last minute to sleep over. Maggie would have gone without brushing or just finger brushed, but the routine was too firmly etched in me to skip it, even for a day. Mine at her house said "GEW" in permanent marker. Hers at my house had a yellow mini hair band wrapped around the handle to identify it, in case the bite marks on the end weren't enough.

Everything else, though, we could share: pajamas, pillows, face soap, phone chargers, stuffed creatures, plantar wart treatments, hairbrushes, and clothes. Now the idea of trading tops *or* bottoms with Maggie is ridiculous. Besides the monumental size difference of our upper bodies, I am three and a half inches taller than Mags, and three and a quarter of that is just legs. It doesn't seem like that big a difference because I am always slouching and she is always standing up tall like she's trying to see over someone's head at a gun control rally.

The last time I wore anything of Maggie's besides a headband was the first weekend after school started in ninth grade. Maude and Mavis had moved in but hadn't become the hoarding slobs they are now. I went to Maggie's after school on Friday, which rolled into Saturday which rolled into Sunday. It seemed too much to wear my Friday clothes all the way into Sunday brunch, so I borrowed a tank and a jean jacket when her mom sent us out for bagels. I was still wearing one of the bras I'd gotten when Mom took me shopping that summer (the last time we ever shopped lingerie together), a pale blue eyelet balconette, cute, not sexy, which in retrospect should have already been dumped in the giveaway pile. I was either too naïve to realize that the thing didn't fit anymore, or too embarrassed to admit it, or both.

Maggie was already off gluten, so I was in charge of choosing a bagel assortment for the Cleave family while she went to the coffee shop next door for drinks, and Max waited with the car running. It would be a lot of pressure even if her family didn't have strong opinions about everything.

"You look like a woman in need of a bagel." The guy behind the counter was probably a year or two older than us, with a mass of thick curls held back by his bagel-shop visor. If this bagel-shop thing didn't work out, he could probably be an Abercrombie model. He gave me a hungry-looking half smile.

"I *am* in need of a bagel. I need a dozen bagels, actually." I returned his half smile with a whole one.

"A dozen comes with thirteen. Most people think it's gonna be twelve, but here it's thirteen. You get a bonus bagel."

Now I would probably say, "It's called a 'baker's dozen' and it's not that special. Everybody does it. *Four*teen bagels would be a bonus." But his cheekbones were so chiselly and his arms looked like they'd been kneading a lot of heavy bagel dough, and I was still hopeful about boys and breasts and bagels. "I love bonus bagels!" I chirped.

I asked for two each of the classics: plain, poppy, egg, sesame, everything. But for the others, would Maggie's mom like flax and apple? Pepper parmesan? Was her brother a cinnamon raisin guy?

"Do you have someone to share all these bagels with?" He puppy-dogged his eyes at me. I ate it up.

I leaned over the counter guessing what kind of bagel eaters the Cleaves were, and liking that this guy was flirting with me, even if his lines were terrible. Pepper parm, cinnamon raisin, this jacket must look good on me. Another sesame, can't go wrong with plain, my hair really does look better when I haven't washed it. Whole wheat's boring, try something new, I wonder where he goes to school. I couldn't decide, except to decide to keep not deciding.

Parents and teachers always loved me. I got along with most girls, unless they hated Maggie enough to be mad at me, too. But boys, especially older ones, had never noticed me. Or at least they never seemed to notice I was a girl. But maybe that was changing. Or maybe it was just this kid in the bagel shop who liked how I was independently deciding the breakfast fates of up to thirteen people. Bialy, honey oat, salt, maybe he's here every Sunday.

At some point, I noticed that while I was peering over the counter at the wire bins of bagels, the hot guy with the plastic serving gloves was staring straight down my shirt, still wearing that same half smile. I followed his look down to my chest to see that not only were the tops of my breasts popping over the tank like a couple of freshly baked bagels, they were spilling out of the bra enough that there was a slice of deep pink areola visible on each side. I wasn't charming and adorable. I was nip-slipping the bagelmeister.

"The rest plain," I said, pulling the jean jacket closed. That's when I discovered that it didn't really close all the way, something Bagel Boy probably realized before I did.

"You sure? Those honey-oat ones are—"

"Yeah. Just plain. And a tub of cream cheese."

"Okeeee," he said. And packed up everything with no more flirty smiles.

I put my own dirty Friday shirt on as soon as we got back to Maggie's.

This doesn't happen anymore because I don't let it happen anymore. I shut down the flirting before it starts, with a big gray sweatshirt and no tolerance for overly friendly conversation. I shut it down before it peers down at Maude and Mavis and either gets stupidly excited or morbidly curious. Before I have to wonder whether it's me or them.

Or I did, anyway, until Jackson showed up in the re-lo binder's number one Starbucks and I let myself wonder.

CHAPTER 9

We are doing a unit on volleyball in gym.

Volleyball includes a lot of jumping.

I avoid unnecessary jumping.

Most girls do a quick change in the locker room—pulling off sweaters, pulling on T-shirts right over their usual bras. It's just gym. I, on the other hand, head to a bathroom stall, take my last deep breath for the hour, and wrestle a black overhead sports bra, at least a size too small, directly over my regular bra. I need all the support I can get. The sports bra squeezes and compresses everything into a single mound—kind of a unibreast. Or a superboob. I pull on my dad's old 2008 Run for the Zoo 5K shirt. He has a good collection of race-day shirts going back years. When I was smaller I used them as sleep shirts because they were worn in and soft and made from that breathable athletic fabric, but this is the only one that fits now. That year when Dad checked in late, there were only XXLs left. Now I wear it pretty much every time I know the Illinois Department of Education's obsession with daily phys ed is going to make me sweat.

Leaving the stall, I stand in front of the mirror. The shirt drapes over the squeezed-in superboob, my shoulders curve forward and in, and my arms cross low. I pull at the shirt, wishing it could just float out a half inch around me on all sides instead of obeying whatever laws of physics or apparel tell it to cling to me. I look like a big shapeless blob, with stick legs poking out below. I look like a giant, featherless chicken.

Which I am, clearly.

"Walsh! Let's go!" says Ms. Reinhold, breezing through the locker room, not even looking at my chicken body. I slump out to the gym, hearing her rounding up stragglers behind me. "Woster, noooo. Jeggings are not gym clothes. You can wear school sweats."

A minute later, Nella Woster and Ms. Reinhold appear in the gym, Nella in a pair of saggy maroon sweats cinched tight around her waist. "Nice sweats, Nella!" yells Griffin Townsend. Nella sticks out her tongue at him and catwalks to the warm-up stretches.

She's not showing off; she can't help having exactly the body that whoever decides what's perfect decided is perfect. She could show up in a clown wig and look hot. I could show up in a clown wig and it still wouldn't be the funniest-looking part of me.

We are divided into two lines to learn the underhand serve. Except for Jessa Timms, who plays on the volleyball team, most people's balls go wide, fall short, or fly high, coming down on the other side of the net like a gently falling leaf, which would give the other team time to sit down with a notebook, track the trajectory, discuss who was going to return it, take a bathroom break, and then smash the hell out of it.

My serves coast just over the net, one after another. Ms. Reinhold nods her approval.

"Let's try some overhand."

Again, a handful of kids make it, most do not. After a couple of tries, I understand where the toss has to be in order to meet my hand at the right point. Most people are throwing too high or too close. Even though I haven't played, the weight and the pressure and the curve of the ball feel right. I'm able to get most of them over the net. Jessa Timms drills every ball like a machine gun, jumping to meet the ball in the air.

Ms. R is watching me closely, and I shift a little uncomfortably. I know she's the volleyball coach, and I know that since the volleyball season changed to winter, not as many girls go out for it. A part of me wants to mess it up, so she stops thinking I'm good, because I don't want to have to explain why I'm not interested in playing any sports.

But another part of me keeps hitting them over the net, swinging my arm harder and harder, because it feels good to be good at something besides math.

"Why don't we try a little real-world practice, gang," she says. She puts half the kids on one side of the net, half on the other, and shows them how to rotate players through. "Just see how long you can keep the volley going." I line up with my class but she says, "Not you, Walsh. Timms, come over here, too."

She pulls us to a corner of the gym. Behind us there are slaps and cries of pain and roars of laughter as people hit the ball with no understanding of technique. Someone shouts "Fuck!" and Ms. Reinhold yells back, "You should not be passing with an open palm. And watch the effenheimers!

"You ever play?" she asks me.

I shake my head.

"I want you to see where the real power in a serve comes from." She tosses Jessa the ball and says, "Show her the run-up, but don't actually hit it."

Jessa tosses the ball up and kind of launches herself at it. I cringe like she's going to spike it down on my face, but she just catches it and grins.

Ms. R has her show me a couple more times, then we both try it. The first time I make the leap, the unibreast heaves up and down, feeling like it's doubling the pull of gravity. The sports bra has pulled halfway up and stopped, so there is essentially a tight horizontal band of elastic bisecting my chest in the middle. I tug it back into place and steal a look at the class, but everyone else is playing or grabbing at Nella's sweats.

Coach Reinhold and Jessa Timms are watching my feet, asking me to jump again and again while they correct the steps. I'm pretty sweaty, and between every jump I have to readjust my bra. There's a pain in the sides of my breasts every time I hit the ground, and the bra is pulling on my shoulders like if you stuffed a backpack with bricks and wore it backward, but I can feel I'm getting it. They decide I'm ready to try an actual serve.

My first try with the ball, I miss it altogether.

The next, it jams my folded pinky and careens directly to the right.

The third, it rockets from my hand and smacks into the ground with enough force to crater the gym floor. (Okay, no, but hard.) The only way it would have made it over a net would be if the net was a foot high and right in front of me, but the sound of that smack gives me a tingling rush anyway.

Reinhold laughs. "Now you get it? It's not about your arm. Power comes from your whole body." I pull both sides of my bra back into place as Reinhold shouts to the class, "That's it—locker rooms." The others leave the balls rolling around the court and file down to change.

"That was pretty cool, right?" Jessa offers me a fist bump before she heads toward the locker room.

"Walsh," Ms. R calls. I turn to her brightly. I assume she is going to ask me to try out for the volleyball team and for a moment I am happy. But already my neck and shoulders are starting to ache from the strain of jumping around, and then I remember what the volleyball uniform looks like.

She doesn't say anything about the team, though. She doesn't even say I did a good job. She asks me for an email address. She has her phone out and says, "I'm sending you a link." She hits a couple things with her thumb and slides it back in her pocket. "It's not strictly school related, though, so don't get me in trouble," she says and winks.

Nella is still standing under the basketball hoop with a few boys around her. Ms. R yells over, "The last one in this gym will take down the nets and put away the balls, and no, I will not write you a late pass."

The boys scatter, except for Griffin. Nella has him by the arm, preventing him from leaving the gym before me. "Run, Greer! I've got him!" she yells and laughs. "Go!"

CHAPTER 10

The summer after second grade, I saw a video of Emma Watson when she had really short hair and I told my mother that I wanted a haircut. Right before school started she took me to get a pixie cut. They clippered up past my hairline in the back, and over my right ear, leaving long bangs on one side, the kind that are always falling into one eye. I remember how light my head felt when I walked out, and how fast it dried after a bath. When I see pictures now, I love it. I look like an adorable little boy.

Nella, who had had superlong hair when we left school in June, also happened to return with a short pixie cut, one side longer than the other. It wasn't exactly the same, because her hair is darker than mine, hers fell into her right eye and mine into my left, and because she already had her ears pierced so no one ever thought she was a boy.

It was close enough, though, that for most of that school year, parents and substitute teachers mixed us up all the time. They'd call me Nella and her Greer (or they'd call me Ella and her Gwen, because we both have the kind of names people don't quite believe). Kids in other grades would say "You look exactly like that other kid." And anybody who didn't know us would say, "Did you plan it?"

With some kids, that would be enough to start a rivalry. The cooler or cuter or meaner kid would resist the comparison. She'd try to distinguish herself or say the other one copied her. It happens when other people try to lump you in with someone else. The two shortest boys in the grade always hate each other. The three kids at the peanut allergy table can't stand each other.

But Nella ate it up. Right away on the first day when we saw each other, she came up to me and said, "Greer! We're haircut twins! WE'RE HAIRCUT TWINS!" and held the sides of my arms and bounced like this was the best news she ever heard, even though we only knew each other from school. "AND WE HAVE THE SAME BACKPACK ALMOST!" Her Fjällräven pack was light green with yellow straps; mine was bright blue with yellow straps.

It didn't make us friends exactly, but for the next few months at least, we were, in her mind and everybody else's, the haircut twins.

So that's why it's especially weird for her to be the most perfect-looking person in my school, and for me to be me. The idea that anyone would ever mistake me and Nella at this point makes as much sense as mistaking a gazelle and a rhinoceros. (I'm the rhino, obviously. A Sumatran—the kind with two horns.)

We both grew out our cuts, because having that kind of hairstyle when you're a kid kind of sucks. There's not enough to make a ponytail, which means there's always hair hanging in your face, which turns out to be annoying as hell. If I hadn't discovered head-bands I never would have made it through third grade. Nella's hair grew faster, and she could actually do tiny French braids by the time fourth grade started. Everything else on Nella grew faster, too, but on her, it stopped where it should have.

We've never talked about it, but I think she still feels like we have some connection. Or at least history. Not enough that we'd hang out or be friends outside of social media. But something. That's how it is with Nella and everybody. She has this way of responding to a person that makes them feel like it's nice to be in her orbit. Not just that they want to date her, but also that they just want to sit by her or joke with her or be her haircut twin. All are welcome in the universe she sits so perfectly comfortably at the center of.

And maybe it's that, even more than the perfect boobs, that I'm most jealous of.

If I could wake up in Nella's body one morning, I might still be an awkward mess. But, god, would I love to try.

CHAPTER 11

Since we came together over Tyler's nut cup last week, Jackson has been stopping to talk before first period every day. German III is three doors down from my math, and we're both usually early. He updates me on adjusting to the new place, and I try not to stare at the cowlick he has over his ear, which is beckoning me to touch it.

We are talking about Quinlan's third grade troubles. Everybody was supposed to make a poster about a state with three facts on the page.

"I remember that project." Quin's school is where Tyler and I went, but a lot of the teachers are different. "Everybody wanted Illinois, so my teacher said no one could have it. I finished Delaware fast and then I did Illinois too."

"You didn't do all fifty?"

"Markers ran out."

"Quin decided she wanted Maine for some reason, but there were already two girls doing Maine, so the teacher gave her Ohio. I think she thought she was being nice, since we just came from there. But Quin drew poops all over Ohio, cut it into tiny pieces, and put them in the guinea pig's cage. And then she called the teacher a moron and walked out."

Judging by the call Jackson's mom got from school, no one else thought it was as funny as I do. I would never have done anything like that. I wouldn't have even drawn a poop on an assignment if I could erase it after. "Your little sister has balls."

"Gross. Also true."

"Wait, how did two kids have Maine? You could have partners?"

"I guess if two people picked the same state." He shrugs.

"Maybe Quin just wanted a partner. Maybe that's why she wanted Maine." What kind of teacher doesn't assign the new kid a partner?

"Well, nobody's going to want to be her partner if she acts like that." He sounds exasperated, like they've been through this before. Like Maine or no Maine, nobody likes the kid who shits on Ohio and shreds it over the class pet.

"They'd want to be her partner if she had Delaware. Cool people pick Delaware."

"I would always pick you for my partner," he says, and all my internal organs stop working. "You'd do all the work."

"Right," I say, and hope there's an all-school poster assignment so Jackson and I can work on Delaware together.

"Almost forgot." Jackson kneels to unzip his backpack. "I have something for you."

I assume it's something boring like a note for my mom from his, but I hold my breath hoping it's Grumpy. I haven't asked about him and I'm not going to. The only way I'm ever seeing that dwarf again is if I break into Jackson's house. Or I'm invited. Hah.

Max Cleave stops in front of us and says, "You coming to the cages?"

Jackson stands up and I see that he's got a balled-up paper towel in his hand. Definitely not a note, but it seems like a bad way to keep a miniature glass diamond miner. Maybe Quinlan stole something else, too. Maybe he's returning Tyler's nut cup.

"Yep. I'll meet you by the west door." The minute bell rings to move the cattle along to class. I don't know what I'm more curious about—the thing he's got in his hand or what he's doing with Max Cleave.

Jackson watches me watch Max walk away. "Off-season batting practice. I guess I'm going out for baseball next spring."

"I thought you played tennis?"

He shrugs. "Might be nice to do a real team sport again."

Apparently, it's that easy for him, coasting from sport to sport, team to team, school to school, friends to friends.

The halls are emptying. A teacher across the hall leans out to shut the door and give us the stink eye.

Jackson holds out the wadded paper towel. "I hope it's not too squished." I take it from him and peel back the sides. It's a chocolate chip muffin. Given to me. By Jackson Oates. "My mom made them." I blink at that beautiful muffin, and I want to stuff it in my mouth all at once, and also never eat a bite of it. "Seemed like something you'd like," he adds, since I still haven't said anything. Of course I like it. It's a homemade muffin chockful of chips, smelling like butter and vanilla and brown sugar. Plus it could have been Quin's class guinea pig fried on a stick and I would still love it, because Jackson Oates wrapped it up in a paper towel and brought it to school for me. But the fact that it's a muffin just pushes everything over the top.

"Thanks," I manage.

"Guten appetit!" And then he's gone, and I'm carrying that muffin into math like a baby guinea pig. (A delicious baby guinea pig.)

CHAPTER 12

Volleyball tryouts are next week. Jessa Timms has reminded me four times. Ms. Reinhold has mentioned it zero times. I told Jessa I'd think about it. I will. I'll think about how I'm not going to try out for volleyball.

I open the link from Ms. R on my phone again. She was telling the truth: It is not school related. Or even volleyball related.

It's a website called Sports Supports.

The logo looks like it was made on a home computer from when my parents were in school. *Sports Supports* is written in a font like NASCAR's, and they've highlighted all but the *U* and one *P* in Supports so at first it looks like it says *Sports Sports*. A lot of the text on the site is yellow against a blue background. It is the cheapest-looking website I've ever seen, including the one Tyler and his friends made in third grade so they could post videos of Matchbox cars smashing into each other.

It is a cheap-looking website that sells one very expensive thing: a sports bra.

Only it's not just any sports bra. It has a name. It's called the

Stabilizer and it says it's designed for "active women with cup sizes from DD to J." It says its "unique design" and "patented fiber blend" "provides multi-angled support and stabilization." It "eliminates neck and shoulder pain," "minimizes movement," "wicks away moisture," and "provides a slenderizing and flattering fit." It comes in one color: beige. There is a picture of it. It looks like a giant knot of ace bandages with two big beige shields sewn into it. It looks neither flattering nor comfortable.

The Stabilizer sounds like the title of a Denzel Washington movie, not like something I'd like to strap my boobs into.

But there are 267 reviews averaging 4.9 stars out of 5.

I've been reading and rereading the raves since I first opened the link:

Age: 30–35

Size: 32 DDD/F

I just finished my first half marathon in the Stabilizer and I can't believe how good I feel! No pain whatsoever. And no adjusting the whole time!!! Everything stayed put. And no monoboob! U won't believe it!! Totally worth the price.

Age: 50–59

Size: 42G

I have tride every lady's bra on the market and when this one came out a friend said "waht can it hurt just try it theres a ga-runtee you can get your money back." I can tell you I WON'T be asking for money back. This is the best bra Ive ever wore in almost 50 years of wearing braziers. I don't do any sports but I have it on all the time except sleep. If their was a white one I would get that to.

Age: 12–18
Size: 32H
Love love love this bra! Okay it's not cute. Like SERIOUSLY not cute. But I haven't been able to wear a Victoria's Secret or Perk Up bra since I was 11. It keeps everything locked down so when I'm running or cheering my boobs aren't flying all over. LOL. Plus everyone asks if I lost weight. Would rather have a bra that works than a cute one that doesn't do the job. And I can always get cute panties!!! LOL

"What are you looking at?"

I scramble so fast to close the browser I end up dropping my phone, and when Jackson bends down to pick it up, I step on his hand trying to get to it first.

"Sorry! I am so, so sorry!" I say, jamming the phone into my pocket.

"You got something inappropriate on there?" Jackson says.

"No! Just kind of, um, private." As soon as I say it I worry it sounds like I'm either sending or receiving nude pictures. I blurt out, "Not pictures, though!"

"Oh-kaaaaayyyyy." Now it definitely sounds like it's pictures. But I can't think of anything else to say that won't make it weirder, so we just stand there outside math in silence.

"Auf wiedersehen, I guess." He shrugs.

There are still six minutes before school starts and I don't want him to auf wiedersehen. I say the first thing that comes to my mind: "I'm trying out for volleyball." No, I'm not. Why would I say that?

Jackson says, "Volleyball?"

"Some schools in our athletic conference wanted to add field hockey, so all the schools had to bump volleyball to winter."

"Nice pun!" he says. I look blank. "Bump?"

"Right! But I probably won't make it. I mean I definitely won't be on varsity. Maybe not JV, either."

It is unlike me to be this self-deprecating, but I already decided I'm not going to do it, because I would not be caught dead in a volleyball uniform, and because there is way too much bouncing. So I'm definitely not going to be on the team that I just said I was trying out for.

"Are a lot of people trying out?"

"I . . . I have no idea, actually."

"So why do you think you won't make it?"

"I don't know. I just didn't want to assume."

"You should have more confidence in yourself." He says it in a funny, whiny voice, like the way a beautiful mermaid girl on a Disney show would talk to her friend who looks like a sea lion. The minute bell rings, but he doesn't go. "Repeat after me: I am."

"I am."

"The greatest."

"The greatest."

"Volleyballerina."

I snort. "Volleyballerina."

"Who ever graced the halls of Kennedy High, so help me Olympic committee."

"Who ever graced yeah whatever."

"Say you're going to make it."

"You're going to make it."

"Say, 'I, Greer, am going to make the team.'"

I roll my eyes at him, but he doesn't budge. We stand there facing off, and I have a feathery feeling, like a tiny butterfly just poked her antennae out of a cocoon in my stomach. Finally, I say, "I, Greer, am going to make the team. Damn it," I throw in for good measure.

"That's the spirit." And he bumps my side with his side, and I am pretty sure I let out one of those ridiculous breathy sighs like when the mer-prince gives the mermaid a pearl and she falls in love with him.

The start bell rings, meaning I am officially late to school despite having stood inside the building for almost fifteen minutes.

"Scheisse!" says Jackson, and bolts.

And now I guess I'm trying out for the volleyball team.

CHAPTER 13

One weekend last spring, Maggie dragged me to a movie with Natalie, Tahlia, and a couple of other girls. My preference for avoiding clusters of teenagers lost out to her promise that Seth Rogen would be hysterical. Whoever said their mom was going to pick us up didn't mention that the mom was working until five thirty, so we were stuck at the mall with this pack of girls for two extra hours, which made Maggie and me feel like the living embodiments of a cliché. (I said this to Tahlia's friend Kiki, who said, "Oh, it's pronounced *click* even though it's spelled with a *q*." Then I felt worse because if I was going to be in a clique, I'd at least want to be in one where everyone knew what a cliché was. And now that I think of it, it was Kiki who assumed that we'd all want to wander around the mall all day. Quiqui is not going to be in my quiché.)

Mags and I trailed behind the other girls for a while, me occasionally looking at a pair of pants, because pants don't make me feel like a mutant, and Maggie reporting which brands used child laborers (most).

It was boring, but fine, until Tahlia led everybody into a store called Perk Up!, which is pretty much a lingerie store for people under twenty-five. Everything is bright, patterned, lacy, and tiny. If you had cataracts and glanced at a table of bras, you'd think you were walking by a tray of cupcakes. The vibe is "Sexy Schoolgirl Pajama Party," and it's the kind of place where if your dad went in to buy a gift card, he'd be followed by mall security for the rest of the day. It's also the kind of place that makes me hyperventilate, especially since I resigned myself to ordering and reordering the same full-coverage, no-nonsense workhorse undergarments online so I don't have to think about it. Not the store for me. The girls all cooed, and even Maggie started leafing through a pile of undies. My breasts grew a half pound each just being in there.

"I'm going to go to the bookstore," I said.

"I'll come," chimed Maggie, scowling at a pair of panties with MEOW printed on the butt.

But as we were turning to leave, I noticed a poster of a girl in a cute plaid bra and matching bottoms, and instead of the kind of skinny where you could identify her bones and major organs, this model had curves. Like big curves. Like she was made of flesh instead of just skin, and kind of a lot of it. PERK'S EXTENDED SIZE COLLECTION JUST GOT BIGGER!

It was a cheap slogan, but in smaller print it said, "Select styles in 26AA to 40G." If that cute bra was in the Extended Size Collection, and the extended size collection extended to my size, by extension, I could have a cute plaid bra, instead of the institutional beige one I was wearing.

I wasn't about to look for it with the other girls there, but the next day Mom dropped me at the mall as soon as it opened, when senior citizens were doing their morning laps and Perk Up!'s customers were asleep in their matching camis and sleep shorts. (Mom thought I was going back for a birthday gift for Maggie.)

"Lemme know if you need help finding anything," the Perk Up! assistant manager mumbled without looking up from the thongs for tweens she was arranging.

At first I couldn't figure out where the "extended sizes" were, but hanging under the display bras in the back there were drawers of extra undergarments, bras nested inside each other like silky matryoshkas. A cups and Bs and Cs and Ds and DDs, all the way up to Gs! And then there it was, the bra de résistance: pink-and-orange-and-cream plaid with a pair of matching boy shorts, in (close to, maybe?) my size. I also picked up a lacy, stretchy overhead bralette in a pale purple, because I was feeling so optimistic about the big girl in the poster and the plaid bra that I momentarily lost my mind.

I took them into a fitting room, where there was a sign that said, LET US FIND YOUR PERK-FECT FIT! and a cartoon of a happy salesperson in smart librarian glasses wrapping a tape measure around a giddy-looking customer with the exact dimensions of a toothbrush. No, thank you.

I tried the purple overhead one first, because it looked so comfortable.

It was comfortable like wearing a scratchy vest made of old dryer sheets and thorns that stopped halfway down your boobs would be comfortable. Okay, that one was a long shot anyway. Doesn't matter.

I picked up the plaid bra. There were only two hooks in the

back (mine had four), and the straps resembled thin pink ribbons you'd tie on a baby's head to signal she was a girl, but the cups were like mixing bowls. It was sort of like if you took the sails off a pirate ship and made them into a bikini.

I hooked the band and slid my arms through the straps. It's a good thing I liked that plaid print, because now I was looking at a lot of it—enough so that the bra actually covered most of Maude and Mavis, without rolls of boobage coming out the sides. It fit! Sort of.

That is, it did until I bent down to pick up the purple bra that I'd dropped on the floor, and both breasts slid completely out of their cups. I stood up and tucked them back in. So it wasn't something I could do a handstand in, but I wasn't much for hand-stands anyway. It wasn't comfortable. Or supportive. Or cheap. But it was enough to feel like I was wearing something a fifteen-year-old would wear, instead of a grandmother.

I leaned forward just a bit. They stayed in.

A bit more. Still in!

I leaned forward as far as you'd need to to hand someone your money if you were buying this bra. Ploop! There went Mavis. "What's going on out here?" she asked.

When I held perfectly still and stood straight, Perk Up! was right—the bra was the extended size that fit over my extended body. But already the skinny ribbon straps were digging a thin wedge in my shoulders, and even the tiniest bounce on my heels had M&M flopping like a mattress on the roof of a Volkswagen.

Essentially, they had made a bigger version of the same bra but had not modified it to account for the different physics of a shape like mine. It would be like if you stacked thirty snowballs on top of each other to make a super tall snowman and expected him to be as stable as the standard three piece. Or if you tied that mattress onto your Volkswagen with a friendship bracelet.

I stared at my plaid-patterned self in the mirror.

This bra didn't do any of the hoisting, holding, or hauling I needed it to do, and Maude and Mavis were hanging troublingly close to my belly button. This was not my Perk-fect fit.

But for the first time since my C-cup days, they were wearing something cute.

"You all set?" asked the clerk, who had given up pricing underwear and was playing on her phone.

I bought the useless plaid bra and the matching boy shorts. I have no idea why. They are in the bottom of my pajama drawer with the tags on and will stay there forever.

CHAPTER 14

"Tyler needs a haircut."

"I need one, too. I can take him to my place."

"He doesn't need a fifty-dollar haircut." Mom means Dad doesn't need a fifty-dollar haircut, either. He has nice hair, wavy and dark and thicker than most of the other dads, but it's not a complicated style or anything.

"Would you like me to just trim him up in the bathroom?" Dad smirks. He tried the trim-him-up-in-the-bathroom route when Ty was little and ended up having to shave his whole head. Everyone assumed that he was the one that brought lice to pre-school and that's why we shaved him. Mom was humiliated. Ty said his ears were cold.

They go back and forth for a while about whether it makes sense to spend fifty dollars on hair that mostly lives under a hat anyway. Mom caves when Dad reminds her that for fifty bucks, they will also give Ty a good, scalp-scrubbing wash, which they wouldn't do at the ten-dollar place and which the boy clearly needs.

I'm anxious for Dad to take Tyler and go already, because I need to talk Mom into ordering a bra from a website that looks like a Ukrainian internet scam, and I really, really don't want Dad to be part of the conversation. One time I had to get pads when he was pushing the grocery cart and I spent the rest of the time wondering when Mom had told him I'd gotten my period, because I sure hadn't.

When the boys are gone, I sit down next to Mom, who is in front of her laptop studying online reviews of feng shui providers to add to her binder of recommendations.

She looks up from her computer. "I'm supposed to find a good feng shui practitioner, but they all look like middle-aged white women." She says it like she's not a middle-aged white woman herself.

I look over her shoulder at the thumbnails, where all the businesses are called things like Four Winds Resources and Pathways to Peace and The CHI-cago Center. "I feel like I should try to make the recommendations in the binder more diverse, you know?"

"What review site is this?"

"Neighbor-to-Neighbor."

"Aren't the only people on Neighbor-to-Neighbor middle-aged white women?" My mom usually complains about the neighborhood app because she sees it as competition, but maybe she still poaches the crowd-sourced intel.

She sighs. "That's why I don't like to use it," she says, still using it. She clicks on a picture of a woman with a long gray braid and a bird on her shoulder: Pamela Holly Desrosiers.

"I'm thinking of going out for volleyball," I begin.

She doesn't look up from the screen. "Volleyball? Do you know how to play volleyball?"

"We did a unit in gym, and I was pretty good at it."

She nods and makes a note in her notebook. "I think that would be good for you. You should have more activities." I know Mom is disappointed that I don't have more "activities." She's an "activities" kind of person.

"Practice would be after school every day."

"Maybe we should try one of them," she says, looking around the house. She must be excited about all the five-tiny-house-icon ratings Pamela Holly Desrosiers has gotten. I wonder what Pam would say about the pile of Tyler's gear you have to climb over to get in the front door. That can't be good for the flow of our energy.

I try to bring the conversation back to the bra. "So with volleyball and everything, I'm going to need a new sports bra."

"Okay. We can go to Master's this weekend." Master's is the big sporting-goods store on the highway. You can buy everything from golf tees and no-show socks to yurts and hunting rifles. It's Tyler's happy place.

"Actually—" I start.

"Oh! This guy looks Chinese!" It's the same excitement she shows when she finds a size 8 Tory Burch ballet flat at a shoe sale. Good deal on designer shoes = appearance of cultural competence. She jots his name down in her notebook. I am glad Richard Lin is not here to hear this conversation.

"Actually," I start again, "I already found one online that looks good. It's got really good reviews."

"Don't you think you should try it on?"

"I've tried the ones at Master's. None of them fit right. But this one online says it's specifically for women with, um, who need more support." This is a subject that Mom and I don't talk about directly, either.

"All right, you want to show me?" she says, turning the computer my way.

I pull up the Sports Supports site and find the page with the Stabilizer. I am very aware of how awful the site looks and for a minute I think I should just go to Master's and get something off the rack and hope for the best. But then I remember the reviews, and they sound real to me, like real girls and women wrote them. No pain, no bouncing, no monoboob . . . I turn the computer back to Mom and watch her face.

She curls her lip like she's looking at a Facebook post of someone's bike accident, the kind with pus and skin flaps. She clicks through a couple of views and says, "Well, it certainly looks *different*." She pages down to read some of the reviews and her expression looks more interested. And then her eyebrows pop up into her hair.

"I know it's kind of a lot."

"Kind of? I got mine at Target for twenty bucks." Mom's sports bra looks like a pink-and-green headband, more fitness accessory than anatomical support.

"The reviews say it's worth it."

"Jeez. How much better can it be than a normal one?" She catches herself, too late. "I mean, ah, like, ah, the regular kind."

I don't feel it coming, but suddenly my eyes fill, and my face is prickly. It's not just that she said "normal one," aka a bra that fits "normal" breasts, the kind "normal" bodies have. It's also that I feel like an idiot for putting so much hope into a stupid sports bra. Like some bizarro contraption is suddenly going to make my body feel and look like other girls' bodies. Like I'm going to start playing volleyball and be really good. And I'll stand up straight, and no one will think twice about my chest and I won't think about it either. And if I have to jog down a hallway because I'm late to class from talking to Jackson for too long, it won't feel like I've bruised my nipples and the skin over my ribs is ripping in two. And I won't be afraid that if somebody ever liked me, my boobs would become some big joke about him, too, until we were both embarrassed about them. But it's stupid to think I can get all that—that I can buy my way to normal—from a website that puts an apostrophe in ASK OUR CUSTOMER'S.

I can't say anything to my mom because I will cry for real. I can't look at my mom because I will cry for real. I can't close the laptop because I will cry. For real. I look over to the shelf where Grumpy isn't and wipe the corners of my eyes with the edge of my hand.

But whatever else she is, Kathryn Walsh isn't stupid, and now she's actually looking at me and not at the feng shui list.

"You really want to try this one?" she says.

I still can't talk, but I nod.

And Mom says, "Go grab my purse from the kitchen."

And the Stabilizer is on its way, with free shipping.

CHAPTER 15

Seventh grade was the year my grandparents moved from Long Island to Florida, and the last time they visited in the winter. Dad and Ty were playing Mario Kart. I was lying on the couch with my feet in Dad's lap, rereading *The Hunger Games,* and half paying attention to the race. My grandparents' flight would be landing in a few minutes, which meant that with the rental car pickup, the hotel check-in, and the drive to our place, we had two hours to make the house and ourselves presentable.

"Fold!"

Mom dropped the basket at her feet, making eye contact with each of us so we couldn't say we didn't hear her before she stepped out of the way of the TV and on to some task she didn't trust us with.

"One sec," Dad mumbled. I slid off the couch, pulled the basket closer, and snatched some of my own things before the boys could get to them. Dad sped Baby Peach over the finish line and leaned down to grab a pair of Mom's yoga capris. Ty clicked through the menus to switch to single player. "Ty. Come on." Dad reached for the remote, but Ty squirmed out of reach.

"It's still waaarrrrmmm," I cooed.

Ty looked sideways at me with a grin. My brother had a weak spot for things just out of the dryer. He dropped the control and tipped the basket over himself.

"Oh my god. So warm. This is amazing." He pulled Mom's lavender fleece over his face and flapped his arms in the pile like he was making snow angels.

Dad rolled his eyes at me.

"Come on, dummy." I grabbed Mom's sweatshirt off him. Dad and I peeled through the laundry, neatly folding and stacking everybody's clothes. Ty could only fold rectangular things, so he focused on matching socks. "Do you wish you lived closer to Grandma?" I wondered about this a lot. Mom's mom died when I was little, and my grandpa and his new wife lived in Madison. But my dad was a long way from where he grew up, and a long way from his parents.

"Sometimes." It didn't sound like a yes, but Dad has always been diplomatic. Now I understand that he loves his parents, but he might love them better from a distance.

"Whose is this?" Tyler held my bra by one strap. I had meant to grab all my underthings from the pile before he crawled in it, mostly because he is dirty and the clothes were clean, but I'd missed this one. It was one of my first—tiny, white, and useless, more like the idea of a bra than an actual bra. The cups were hardly cups at all, because they didn't need to be. They'd poof out from my body like an unfilled balloon if they were any bigger.

"Mine." I grabbed it from him.

"Greer has bras?!" Ty said it like it was a scandal. "Oh my god."

Ty's mouth was open, and he looked at my dad, like was he not hearing this?! Dad shrugged his shoulders like he did not understand what Ty was getting at, but he was trying not to smile.

"Yeah, that's what happens, Ty," I said. "Girls wear bras."

"And that's your bras? It doesn't look like Mom's." I swatted him with it. It took a long time for Ty to stop calling one bra "bras." I guess because there was space for two breasts he assumed it was supposed to be plural. He might be right. We call pants pants. A pair of bras? Maybe. Now I'm sure Ty knows the terminology, but he doesn't talk about bras in front of me.

The weird thing is that I was less self-conscious about it then, when if Ty had really been observant, he might have noted I had nothing to put in the bra, than I am now, when the need is undeniable. Or maybe that's not weird at all. Maybe that is exactly why I'm more uncomfortable now talking about bras. Because the idea of breasts is something you hold in your mind. The reality of breasts is something that sits in the middle of your chest, right there between you and your little brother. Right there in your bras.

I buried the bra in the Greer pile and launched myself into Ty. I sat on his chest, my knees pinning his arms, until I wrestled a pair of his own underwear onto his head. "Look! Tyler wears UNDERWEARS? Dad! Can you believe this? Look at Ty's underwears! Oh my gaw-ahd!"

That picture was Dad's lock screen, until Mom told him to put something more appropriate on it. His current screen is a picture of me and Ty at a restaurant, leaning our heads together but not touching at all.

CHAPTER 16

The minute bell rings and Jackson still hasn't shown up. I plod off to class, disappointed. Everyone else looks nervous. We have a test today.

Carlisle Patone has sharpened his pencil to a laser and is writing in a four-point font so he can get the most information on the page of notes we are allowed to keep.

"That's just going to make it worse. You're not going to be able to find anything," I warn.

"Easy for you," says Carlisle, and keeps transferring nonsense from his notebook to the cheat sheet. Someone should put Carlisle out of his misery and bump him back to Algebra II.

Three boys are passing a calculator back and forth and laughing. Most of us discovered the list of words you could make by flipping the calculator upside down in fifth grade, but there are a few kids who still find it amusing to come up with equations whose answers spell out funny words, even on a multifunction calculator that has an entire alphabetical keyboard mode.

7734 = hELL

8075 = SLOB

3722145 = ShIZZLE

312237 = LEZZIE

Here's what I don't understand: If they can CGI a chimpanzee so realistically that my grandpa won't stop talking about how the movie studios could train those monkeys to fight on horseback, why can't Texas Instruments create a graphing calculator where no one thinks 58,008 reads "BOOBS" upside down? Or more correctly, "BOO,BS" upside down?

Maybe the engineers at TI are adolescent boys. Adolescent boys who were too smart for school math, who had to go to special math college and then got jobs making calculators.

I catch Kyle Tuck motioning to me, and I assume he's come up with some equation that equals 5319918. Breasts—especially especially big or especially small ones (5578008), and especially especially mine—are endlessly amusing to Kyle.

For a smart kid, he really is dumb.

The test is easy. I only need my half-size cheat sheet on two problems. I'm the second one done, a full forty minutes before Carlisle. I fish my phone out of my bag to play Zombie Sudoku (which is just Sudoku, but instead of numbers, you fill in the blocks with nine varieties of undead) under the table. Technically, we're not supposed to have them in class during a test, but there is nothing else to do.

Right away I see that there is a picture from Jackson. I pretend to be adjusting my shoelaces so I can lean close enough to my phone to see it.

It's his forehead, and there is a red line above his eyebrow about an inch and a half long, with a whole row of stitches squeezing it together. Tyler has had so many gashes on all parts of his body that I can tell Jackson's stitches are expertly done, and I say a silent thanks to Relocation Advisor Kathryn Walsh for including Best Emergency Rooms in her list of recommendations. She may have saved Jackson's beautiful forehead.

> What happened?

Qmonster.

> Quinlan did that??

Yep.

> ???

My mind is reeling, in part because I'm wondering what that grumpy Grumpy thief did to him, and mostly because he just texted me a picture of his stitches. Before I can respond, he writes

> We're leaving the ER now. I'll tell
> you at lunch?

Lunch? He knows he's not texting Max Cleave, right? He's not texting the taco truck?

"Greer? Do you have a phone out?"

The whole class, the ones done with the test and the ones not done with the test, looks at me like I've just been caught standing over a murder victim with a bloody knife in my hand.

"Bring it here, please."

I keep my head down so no one can see my expression as I

bring my phone to Ms. Tanner at the front of the room. I have never been in trouble in math or in any other class that anyone can remember. They think my cheeks are hot because I am ashamed. They are wrong.

Ms. T puts my phone in a basket she keeps on her desk for just this purpose.

But not before I send back an emoji of a lunch box and a thumbs-up.

CHAPTER 17

"What are you doing? Come on," demands Maggie. She's holding a tray with school salad (one leaf of lettuce, four baby carrots, and a giant foil packet of Ranch) and a yogurt drink. Natalie and Tahlia drift up to us with their own collections of food. This is who I've eaten lunch with since eighth grade, and probably always will, whether or not any of us likes it. That's just how lunch goes. I usually nab a small circle table for us because I bring lunch and can get there first, but today I am standing on the edge of the lunchroom looking for Jackson.

"Jackson got stitches this morning and he said he'd tell me about it at lunch." I can see Natalie raise her eyebrows at Tahlia: interesting new development.

Maggie takes it in stride. By now she's met Jackson and she seems to be buying my story that he is more or less a client of mine. "Okay, we'll grab a table. Bring him over when you find him." She beelines for the last empty circle with the other girls in tow. She smacks her tray down seconds before a couple of juniors get there.

I was not picturing that I was going to sit with Jackson *and*

Maggie *and* Natalie *and* Tahlia. I was hoping for something more like just the two of us, at a wrought-iron café table in a sun-dappled grotto in Italy. But there's only the mayonnaise-dappled cafeteria at Kennedy, no grotto, and it's too crowded to take up a whole table for just two people anyway.

I spot him across the lunchroom. He's got a square of gauze taped over half his forehead, which catches people's attention. Maggie's brother and a couple of other guys stop him and I can read his lips saying, "Eight stitches." They all laugh and Max puts his hand on Jackson's shoulder, like busting his head open is a great accomplishment. For a second I think he's going to leave with them, but I see him point my way and soon he's threading his way through the crowd.

"Hey," he says, with a pretty bright smile for a kid who just had his head sewn shut.

"We don't even get to see it?"

"They said to keep it covered. Plus it's pretty gross."

"You should tell everybody it's a new tattoo."

"On my forehead?"

"It's *your* tattoo."

"Greer!" Maggie calls. We look over and she's patting one of the two empty seats at her table.

"Maggie saved us seats."

"Cool," he says, unfazed, and leads the way to the circle of girls. Turns out he's got chem with Tahlia and English and math with Natalie, so everyone knows everyone else.

Jackson doesn't have a lunch. He says he's on "like twelve

thousand milligrams of Tylenol" and he's pretty sure he'll throw up if he eats anything.

"Tylenol? There's not something more hard-core if you crack your head open?" I watched a video of a girl talking about her breast surgery where she said they gave her pain medication that made her feel like she was eating her way through a cloud of flavorless cotton candy, but at least her chest didn't hurt as bad while she was on it. I am hoping someone will invent a drug that takes away all the pain and tastes like regular cotton candy before I ever need it.

Jackson reaches over and takes a piece of Pirate's Booty from my bag. "As long as you haven't had your eye gouged out with a grapefruit spoon or something, they try not to give out anything you might try to sell."

"That was weirdly specific," I say. I pick up a piece of Pirate's Booty; Jackson plucks it right out of my fingers and grins at me.

Natalie says, "That happened to my cousin!"

We all turn to her in shock. Maggie says, "Your cousin's eye was gouged out with a grapefruit spoon?"

"No, he had his wisdom teeth out, and he sold all the pills they gave him."

Maggie rolls her eyes.

"Did he get caught?" Tahlia asks.

"No, but it hurt really, really bad and then he couldn't take anything except, oh, well, Tylenol."

Everybody looks at Jackson again. "It's not that bad. And they did give me the really serious Neosporin." He pulls a white tube with a pharmacy sticker out of his bag and holds it up. "This stuff is hospital-grade. Not that punk-ass CVS Neosporin. Mine kills Ebola!" Natalie laughs loosely, her suffering cousin forgotten, and Tahlia giggles to catch up to her. I feel a little pinch in my stomach, because I can see how much they are drawn to him and how good he is at making that happen. I knew it wouldn't just be me, but I didn't want it to be them.

Jackson lowers his voice. "But seriously, do you think I can sell this? It's pure, man. A hundred percent . . ." He turns the tube over in his hands. "Actually, I have no idea what it's made of. Uranium? Vibranium?" He looks completely confused, and now even Maggie is laughing, but I can tell hers is genuine because she's dribbling yogurt smoothie down her chin. "Greer, could you take this to your private lab and analyze the chemical components for me?"

I throw a puff at him, which he tries to catch in his mouth and misses. He makes a shame face at me like it's my fault he can't catch, and the pinching feeling turns into a warm spot, like a tiny butterfly has just peed on my liver.

"But what happened to your head, though?" Natalie spills out. If the tube of prescription antibiotic ointment leaked enriched plutonium that turned Maggie and me into radioactive pudding right now, Natalie and Tahlia wouldn't notice. Tahlia is literally holding her breath until Jackson speaks again.

"He got a tattoo. It says 'New Kid.' "

Jackson makes a show of rolling his eyes at me, but he knocks his knee into mine under the table.

"My sister hit me." By now he is seriously inhaling my Pirate's Booty. "Maybe I am hungry."

I twist the bag toward him. "Did you deserve it?"

Jackson smiles at me. "She thinks so. I was trying to finish my *Heart of Darkness* essay before school—"

"I haven't even started mine!" squeals Natalie. Jackson pauses to give her a sympathetic cringe, and she is sucked right in.

"And Quin brings over Operation—you know that game? It's not even worth it to say no to her, because she'll keep at you until she wears you out. Greer's met her. She knows." The other girls shoot me a slightly curious, slightly jealous look, and the pinchy/piddling butterfly stands up and sticks her tongue out at them. "She goes first and the thing buzzes immediately. I get my piece out, and it's her turn again."

"I can only get the little basket out!" shares Tahlia.

"I can't even get that!" says Natalie.

If Jackson was a cute girl telling this story, and Natalie and Tahlia were boys, they'd be bragging about how good they were at Operation (or soccer or Call of Duty or parkour or whatever) instead of how bad they were. Maggie rolls her eyes. She's thinking the same thing.

"It's actually not a basket. It's a bucket," says Maggie, annoyed.

"She buzzes, but I let her try again. And again. And again. She's terrible at it. I think she gets some kind of rush from making the guy's nose light up. I'm trying to do my homework, so I let her keep going. But then she gets mad at me because she says I'm not really playing with her. 'Watch, Jackson! You have to watch my turn!'"

Tahlia is leaning so far forward I can see down the front of her shirt. It's a plain white fitted Henley with little black buttons, nothing fancy, but I can see the top of the lavender lace cups of her bra and the breasts that are snuggled in like twins at a Perk Up! sleepover. Cute. Perky. If anyone ever managed to sneak a peek down my sweatshirt, they'd see a bright white granny bra, completely plain except for a satin bow the size a mouse would tie onto a birthday present stuck right between the humps. Like if you planted one dandelion in front of a nuclear power plant to make it less industrial and more pretty. I cross my arms in front of my chest and lean back in my seat.

"Finally, she gets out the last piece—somehow with only one buzz—"

"Was it the basket?" asks Tahlia.

"Bucket," corrects Maggie.

"Heart." I can't tell if he is a performer and this table of girls is the audience, or if he is a performer and we are all the instruments, but he is definitely a performer. Of course it would be the heart. "And then she says, 'I win! Now I get to pick a prize from you.' And then I see that she's already got"—there is just the tiniest pause that no one else notices—"something from my room. I take it back, and five minutes later she comes in and nails me in the face with a can opener."

"Oh my god. She sounds exactly like my little cousin. She's so annoying," begins Natalie. The girl has a lot to say about her cousins today. But Maggie's face is scrunched up like she's thinking hard, and I'm pretty sure I know what she's thinking. "This one time at Christmas—or wait, maybe it was Easter—"

"Jackson, that's messed up," interrupts Maggie.

"I know, right?" he says.

"No, really. It sounds like she's—" And I can hear it coming and I say a silent prayer to Maggie under my breath. *Don't call Jackson's sister a psychopath. Don't call Jackson's sister a psychopath.* The two of us binge-watched three seasons of a series called *In the Mind of a Maniac* last summer and Maggie's been on the lookout for psychopaths ever since. *For the love of all that is good and pure and holy in the world, don't call Jackson's sister a—* "Angry. Really, really angry."

At least she didn't say psychopath.

"Maybe." Jackson shifts a little, lays off my lunch for a second, looks down. I remember the other things I've heard about Quin, and how the first day I met him she refused to leave the car because she was mad about another move. Maggie might be right. Even though I don't think she should take that out on Jackson's beautiful forehead, part of me gets why she would be angry. At everybody.

And I think this is maybe what he's thinking, too, and I think this is why he doesn't seem especially mad at her. If Tyler even accidentally hit me like that, I'd be demanding that my parents take him to the vet and put him down, but Jackson is just staring at the tube of nitroglycerin or whatever it is, and folding one lip over the other, while everybody else waits for him to make this moment fun again. Charm us, Jackson! That's what we want from you!

"Have you ever thought," I finally say, not taking my eyes off him, "she might be a werewolf?"

He looks up, and smiles with just his eyes. Grateful. "I hadn't, but now that you say that, it does make sense. The violent outbursts, the howling, the constant hair brushing . . ."

"The ruthless approach to board games," I add. "My mom probably has a support group listed in her binder."

"Do you think we should try cutting out gluten?"

"I don't know. Maggie, is that working for you?"

Maggie throws a baby carrot at me.

"What are you guys even talking about?" chirps Natalie, who has lost track of the conversation, and more important, where she and her cousins all fit in it.

Guess what, Natalie? You don't, says my cocky butterfly.

The bell rings, giving us four minutes to get to next period. Tahlia tugs Natalie up. "Come on. You always make me late."

Maggie carries her tray to the recycling station.

"Thanks for finally sitting with me, Greer," Jackson says.

"Well, I felt sorry for you with the head injury and the were-wolf sister. And being new and friendless and from Cleveland and all that." Jackson tilts the empty Pirate's Booty bag my way. Classic big-sibling trick: pawn off the garbage on the other kid. I throw up my hands to refuse.

He heads toward the second-floor stairwell, but not before turning around to add, "I guess tomorrow I'll sit at the counter and write wistful poetry about your Booty." I turn tomato red, and the tiny butterfly shits herself.

Maggie slides next to me and looks back and forth between me and the disappearing Jackson. She smirks, but doesn't accuse me of anything. "He's cool. But the sister sounds like a psychopath."

"Mmm-hmm."

CHAPTER 18

Volleyball tryouts are starting and the new bra hasn't arrived. I'll make do with my sports-bra-over-regular-bra-under-giant-shirt strategy. Maggie is excited that I'm trying out. She says she always thought I'd be good at team sports because I'm good at following directions and remembering rules. I draw a frowny poo on her arm in blue pen. And then she adds that I'm strong, because Mags can't lift anything heavier than a twenty-ounce kombucha, which makes me seem like a weightlifter. I think she also feels bad because she's at play practice every day, and I go home alone to lie half naked in my room. (She doesn't know that's what I'm doing, but she figures the alone part, and she likes the idea of me having something to do.)

Tryouts last the week. Jessa explained there are practices every day after school, and Ms. Reinhold and the team captains evaluate people as they go. Two years ago, a newbie like me wouldn't have had a shot, but now that volleyball shares a season with basketball, Jessa says they lost some good players.

There are a ton of warm-ups before we get near a volleyball:

burpees, mountain climbers, squats. None of them are easy, and all of them make my superboob swing around like an accident-prone trapeze artist. I keep yanking both bras back in place, but one of the straps underneath gets twisted and starts rubbing.

The worst drill is something the girls from last year call "sprinting to hell and back." You run one length of the gym, bend down and touch the line, run back, touch the line, then run three quarters, touch the line, run back, and keep shrinking the distance until it's only a few feet—and then you start lengthening it again until you are running the whole way again. It's horrible.

If it was gym class, a few guys would go all out and race, but most people would trot along next to a friend and never even bother to touch the line. But these girls (a) know they are being evaluated for both skill and attitude; (b) are fiercely competitive; and (c) might be a sleeper cell trained on Themyscira to defeat the Patriarchy using only brute power and headbands.

It's impossible not to get caught up in it. I watch the first group go, and when it's my turn, I'm right there in the mix, heart pounding, shoes squeaking, racing for that line like I'm Katniss Everdeen and Prim's life depends on it. I sprint up the gym, pivot a foot in front of the line, and smack my hand down, then shoot the other direction. It's murder on the knees, and one girl who hasn't tied her shoes tightly actually slides right out of them on the second stop. As the drill goes on, the line begins to stagger. I'm behind a couple of girls, but ahead of the main pack. Maude and Mavis are not happy, though, double-corralled in their school-day bra and the sports bra. They are hot and sore, and the twisted spot is hurting like crazy. It feels like a piece of tree bark rubbing against a blister. I put one hand up to hold the strap away from my skin, and by doing this I can use that forearm to hold back some of the bouncing as well.

Turning into my final full-length run, I am right on the heels of Jessa. She's throwing her whole self into it, and I'm trying to keep up while carrying an armload of angry kittens (with claws). We finish the drill and sink against the wall to watch the third group of runners.

"What's with the arm?" she pants between sucks on her water bottle.

"My bra strap is bugging me."

She nods, as though she has any idea what I'm talking about. Jessa's not little, but it looks like every part of her is solid muscle. I doubt her breasts try to go anywhere the rest of her isn't going. "I'll give you some Glide."

I look at her blankly.

"It's, like, this gel that you use wherever stuff rubs." I am still staring at her blankly. "A lot of people use it with new shoes. I use it on my thighs. They rub together when I run."

"Thanks," I nod, and Jessa gets up to roast another player about her poor sprints to hell and back.

And right there, Jessa Timms and I have had the most intimate conversation about our bodies that I've ever had.

CHAPTER 19

"Melinda Oates sure thinks I'm a lifesaver," says Mom, swirling the wine around her glass. She never drinks more than a few sips of it. She's usually too busy talking.

"Who's Melissa Oates?" asks Dad, at the same time I say, "Why are you a lifesaver?"

"Melinda, not Melissa. Melinda is a client of mine, and the reason that I'm a lifesaver is because she's moved seven times in fifteen years and she says she's never had the kind of relocation support she has had here."

Dad forks a spear of asparagus off Mom's plate. "That's great, Kits." This is his name for her, which no one else is allowed to use. "I hope she finds someone half as good as you next time." Mom beams.

"Why would there be a next time?" I ask. I'm annoyed at myself for the tiny panic I feel.

"Somebody moves seven times in fifteen years," says Dad, "I doubt they'll stick around suburban Illinois forever." He puts a little extra emphasis around "Illinois," just enough to make me wonder if he wishes he were somewhere more interesting than the middle of the country.

It hadn't occurred to me that Kennedy might not be the last school Jackson will be the New Kid at. I figured once they got here, here was home. But maybe some dumb girl in Cleveland thought that, too.

Mom is not fazed by this, because to her, the Oateses are clients. Companies pay Relocation Specialists to help with moving in, not moving out, so if they stay or go is irrelevant. In fact, my mom needs families like theirs to keep uprooting all the time so she can get their three-month settlement-support contracts.

I'm distracted by the thought that Jackson won't be around long enough to fall in love with me. I have no experience with anybody falling in love with me, but I suspect that it might take a long time. On the other hand, if he is going to move, maybe he'll move before he falls in love with somebody else, so there's a silver lining.

"How's volleyball shaking out, G?"

I shrug. "There are eight or nine girls who are awesome, like Olympic-ly awesome. And there are some freshmen who have never played anything that wasn't on a PlayStation. And everybody else is in the middle."

"Which part of the middle are you? The top of the middle?"

"I'm okay," I say. What I don't say is that I felt better about the whole thing before Coach Reinhold yelled at me for missing a perfectly easy hit because I was adjusting my bra. Or that my blocks look bad because I'm holding down my giant T-shirt while I jump. I'm not exactly a superstar out there.

But now that I've been to all those practices, I want to play. Except that at the end of every practice, my breasts ache like they've been squeezed in an elevator door. And my shoulders burn from the weight. And now there are rashy red spots under both arms where the bra has been rubbing.

Plus there's that uniform.

It will be much better if I don't make the team. Then I can concentrate on the things I am comfortable with: wrecking the curve in math; keeping Maggie from starting a revolution; and making fun of Tyler. And secretly obsessing over Mom's client's son.

"I'm sure you're better than okay." He goes to squeeze my shoulder, and I shift sideways out of habit. "Where's your confidence?"

In math class, I think.

"Can we get me some shoes tonight?" Tyler says it with his mouth full of bread, like "Caweegehmeshmoosdanite?"

"You need shoes again?" Mom puts half her chicken on Tyler's plate. He doesn't have giant breasts making him look "heavy," so Mom thinks he's too thin.

"Yah," he says between chews.

"Does it have to be tonight?"

"Yah." He swallows and says, "My gym teacher says I can't bring those shoes into her presence again."

"What does that mean?"

He says, "I dunno," but without any actual words, just that little melody that always goes along with "I dunno."

Mom goes out to the front to investigate the shoe situation. A second later we hear a cry like she's found a dead body. "Oh my . . . Oh my god . . ." Worse. Like a client has found a dead body and she doesn't have any five-star dumpsters to ditch a corpse listed in her re-lo binder. Dad runs out to help and he says, "Jesus effing . . ."

Ty and I stay at the table. "They that bad?" I ask.

"I guess."

"Did you get them wet or something?"

"I stepped in the creek a couple days ago, but I put 'em in a plastic bag so they wouldn't get everything else in my locker wet." He sounds proud that he took such good care of his shoes.

"Tyler, you've got to take wet things *out* of the plastic bag so they can dry. Otherwise stuff starts to grow in them."

We hear my mother cry out, "HOW is this even POSSIBLE?" and my dad shout, "Just get them out of here!"

"What kind of stuff?"

"Bacteria? Mold?"

"That's nasty," says Tyler, as though I'm the nasty one.

The front door opens and closes, and my parents pass through the dining room on their way to the kitchen to boil their hands.

"I can't get that smell out of my nostrils," Dad says, blowing his nose into his napkin again and again.

"Tyler, those shoes were a hundred and twenty dollars."

"Is that a lot?"

"When they last less than a month it is," Mom says, exasperated. "Let's go. Master's closes in an hour. Oh my god. Now I can smell it in here. Did you wear those socks with those shoes today? Get rid of them too." She drains her whole wineglass for once. "IN THE GARBAGE, TYLER. NOT ON THE TABLE. Oh, Greer, that package you ordered was on the front step." She tosses a padded envelope at me.

"What'd Greer get?" Tyler whines as he follows Mom out.

The Stabilizer has arrived.

CHAPTER 20

This is how I usually put on a bra: Pull it around my waist like a belt. Hook each of the four hooks. Twist it around. Poke my arms through the straps. Lift the front up and over. Tuck everything in. I can't reach around back to hook it while it's already covering me like you're supposed to, because the whole thing is too tight. I don't have the lats to pull it together.

There is always a half-inch gap between the bottom of the bra and my body, because the cups aren't actually big enough. My boobs squeeze out and over the sides like an overfilled muffin tin. Instead of a sexy little dip of cleavage like you'd see in a Victoria's Secret ad, mine looks like a butt crack going straight up to my neck.

Right away the Stabilizer looks different from my old sports bra. There are several sets of hooks, and the straps are threaded in and out like one of those pot holders you make on a toy loom. If you pull on one part, it shifts and tightens all the other parts. Imagine levers and pulleys and stretchy belts. Imagine if M. C. Escher and Rube Goldberg designed a bra.

Fortunately, it comes with directions. Yes. Directions. For a bra. Unfortunately, they are a little hard to follow. There's a page of illustrations of a woman adjusting all the dimensions, and the address for a YouTube video "for more ways to wear the Stabilizer." But first I have to actually get inside the thing and how to do that isn't as obvious as you'd think. I wrap it around my waist and put my arm through a hole, but there's not another hole that looks the same for my other arm, so that can't be right. I flip it over, thinking maybe it's upside down, but now all the hooks are facing in. I stare at the illustration, trying to match up the crisscross of the various straps with the tangle of spandex in front of me.

I try every combination of looping, tying, and strapping, until I more or less get it on. The hooks come around the sides instead of the back, and when you cinch the straps that go over your shoulders, they also adjust through the cups. It's generally bra shaped, but a very complicated bra. Like if the engineers at SpaceX invented a bra. It would be ten times easier to get it all perfect if I had another person here, but the only other one home is Dad and neither of us wants to make my new sports bra a family project.

Once I'm in and adjusted, it feels pretty good. It's tight, for sure, but not so tight I can't breathe. When I wear my too-small sports bra over my too-small regular bra, it feels like a boa con-strictor. This is more like a bear hug.

I do a little jump. It feels okay. I do a bigger one. I can't quite tell, so I jump up and down a bunch of times in a row. They aren't flopping! It's not like they're not moving, because I'm not made of stone, but they are moving with me, like my arms do, like my nose does. Like they are part of my body and not just a purse or a couple of sacks of potatoes I threw over my shoulder.

I lift my arms above my head. The fabric stretches, but it doesn't ride up. I wave my arms over my head like I'm trying to get the attention of a rescue plane, but everything stays where it's supposed to. When I put my arms down, everything is still where it's supposed to be. Nothing rubs wrong, either. The fabric is soft.

And the people on the site were right: There are distinctly two breasts, not one monster one. This is a relief, because I've been having to use Jessa's Glide between Maude and Mavis, and even still, they are red and raw.

"Greer?" my dad yells from downstairs. "Want to watch the *British Baking Show* with me?"

"I'll be down in a minute!" Part of me wishes I could show him the thing because he loves gadgets, but the other 99 percent of me plans to keep this feat of engineering to myself.

I try something I haven't done in years: I turn a cartwheel in the space between my bed and my closet. I whack my leg on my nightstand on the way down. It hurts like I've cracked my shin bone in half, but my breasts feel great. I don't even have to tug the bra back down.

In the bathroom mirror, it looks like I've fallen through the webbing of a lawn chair and gotten tangled up, or like I'm a sporty mummy. But I feel more like I've put on a safety net. And if you attached a cable to it, maybe I could even fly.

CHAPTER 21

Kate Wood and Jessa find me before math. It's the last day of try-outs. Coach R will post the rosters on Monday. Kate's heard a bunch of rumors from her sister, who is one of the varsity captains.

"Emma says seniors are automatically on varsity, so Eva Frank and Arianna whatsherbutt will be on varsity even though they suck. I mean, not to be mean or whatever."

"That's fine." I shrug. "I didn't have a shot at varsity anyway."

"But that means that somebody who would have been on varsity will take a spot on JV!"

"Right, but those seniors who would have been on JV move up to varsity, so the numbers are the same."

Kate ignores my logic. She thinks we should be worried about this news. Maybe they use a different kind of math in sports where twelve girls on one squad does not equal twelve girls on another. She starts in on a bunch of hypothetical volleyball rosters. It's more complicated than the electoral college.

Someone bumps the back of my knee, the kind of thing that makes your legs fold but doesn't knock you over. Jackson doesn't say anything, just waves as he keeps going, not wanting to interrupt the volleyball summit. The redheaded girl who always tries to drag him to class early to conjugate verbs will be whatever the German word for *happy* is. I watch him like he's a birthday balloon disappearing into the clouds. Kate doesn't pause for a second.

"And Nasrah Abdullahi will for sure make it 'cuz she's so tall."

Nasrah is a ninth grader who has never played either, but she's almost six feet and a pretty amazing athlete. Jessa says Reinhold practically drooled when Nasrah walked in to tryouts.

Jessa and Kate are going through the list of girls at tryouts, trying to determine where our real competition is. Or really, where my competition is, because Jessa is awesome, the best of the underclassmen, and Kate's been playing in a competitive league since she was ten.

Way down the hall, Jackson is stopped outside of class with Red Hair. She's leaning on him and laughing, like he's telling some hilarious story. I wonder if he's telling it in real German or the kind of funny broken German he uses on me.

"There's one other thing that Emma said. About you." Jessa brings me back to real life.

"What?"

Kate says, "She said they were talking about all the new girls and the thing that everyone said about you was that you might be good, but it's like you just aren't comfortable or something. Like you're distracted."

"I'm not distracted." Of course I'm distracted. It's like I'm juggling two extra volleyballs out there. "Maybe I'm a little nervous."

Kate shrugs. "I'm just saying what Emma told me. And I know for a fact that Reinhold is big on attitude."

"Attitude? Who said anything about attitude? I've got an AWE-SOME attitude." I am sure my attitude does not sound awesome.

"Not attitude, exactly. Focus," corrects Jessa. It occurs to me that it was Jessa, not the coach, who wanted me to try out. It matters to her that I do well. "Just make sure you seem more focused today."

Are they kidding me right now? I've been thinking of nothing but volleyball—well, volleyball and Jackson—well, volleyball and Jackson and whether my ribcage might actually shatter if my breasts get any heavier—for the last week.

"I am focused. I've got awesome focus. I'm like a laser." I make the *pew-pew* sound, even though I know perfectly well that real lasers do not make *pew-pew* sounds or any other sound for that matter. They're light waves. The minute bell rings and I am so laser-focused that I barely even notice as Jackson ushers the flirty Fräulein into class. "A LASER!"

CHAPTER 22

I am not focused. How can I focus?

I used to be able to focus. I didn't think about my body; it just came along for the ride. I didn't think about what I was going to wear, as long as it wasn't scratchy, itchy, too hot, or too cold. I let Mom do most of the shopping, and Mom has good taste. It worked for me. It worked for both of us.

Now Maude and Mavis take up anywhere between 25 and 100 percent of my thinking most of the time (how they feel, how they look, whether anybody can tell how enormous they are, whether they are going to knock into a shelf of wineglasses at Macy's). School, volleyball, the ever-evolving state of the universe and everyone I know or care about in it, and Jackson have to share the rest. Not exactly focused.

In sixth grade, when everybody else started wearing skinny-strapped bras or camisoles under their tops, I did, too, even though there was no physical reason for it. Mom brought them home, and I put them on. Other girls got slightly thinner, then slightly thicker, but I stayed flat as a pancake.

Flatter. A crepe.

It didn't bother me, because everything fit fine and felt fine. I still felt more like a kid than an almost adult.

Everything changed in one day during the summer between eighth and ninth grade. I put on a bathing suit and came downstairs to wait for a ride to the pool. Mom took one look at me and said, "Is that the only bathing suit you have?

Two B-size breasts had appeared overnight. B+ even.

Not really, because breast tissue does not instantly inflate like a life raft on a whale boat. But I hadn't noticed that they'd gotten so big until my mom pointed out that they were nipping out of the swim top that had fit perfectly when we'd visited my grandparents in Florida the winter before. That is, I didn't notice them until someone else pointed them out to me.

I suddenly had something new to think about.

And I didn't hate that. Not at first.

A few weeks later, though, they were Cs (you can ask Prince Bakersdozen at the Ninth Avenue Bagelry), and by Halloween they'd hit D. And then they kept on going. It was like *Little Shop of Horrors*, except in the middle of my own body. I should have called them Audrey, like the maniac plant, but there were two of them, and besides, I knew a kid named Audrey and Audrey was fine and petite and delicate. This was not an Audrey situation. This is a Maude and Mavis situation.

Maude and Mavis are big, gruff names for big, gruff body parts. Flabby and pale and hangy names. Old lady names.

Ugly names.

My best guess now is that they might be H cups. H. *AAAAYTCH.*

32H. I'm not 100 percent sure, because even if you watch a dozen videos on how to measure, it's much harder to do on yourself, especially if your breasts tend to hang low. Then the measurement is misleading. Have I considered having my mom or a friend or a stranger in Victoria's Secret measure me, as every perky-boobed, bra-curious woman on the internet does? NO FUCKING WAY, but thank you for the suggestion.

The exact size doesn't matter that much anyway because once you get past a couple of Ds, bras are expensive, hideous, or hard to find. Or they pretend to be the right size but don't actually hold anything up, in, or still.

Here's what you don't see on the internet: Me, smashing Maude and Mavis into the four-hooked holster, size 34DDD, I included in the Zappos cart when Mom told me to order some "dressy sandals" for a client's kid's bar mitzvah. Props to Zappos, which makes it easy to leave your rejects on the front step for the UPS driver, but since I could hook the thing and my boobs didn't fall out of it, and I didn't want to talk to my mom about why I kept getting and sending Zappos boxes instead of walking into any store and grabbing something off the rack like she does, I tossed out the return label and called it good enough. (The shoes didn't fit right either. At least the bra didn't give me a blister.) Plus if you consider the size in algebraic terms, it's $34d^3$, which sounds about right.

I have two main bras, identical except that one's white, one's beige. (It actually said "nude" on the tag. I wonder if Fabergé, maker of fine undergarments for women, knows that not all of their customers are ecru?) They didn't fit right when I ordered them last year and they really don't fit right now. The style says "minimizer," but the only thing minimized is my lung capacity. My breasts squeeze out in every direction, the band feels like I borrowed a belt from an American Girl doll and cinched it around my ribs, and from the waist up I look like a combination of a postnuclear mutation and the spell Harry Potter used to blow up Aunt Marge.

So that's what I think about when I'm supposed to be thinking about a serve. Or a block. Or world hunger. Or a boy.

All the cute tops Mom bought for me over the last couple of years are packed into a tub, and I spend most of my time tucked under a big gray hoodie.

Mom and I don't talk about it. I don't blame her. It's me. Sometimes she'll say something like "You never wear that orangey boho top I got you."

"I don't really like it," I'll say back. Either she doesn't notice or pretends not to notice that there's no way I'm going to fit into any of my old things anymore. Or maybe she has noticed, because she only asks about the biggest and flowiest things. But that orangey boho top would hang off my chest like a tablecloth at an autumn wedding. It's packed in the bin with everything else.

Once in a while Mom will look at what I'm wearing, usually something I've been wearing the whole weekend. Big, plain, loose, dark, unnoticeable. That's what I'm going for. She'll say, "Want to go shopping for some new things?"

"I'm good," I'll say. I'm not good, though. I'm not good at all.

CHAPTER 23

Each period is supposed to be fifty-five minutes, but seventh period lasts at least an hour and a half. Once, Kurtis and Omar explained a theory about how there are forces acting on Earth's rotation: Instead of a consistent 1,040 mph, the speed is constantly changing; we don't notice it because our very existence is bound by the relationship of time and space. They said even our thoughts can change speed, based on the actions of these forces. The thing you are thinking right now could be only a blip or you could have been reasoning it out slowly over hours, but you'd never know.

That whole conversation was probably the longest Kurtis and Omar ever had with a girl, even if it was only me. It might have gone fast for them, but it was very slow for me. The force plays tricks on people.

I think of their theory of time when AP US History drags on. I used to think it felt slow because it was the last period of the day or because Mr. Feiler reads the textbook out loud to us at a rate of a page an hour. But the idea of a malevolent time force screwing with me at the end of the school day makes more sense.

The good thing is that Maggie's in this class, and if time stops altogether, at least I'll have a friend with me until it starts up again. (Kurtis and Omar would go bananas if they heard me say that. "That's not how it works!" they'd say, and then I would have to gently explain that I don't really care and I don't want to hurt Kurtis's and Omar's feelings.)

The point is, the clock is barely moving. I am anxious to get down to the locker room to put on the Stabilizer and make all the adjustments before the last day of tryouts. I need to be focused, apparently, and the best way to do that is to ensure that Maude and Mavis are battened down and there's plenty of Glide for all my rubby parts.

After five hours of Feiler, even the universe gets bored of toying with me. The bell rings.

"Break a leg," Maggie says. "Not literally."

"You too," I say. "Literally." Maggie is on her way to musical practice, and a broken leg might be her only ticket out of it.

She tried out, got a good part, and then threatened to quit because the plot of *Seven Brides for Seven Brothers* is "sexist, demeaning, and heterocentric." The basic idea is that the brothers are a bunch of bachelors living in the backwoods of Oregon in the 1850s. One day they go into town, meet some women they like, and more or less carry them back to their shack in the middle of nowhere. Even though they are essentially hostages, the women teach the brothers not to be slobs and everybody falls in love. You would think the school might find us better musical role models, like Sweeney Todd, who kills people and sends their bodies to the cannibal baker downstairs.

Maggie's parents wouldn't let her quit, though. "You need more extracurriculars for college applications," said her dad. "Then *be the change*," said her mom. So now there is one grumpy bride in the cast who argues about pretty much everything. You'd think they'd kick her out, but she has an amazing voice, and there aren't many strong altos.

"If you're still here at the end of play practice, Max and I can give you a ride home."

"Thanks. We'll see how late she keeps us. Maybe she'll boot me right away."

"Then come join the cast of *Seven Types of Male Tyranny and Operatic Misogyny!*"

She must have been working on that line for a while. The truth is, even if I was the greatest performer in the world, the costume crew could never get me into one of those corsets. And speaking of corsets, I'm off to the locker room to strap on the Stabilizer.

CHAPTER 24

If it was hard to do in my room, with plenty of space, a mirror, no one around, and all the time in the world, getting this thing on in a bathroom stall in the middle of the noise, steam, and anxiety of a high school locker room is almost impossible. I feel like Houdini's drunk cousin trying to escape one of the master's tricks without touching a toilet seat.

It's all fine except for one strap, which I now see I should have hooked first. If I pull the fabric around with my right hand and twist all the way with my left shoulder, I can almost get the hooks to reach, but not quite. It feels like a blood pressure cuff inflating around my lungs.

Voices are fading. The locker room is clearing out. The last one to the gym floor has to take an extra lap. If Coach R already thinks I'm not focused, I can't show up late with one boob on the loose. That will seal the deal. But I don't even have the old sports bra with me.

"I got 'em at Master's. They're, like, twenty-five bucks." It's

Jessa's voice, leaving the locker room, telling somebody about either inexpensive shoes or expensive socks.

I step up on the toilet seat so I can see over the stall door. Not shoes or socks. Kneepads. She's showing someone her new kneepads, bright white, like part of a stormtrooper's uniform.

There are only a few stragglers left lacing shoes or locking lockers. Jessa and her kneepads will soon be out the door. I will be alone, and no closer to latching my safety belt. I would like to shrink down and die, but I say, barely louder than a whisper, "Jessa?"

Jessa Timms has eagle ears. She whips around, looking for the source. "Jessa!" I say again.

It's got to be odd having a teammate beckon you from a bathroom stall, but Jessa tromps up like this kind of thing happens all the time.

"Hey, Walsh."

"I'm sorry. I feel really stupid. Could you help me with something?"

"You need a tampon?"

"No." I hop off the seat and crack open the door. "I can't get this strap hooked."

Jessa wedges into the stall and hoists the strap into place. "Middle hooks?"

"I guess." She neatly hooks the row. I had only been able to reach the far hooks last time, but it's even snugger now. It's such an improvement that I decide it's worth a little more embarrassment. "Could you move the other side up, too?"

Jessa adjusts the hooks on the other side and I twist from side to side. It feels good. She takes a step back and says, "I've never seen one like that."

"I just got it," I say, feeling self-conscious. I pull the Zoo Run tee over my head. "It's made for people with—it's supposed to be better support."

"It looks like it." She leans around me to check out all the angles. There is no part of Jessa that is embarrassed by this conversation, and it makes me a little less embarrassed, too. "Mine's just one of those pullover ones but it smashes 'em both into one big one."

"That's what my old one was like. Uniboob."

She laughs like she's never heard anyone call it that before.

We are the last ones into the gym. Just by accident, I am a step ahead of Jessa. Coach Reinhold says, "Take a lap, Timms!"

Before I can object, Jessa is off running, like she was planning on enjoying a trip around the perimeter anyway. From ten yards off, she turns, points to her chest, and yells back at me, "Hey, Walsh! Watch out for the Uniboober!" She laughs at herself the whole rest of the way around.

CHAPTER 25

The tryout is better than I could have possibly imagined. I play better than I ever have. I just feel *good*. I'm comfortable and smooth, and when I play hard it doesn't feel like any part of me is about to tear off.

Because I'm not messing with my shirt between every play or limiting my moves to keep my boobs in place, I start to notice things I hadn't noticed before. How the ball spins differently when Kate serves than when Nasrah serves. How Sylvie Suprenant and Khloe Vang-Ellis do a fingers-only handshake every time one of them hits the ball. How Kaia Beaumont apologizes all the time. How if you watch the way other people move, you can start to anticipate what comes next.

It's like I've been looking either at the ball or at myself the whole time, and when I finally look up, there's a whole different game going on.

I'm still in the middle of the group, but maybe the high middle. When Coach Reinhold yells at me, she's not yelling, "Where were you? You shoulda had that!" or "Come on! FOCUS!" or "Stand the hell up, Walsh!"

Instead she's saying stuff like "BIG hands on those. Thumbs should be UP" or "Left-right-left-jump, Walsh" or once in a while, "Yes! That's it!"

Coach will post rosters before school Monday, but there is a lot of guessing and assuming as soon as she heads back to her office. Girls are taking turns saying things like, "Are you serious? You did great." "You'll definitely make the team." "I was terrible. Did you see me block that shot with my FACE?"

"Walsh!"

I turn to Jessa, who gives me a hard high five and a fierce nod that is Jessa sign for "Nailed it!" I'm weirdly proud to have made Jessa Timms proud.

I grab my stuff without changing and head to the auditorium to see if I can still catch a ride with the Cleaves. It will save me trying to untie myself from the Stabilizer in front of anybody. I'm pretty sweaty, but it's a short ride, and since I'm completely invisible to Max Cleave, he won't even know where the smell is coming from.

Mr. Coles is at the piano in the auditorium. He retired before we started at Kennedy, but he comes back to help with the musical every year. He looks happy behind the piano, like high school students singing show tunes is the sweetest sound in the world. They aren't working on choreography yet, just singing. A half dozen students are in this number, trading back and forth between solos and choruses.

They sound good, even if it's not my kind of music. Maggie is in the middle of the girls, scowling. I'd be afraid of that face, but they keep singing, and when her parts come up, she puts on a moony musical-theater smile like the rest of them. Maybe as long as she is singing, she's not thinking, and if she's not thinking, she can enjoy this crap.

Then Aidan Neal takes his solo, which includes a line about pursing lips, taking aim, and "bagging the sweetest kind of game."

No one else is watching Maggie's face like I am, so when she slams her palm on the piano and says, "Oh my god! Is no one else hearing this?" they all jump. The kids who know her well roll their eyes; the kids who don't look at her like they are genuinely confused; and Mr. Coles beams because all drama is good drama. "How are we still doing this play?" Maggie yells.

"Tell us what you object to, Ms. Cleave," says Mr. Coles.

"Yeah, what NOW?" snarls the senior who is playing Milly, the lead girl.

Maggie is incredulous. "Are you kidding? 'Take good aim'? 'Bag the sweetest kind of game'? GAME? BAG? They are advocating treating women like animals. Is a hunting metaphor really the kind of message you want to be sending?"

Aidan Neal looks down at his music. He looks guilty, like he made up the words instead of just singing them.

"If you hate the play, why did you even go out for it?" says the Milly.

Mr. Coles smiles brightly. "It's rather old-fashioned, isn't it?"

"Uh, yeah," says Maggie.

Mr. Coles nods his head. "I agree with you. Showbiz can be

quite traditional and even misogynistic. That is the frustration of Broadway."

"There are other plays, you know, that aren't so offensive."

"Anything you want to recommend for the future?"

"*Urinetown? Avenue Q?*"

Mr. Coles laughs. "Those are excellent! Loved them both! *Book of Mormon*, too, if you haven't seen it. But many people find them offensive for other reasons."

"How about *Wicked*? I've seen that and it's very empowering and feministical," chimes another cast member. Maggie looks skeptically at this uninvited ally.

"That music is complicated, even for professionals, though I'd be willing to try it. The licensing is terribly expensive, too. Beyond our budget!"

Mr. Coles calls it quits for the day. He suggests that people spend some time really diving into the script. "Think about it in the context of the times, not that I'm excusing it. What would your characters want and need? What are their opportunities and limitations compared to yours today?"

It's a classic teacher trick. Put extra work on the complainers, and pretty soon the complaints die down. But Mr. Coles is underestimating Maggie Cleave.

CHAPTER 26

"You sounded great, except I think that girl who's playing Milly wants to kill you now."

"Lizzie Barnes. She already wanted to kill me. Mr. Coles took a bunch of Milly's solos and gave them to my character because Lizzie straight up sucks."

"There's a lot of drama with the drama kids," I say. We are wandering through the student lot to find Max.

"SO MUCH DRAMA," Maggie says, even though she is contributing at least a quarter of it. "I should have done volleyball with you. How'd it go?"

"Pretty good. We find out Monday." When we finally spot Max's car, there are already several people in it. "Um, does Max know you're taking me home?"

"He won't mind."

But when we get to the Ford Focus, in addition to Max there are two seniors and one sophomore inside.

Did you know about this, Maggie?

"Hey." Jackson smiles and slides to the middle.

"We're taking Greer home," Maggie says to Max.

"Cool."

Maggie squeezes tight into Jackson, leaving me three inches to wedge myself. They all smush harder, but these are big guys and it's not going to work. "Just sit on top of me," Maggie says, patting her lap.

I am not sure, but I think Jackson turns slightly pink. I'm sure I do. I stand there, blinking at her for a minute, until she says, "Fine, I'll sit on you," and leans forward so I can get under her.

Now I'm wedged between Jackson and the door, with Maggie's bony butt poking into my thigh. Her legs are draped over Jackson's. I am simultaneously glad I am not sitting there and jealous that she is.

Up front they are talking about the disappointing end to the World Series, and who should be traded to whom. The kid on the other side of Jackson hasn't looked up from his phone the whole time. Maggie's on her phone now, too. Jackson and I can't take ours out because there's a girl in our laps.

"Tryouts?" Jackson says.

I nod and squeeze my arms in even tighter, trying to preserve the millimeter of space between us. I've been wearing the same Zoo shirt at tryouts every day and it's beginning to smell like the zoo. If I wasn't already sweaty from practice, I'd be sweaty now, because I don't usually like people touching me, and now one is literally on me (thank god it's Maggie) and the other (oh god it's Jackson) is one fast turn away from careening into me.

"When do you find out?"

"Monday."

"You doing anything this weekend?"

It's very subtle, but I notice Maggie's body tense. She doesn't look at us, but she's holding perfectly still, like she doesn't want to miss my response.

"I, um, I'm, I have to help Maggie rewrite the script for the musical." She raises her eyebrows at me. I swear my shirt gives off an entire wave of stink.

I am wrong about Max Cleave not knowing I exist. He jerks to a stop in front of my house without asking which one.

"Good luck with the script," says Jackson, as I peel myself out of the back seat.

"Yeah, Greer. I'm looking forward to your help," says Maggie, who has scored herself an accomplice.

CHAPTER 27

None of the furniture is where it was when I left for school.

The couch is where the chairs used to be. One chair is next to it, instead of facing it. The other chair is missing altogether, and the rug is rolled up in the corner. Everything, including the end tables, is lined up in a row.

I walk through the living room to the dining room, where the table has been rotated 90 degrees. My mother is chewing on the side of her thumb. She won't bite her nails—she keeps very nice nails—but she will chew on her actual fingers if she's really bothered.

"Hi?"

"Oh hi, sweetie." She doesn't look at me. She tips her head sideways and frowns at the table. She should frown. There is no space to get around the sides, like if you tried to shove a shoe in a shoebox the perpendicular way.

"Did you try out one of those feng shui consultants?" I bet it was the lady who had a bird on her shoulder in her headshot.

"No, I just read a couple of articles and tried some things myself."

Even better. Mom is a feng shui consultant.

"I think the table was better the other way," she says. "Or we need a shorter table."

"It was good the other way. It had a nice flow," I add, and pick up one end of the table. The two of us reorient the dining room and the world feels slightly more logical again.

She looks satisfied and walks me back to the living room. "What do you think about the couch there?"

"I guess it's fun to change things up sometimes," I say. One of the bookcases is half emptied; the books are stacked in three piles on the floor. Snow White and six dwarfs are still where they've always been, and I wonder if I'm ever going to see Grumpy again. Maybe one of the other dwarfs has had to take on his personality to keep things in balance. Maybe Bashful has started acting like a dick.

She takes my comment to mean I approve. "Yeah, I think so. Just get out of your comfort zone." For Kathryn Walsh, moving the couch represents a move from her comfort zone.

"What are you doing with those books?"

"Oh! I'm de-cluttering."

"Books aren't clutter, Mom."

"When there are so many of them, they are."

I completely disagree. I start sliding the books back onto their shelf. Most of them are my old ones.

She goes on. "Have you heard of the book *The Life-Changing Magic of Tidying Up*? It's about the Japanese art of organizing."

"You read that?"

"I didn't read the actual book . . ."

"But you watched the show?"

"Not really, but I get the drift."

Perfect. My mother believes she has gotten "the drift" of an ancient Chinese philosophical view of space and energy flow and a modern Japanese take on what to put in a garage sale, and has arranged our house like a weird obstacle course. "Well, please don't 'tidy up' my books."

"You're supposed to get rid of all the things that don't bring you joy."

"Does that thing give you joy?" I say, as Tyler blows in like a blast of nuclear energy.

Tyler doesn't even notice that the furniture is all wonky. He just drops all his crap where there isn't a rug anymore, sniffs the air, and says, "Are we having cabbage for dinner?"

If Tyler can smell me, I really need to change this T-shirt.

CHAPTER 28

I reach for my phone when it beeps and remember that I plugged the heating pad into the outlet next to my bed last night. I might have been too enthusiastic at tryouts on Friday, because it's Sunday and I'm still sore.

So the phone is all the way over on my dresser, beeping. "Accio phone."

Still a Muggle.

The things that hurt hurt even more when I drag them out of bed. Dad says there's a good kind of sore, the kind you feel when you gave it your all. If that's true, Jessa must feel delightfully agonized all the time. He neglected to mention that sore is still sore.

Beep. Ow.

In big, bright, uncaring numbers my phone tells me it's 7:06 a.m. on a Sunday, which is not a time that the people who ordinarily text me would text me.

In small, beautiful, mysterious letters it tells me that Jackson Oates is congratulating me. I don't know for what. For getting a text from Jackson Oates?

Congrats!!!

For what?

Glad you're up. Didn't want to
wake you

Why are you congratsing me?

His thought dots take forever.

You're a volleyballerina!

Volleyball emoji, ballerina emoji, volleyball, ballerina, volley-ball.

The butterfly that hatched when I met Jackson wakes up annoyed, but the second she sees the messages, she starts jumping up and down and clapping her wings together. I haven't peed yet, so I wish she'd calm down, but neither one of us can. I want to believe him, but I can't figure out how Jackson would have inside information I don't have. I've taken too long to respond, so he writes again:

It's already posted

I yank my computer off my desk and pull up the school website. Athletics has its own page but there's nothing there besides a note congratulating girls varsity soccer on winning the conference finals. I find the tab for volleyball, then instead of just having the list up, there's a PDF for Varsity Roster and a PDF for Junior Varsity Roster. I click on the JV one, and it opens a spreadsheet with a list of names. There, near the bottom, is *Walsh, Greer Eleanor. Soph*. I made the team? I made the team! The bottom of the team, but still, I made the team! And then I look at the rest of the list and realize that it's alphabetical—Kate Wood is after me—so I'm only the bottom of the list because of Walsh! I'm on the team!

Jackson keeps sending GIFs of fist pumps and runners crossing the finish line and one of SpongeBob giving me the thumbs-up. I will love all of them later, but right now, they are getting in the way of me scrolling the list and quadruple-checking that it's really the real list and not some list of rejected players that I'm on.

Nope. I'm really there. And so are Nasrah Abdullahi and Kate Wood and Sylvia Suprenant and a bunch of other good players. And Jessa is listed as captain! I check the varsity list and see all the people I expected to see.

I didn't realize how much I cared until I saw my name on this list. This is the list. And I'm on the list. Now I can't stop smiling. The Stabilizer and I are on the team. Maude and Mavis are on the team. We're all on the team!

I page through the emojis and GIFs to find a good one to show how excited I am. They are all stupid. On a whim, I take a selfie. In the background you can just see a corner of the whiteboard Maggie and I were supposed to use to map out ideas for *Seven Brides* but which turned into a hundred games of Hangman; a bookshelf full of books, dusty Rubik's Cubes, dustier stuffed animals, tiny boxes and containers, and a Bluetooth speaker; and my crumply bed.

In the middle of all this, me, with my mouth and eyes wide open like I've just won my own private space shuttle. I don't have the stiff look I usually do in a picture, when I'm so uncomfortable that someone is permanently recording what I'm wearing and how I'm standing. I look happy. Just plain happy. My hair and face are all 7:06 a.m. on a Sunday, but still, it looks exactly how I feel. It's how I wish I looked all the time. Before I can change my mind, I hit send.

A half second passes and Jackson sends back a heart emoji. I wouldn't even want to see my expression if I took a selfie now. Probably like a startled moose who is about to either be run over by a motor home or has found her way to a secret forest of willow branches and blueberries. A startled, happy, volleyballerina moose who still really needs to pee.

CHAPTER 29

Practice has been brutal, but we are all getting better and stronger, and people are starting to work together really well. We know who will go for an impossible dig and who will save her knees if it's a lost cause. We know who will blame the setter and who will blame herself for a bad hit. We can tell when someone needs a Lärabar, and we know if someone hands us one it means we're acting hangry.

I still won't change in front of any of them.

I've got a system for getting in and out of the Stabilizer, but it involves some arm waving and pinning myself up against a wall. I duck into one of the single, all-gender bathrooms on the third floor on my way down from Mr. Feiler's room. I've worked a couple more T-shirts into the rotation, too, so I'm not just practicing in Run for the Zoo all the time.

But today is uniform day. The first game is tomorrow, and Coach had to rush the order to get everything on time. Everybody else is thinking about the game and how that's going to go with so many new players. Kaia Beaumont, Nasrah, and I are still trying to understand substitutions, and I swear they are making up new rules every day. Every time someone says we're not ready, Jessa tells them "We were BORN ready!" and then explains that Chatham High School is famously terrible and so there's nothing to worry about.

That's not what I'm worried about. It's the uniform.

Coach R is sitting on an overturned five-gallon paint bucket straddling a big cardboard box. She pulls plastic bags out of the box and reads the label on each. "Cappell? Where's Cappell? Make sure everything fits." She tosses a bag to Cappell, who just steps to the side, whips off her shirt and slides into the uniform top. It's a long-sleeve V-neck, and it's not the washed-out maroon of the school swimsuits. It's deep and rich, like a more expensive version of red, and the sleeves have got gold creeping up from the wrists so that right around the elbows it's like an oil slick of the two colors. There's a gold 11 in the middle of the chest and Kennedy in script.

It's awesome.

"Woot-woot!"

"This just got real!"

"You look fierce, girl!" say the varsity girls, while Coach keeps handing out uniforms.

"Patel? Anyone seen Patel? How 'bout Vang-Ellis? Vang-Ellis, make sure everything fits. Suprenant— Oh, you're right there."

One by one, the mismatched jocks of Kennedy High become a maroon-suited army. The minute that jersey slides over their heads their ponytails get tighter, they stand a little taller, and they look, well, this is going to sound obvious, but they look like a team. An unstoppable team.

But as cool as that is, it's also getting harder to swallow, because I'm looking at these girls admiring each other in their uniforms (now people have started dropping their sweats and sliding into the tiny little butt-hugging black shorts, too) and realizing that those shirts are even tighter than I thought. They are made out of fabric like a compression shirt—the kind of squeezy thing Ty wears under his lacrosse uni if it's a cold early-spring game.

I asked Coach to order me the largest they had, but these things are made to be formfitting. Even twiggy Mena Patel's shirt is tight, and I would have thought a toddler size would be blousy on her. There are only a few uniforms left to pass out, and part of me is hoping that mine is missing from the order, so I can play in my Zoo tee.

"Lah-HEE!" yells Jessa, drawing everyone's attention to Nasrah Abdullahi, who looks like a Nike ad. She keeps her legs covered, so they've given her black leggings instead of the short-shorts, which make her already long legs look a mile high. The shirt just barely rounds the curve of her butt, and even the sleeves hit the exact right spot on her wrists. Everything fits her perfectly, like the designers at Custom Team Gear, Inc. had chosen her as their model of what the ideal player should be in every dimension and then sewed a uniform around her. She happens to be wearing a plain black hijab instead of the teal-and-yellow one she sometimes wears, so it looks like part of the uniform, too. She looks like a professional athlete.

If I was on the other team and that girl walked onto the court, I think I'd forfeit. I'm glad she is on my team.

"Walsh! Try your uniform on, make sure everything fits." I

grab the bag, trying to feel hopeful. Everyone else looks so good in their gear. The rest of them are taking selfies, posting group shots, and sorting through the socks—there is some argument about whether we should wear the maroon or gold ones tomorrow—so I slip into the locker room instead of changing in the gym like everyone else.

Behind me, Coach is saying, "Ladies! Let's get to work! Change out of those jerseys so we don't sweat 'em up before the game tomorrow."

Alone in the locker room, I hold up the jersey. 18! My number is 18! It's just a coincidence, but my birthday is May 18. I love the number 18. The fabric is slippery, like the edge of my old blankie, and I love the way the gold 18 stands out against the maroon. The oil slick design on the arms looks scientific, like some engineer calculated the mythical viscosity of color to determine how they'd flow if forced together.

But it looks . . . small. Smaller than the tops that are already packed into the "outgrown" bins in the basement. Smaller than anything I've put on in a long time. Smaller than I'd be if I only had one giant boob. Much smaller than the space I need for two of them.

But I really want to wear this uniform, more than I've ever wanted to wear anything else. I hold my breath and slide my head through the neck hole and my arms into the sleeves.

And that is as far as it goes. The shirt bunches at the level of my armpits. I tug and unroll it to pull it over my chest, but it is not going anywhere easily. This fabric must be for some industrial use. It is not as stretchy as you'd think.

I press one breast in and tug that side of the shirt down, then work on the other. I get it over the cups, but it is pulled so tight the *Kennedy* is warped; the lowercase *n*'s are as big as the capital *K*. I can't get the bottom of the shirt low enough to meet the top of the shorts. If I lift my arms, the thing rides up another inch and stays there. Plus I look like I'm about to explode. This is how comic makers would draw a girl Hulk; it wouldn't be her muscles, it'd be her boobs that would burst the seams.

I stand in front of the mirror.

Shit.

I can't wear this thing.

Even if I didn't care how it looked, I can't *move* in it. If I bend forward at all, it inches up my belly. If the coach thought I was "unfocused" when my bra was riding around, she's not going to want to send me out there tugging and twisting and pulling just to keep my ta-tas covered the whole game. It'd be handing the other team a win: Never mind looking for an opening, just hit everything to the one who can't keep her shirt on.

I cannot wear this thing.

Here's how tight it is. Imagine a full-grown man trying to fit into a baby onesie. Imagine a hippopotamus wearing a dog sweater. Imagine an article of clothing so tight it can squeeze tears out of your eyes. Because it does.

I can't wear this thing.

And if I can't wear the uniform, I can't play.

I rip off the shirt. Or really, I peel myself out of the shirt, because getting it off turns out to be almost as hard as putting it on. I shove it back in the plastic pouch and sit down hard on the wooden bench.

I want to sneak out now and never come back, but the only way out is through the gym. And this is the only high school in Mom's binder.

I put my dad's T-shirt back on. I made the team, at least. That'll have to be enough. I'll go up to practice for the last time, and tonight I'll email Coach Reinhold that I'm sorry but I need to concentrate on my schoolwork and she should put somebody else on the team in my place. They can keep my $130 activity fee. The other players will think I'm a flake, and if I am ever starving, they'll throw an empty Lärabar wrapper at me and say, "I remember you. You quit the team before the first game." But at least I will die with dignity inside an extra-large sweatshirt that's never been sweated in.

And Jessa. What is Jessa going to think?

Back up in the gym, I look for a partner for the next drill.

"Walsh!" Jessa yells. She is standing with Coach R. I jog over to them, wiping my eyes with the side of my hand.

"We're going to start you tomorrow as outside hitter and Nasrah as right side," says Coach.

"Um . . . well . . . ah . . ." They both stare at me, because the right response is "Great!" and a bounce back to the drills. My face turns maroon, and not the good kind of uniform maroon.

"Outside means you're on the left," offers Jessa.

"Yeah, I know that. I just, I'm not sure if I'm going to make it."

"WHAT?" snaps Jessa.

"I don't have tomorrow as a schedule conflict for you," says Coach, checking against her clipboard.

"I know. Sorry. I'm not sure I'm going to have time to play—"

"AT ALL? Are you QUITTING? NOW?" Jessa steams.

"No! I mean . . ." What I mean is yes, but I can't say it. I love this team. I don't want to quit.

"Jeez, Greer. Were you just at practice for fun? Did you ever even want to be part of this team?" Jessa is angry. Not just angry. I think she's hurt. She has pushed for me from the start, went out of her way to help, and defended me when everyone else, including the coach, thought I was "unfocused." She thought I was part of the team, and the team, to Jessa, is everything. And now I'm bailing. "You didn't even put on the uniform."

My face must give something away, because Reinhold, who has been letting Captain Jessa tear me a new one, puts her hand in front of Jessa before she can say anything else.

"Did you try on the jersey, Walsh?" She says it in a casual way, like she's asking if I've seen a new Mission Impossible movie. Like, "Just out of curiosity, did you wedge your monumental breasts into that sausage casing?"

Mmm-hmm, I hum. I can't open my mouth to talk. Air will enter my throat and it will stop there.

"Did it fit okay?"

I blink really hard and really fast. I shake my head even faster.

Jessa frowns. Reinhold yells over her head, "Assistant Coach Vallejo is in charge," and then to me, "Let's see." She doesn't wait for a response, just heads into the locker room. I scramble after her, and Jessa does, too.

It's almost as embarrassing to take my plastic bag into the toilet stall as it would be to try to change in front of them, because it means I'm some kind of super prude, which most of the girls aren't. But I do it anyway, because I can't bear to have anyone see me grunt and struggle to pull that thing on.

When I come out of the stall, the two of them stare at me. Coach furrows her eyebrows and squeezes the sides of her mouth with one hand. This is how she looks when she's thinking about strategy.

The fact that neither of them says, "What's the problem? It looks great!" confirms that it is as bad as I thought. I squeak out, "It's really tight," and wipe the embarrassment sweat off my lip with those silky oil-slick arms.

"Don't they have a bigger size?" says Jessa, which would be the obvious thing to think if you had not been down this path with a million shirts. In order to be big enough at my biggest point, the whole thing essentially has to be a four-person tent. The sleeves would be down to my knees, and the V-neck would plunge to my belly.

"Timms, run up and get people going on threes and twos." This is a passing drill I love. A passing drill I won't ever get to do again. "Walsh, come with me."

I don't know where we're going, maybe outside to push me in front of a speeding Highlander, but that is the power of a good coach: She says, "Come with me," and you follow. I maneuver out of the uniform top and back into my tee while walking.

She walks faster than most people run.

We end up in the Family and Consumer Sciences wing.

Coach Reinhold knocks on a door with an embroidered sign that says THERESA KERSHAW-BEND. When it opens, Coach says, "Hey, Tess. You got your sewing machine down here?"

CHAPTER 30

Family and Consumer Sciences includes classes like Culinary Explorations, Personal Finance, Independent Living, Child Development, Fashion and Design, Fashion Management, and new this year, Food and Fashion Blogging. Theresa Kershaw-Bend teaches all the clothing-related classes, plus the financial stuff. Another teacher handles food and children, and our IT specialist teaches the bloggers because she has a hundred and ten thousand Pinterest followers.

Coach R tells Ms. K-B that we need a uniform that fits and we need it quickly. It's interesting, this "we," especially since ten minutes ago I was ready to sneak out of the locker room and never return. She says we might be able to special order something bigger, but it would probably be all wrong, it would take too long, and the school activities budget doesn't accommodate special-order items anyway.

"I'm sure we can figure something out," Ms. K-B says, holding up the jersey. As though it's as easy as that. "Anything else I need to know?"

"Try and make it match?" Reinhold says.

"It won't be exact, but I'm sure I've got some maroon and gold back here." She swings her head toward the shelves full of clear storage bins, remnants of cloth folded and stacked inside.

Coach heads back up to the gym while I stand there in my Zoo tee feeling conspicuous. My cheeks are still hot and I'm sure my eyes are pink. Ms. K-B buzzes around the room, grabs a notebook and pencil from her desk, and drapes a measuring tape over her neck. I know what that measuring tape is for and I know what it's going to say. I steel myself. She stands in front of me and smiles. "First year on the team, or have things changed since last year?"

"First year."

"Let's see what needs doing," she says, sliding her glasses on a beaded chain from around her neck to the tip of her nose. "Arms straight, please." I am a stranger in Ms. K-B's domain but she's looking at me like this is the most perfectly natural thing in the world to her. As though imperfectly shaped people stand in front of her tape measure every day. As though I am a problem to be solved—only somehow not a problem where something's wrong. More like a math problem. A puzzle. A collection of unique properties with a unique solution. And I relax a little.

"And things have changed *a lot* in the last couple of years," I add. She laughs, and I do, too.

She starts by pressing one end of the tape at the tip of my shoulder with her thumb. She lays it along my shoulder to the base of my neck, holds that spot with her pinky, and smooths the tape down my other shoulder with her opposite hand. Even through my T-shirt, her fingers are cool, and I get a sprinkle of goose bumps when she touches my neck. She holds the tape against both my shoulder blades next and scratches the numbers into her notebook. She moves around me gently, but without any hesitation or apology, measuring, marking, murmuring to herself. "Thirty and a half . . . Nine and seven-eighths . . . And let's make sure the left arm is the same . . ." she says, filling the page as she goes.

It should be awkward, having this stranger touch and wrap and measure me, but she doesn't act like it's awkward, and somehow that makes me trust her. We haven't gotten to the worst part yet, though, the part where she measures my chest and her eyebrows shoot up on their own. The part where she feels sorry for me and I feel ashamed.

Now she's in front of me, reaching her long arms around to lasso me in her tape measure. "We should be okay over the shirt," she says, as much to herself as to me. "It's pretty thin." She maneuvers the tape around my rib cage, just under my breasts, and tugs it tight. Then she gives it some slack, lifts up just to the biggest part of my boobs—the biggest part of me.

"Don't hold your breath. It messes up the measurement," she says. I didn't even know I was doing it. I exhale and feel everything relax a little. She tugs the tape so the end lines up with the numbers, and suddenly we are done. Minutes. Seconds. If she cringed at the measurements, I missed it. If she doubted those numbers could possibly be right, that she was accidentally reading centimeters instead of inches, I missed it. If she is anything but confident that she can fix my jersey, I am missing that, too. She's already pulling out bins, leafing through for leftovers of material that will work. "Alrighty then. Game is tomorrow?"

"Right after school. But if you can't—"

"Can you stop by during lunch, in case we need to make any more adjustments?"

"Sure, but you really think you can make it work?"

She looks down at the numbers in her notebook. "I've got everything I need." She taps the page with her pencil.

"Thank you so much. If you can't—"

But she's already back to work fishing fabric out of her neatly organized bins. "Greer. I got this."

CHAPTER 31

There's a lot of braiding, straightening socks, and checking tiny shorts for underwear lines. A couple of girls brought rolls of gold wrap to use for headbands, and people are taking turns being crowned. Nasrah's mom has embroidered her number—25—on one edge of her hijab in gold thread. Jessa's marching around in her First Order kneepads, psyching up everybody.

People are too focused on getting ready to notice my jersey, but I love it. I *love* it. Ms. Kershaw-Bend should be in my mom's re-lo binder as a master seamstress/uniform superhero. She split the side seams and took out the whole back section. She used that fabric to create "darts" or folds where breasts go. Like the pointy part (two pointy parts!) a dress has, instead of being like a T- shirt that assumes you are shaped the same in the back and the front. She found some maroon mesh from an old football uniform to fill in the parts she cut out from the sides and back and lined it with a piece of gold (Glinda the Good Witch's dress from the 2004 production of *The Wizard of Oz*) so my bra wouldn't show through the mesh.

So now the Frankenjersey fits properly everywhere, and it still looks all right. It makes its way over my chest, but it narrows again below, so it's not billowing out like a table skirt. It rounds the curve of my butt like it's supposed to instead of stopping at my belly button. And I can twist, turn, and spike without my uniform riding up to my neck. Or if I can't, it's not because of the shirt.

Do I still look like I've got oversize knockers? Of course I do. Would I be willing to wear something this shape-revealing to school or in a face-to-face (or chest-to-chest) conversation with Jackson, Max, or any other boy I know? No, I would not. But standing in front of the mirror pretending to wash my hands instead of checking myself out, I think maybe it's going to be all right. I asked Ms. K-B to leave it looser than the others, but it's not huge. Just big enough. I think maybe my chest won't be the most notable thing about me. I think maybe I won't think about it so much.

When we come out of the locker room to warm up, the people in the bleachers stomp their feet and cheer. A few years ago the school got a new band director who was livid when she found out that the pep band only ever played for football and boys' basketball. She started sending small groups of band kids to all home sports as well as debate and robotics competitions. Somehow, it actually made people start to notice all the other things that happen around here. It's not a full house, but it feels like a lot, especially since I've never played in front of anybody but the team.

People are looking for their parents or their friends in the crowd and you can see that it makes them a little springier once they find them. Maggie is at play practice, Dad's at work, and Mom has Ty at his violin lesson, so I know none of these people are here for me personally. On the one hand, I'm glad because I'm nervous; on the other hand, it would be nice to have my own fan. I want both of those things: to be invisible and visible.

The mini-pep band is playing a Beyoncé medley, and Jessa grabs me and Sylvie and starts dancing like a Single Lady. We laugh till we cry. And then through the chorus of voices I hear him. "Walsh! Eighteen!" I peek into the bleachers and wave. Jackson is sitting with Max Cleave and a couple of other guys—Max just started dating Emma Wood, so I know that's why they're here. Still, though . . . I take a deep breath and resist the temptation to pull my sweaty Zoo shirt over my jersey, and do my best to strut with Jessa to our side of the net.

"Let's go Kennedy! Let's go Volleyballerina!"

Well, now you know what's under the sweatshirt. Jackson, meet Maude and Mavis.

CHAPTER 32

The best thing about my first volleyball game wasn't scoring a point on the very first ball that came to me. It felt good, but it wasn't remarkable. More of a relief. Chatham had left a giant hole right down the middle. It was me doing my job. No one went crazy because it was how it should have gone down.

The best thing wasn't finding out that the girls on the court pull together between *every* point, even when the point isn't ours, for a back-patting huddle or a fist bump. Or discovering that by the time we were seventeen cumulative points in, it had already started to feel normal. That instead of wincing when I felt someone's hand on my back, I could reach out and touch hers, too, and it made us both a little better.

The best thing wasn't that Jackson was there, yelling dumb silly things in German and English, or that there was a text waiting for me afterward telling me that I should give up academics and plan on getting a volleyball scholarship to Volleyball University. And I didn't mind that he had to leave before Varsity was done so I didn't get a chance to talk to him afterward, because there was nowhere I would rather have been than in the locker room with the JV girls.

The best thing wasn't that we won. (But we did.)

The best thing was this one moment, a few seconds, really, that looked like a disaster to everybody else. Kate got under a ball, but just barely, and sent it wide on our side of the net. Sometimes they go sideways, and there's nothing you can really do about it.

But when I saw it sailing out of bounds on my side, something clicked. Not like it clicked into place—more like it clicked out of the way. There was the ball, and there was me. I didn't stop and assess the variables or think about positions or trajectories or my jersey or Jackson or getting hurt or how it would look or if I might fail. I didn't think about anything. I just went for it. I saw the ball, the impossible ball, and dove. And then I was sailing sideways, too. I didn't save it; the thing caromed off my forearm into the stands, knocking Jessa's dad's popcorn out of his hands. And then when I finally hit the ground, face-first, I slid and slammed my shin into the ref's stand, shaking it hard enough that she had to grab the rails to keep from falling off.

It felt amazing.

Not that part with the ref's stand. That hurt like hell and has turned into a throbbing blue egg. I'm not some weirdo who likes pain.

The amazing part was right before that, when my body wasn't only cooperating, it was leading the way. When every muscle and joint and skin cell came together under the same current and did what they were meant to do: Move. Touch. Fall. Feel. Fly. And I thought, *This is what a body can do.*

That was the best part of the game.

"You okay?" Nasrah asked. She pulled me to my feet, wincing like she could feel the bruise forming, too.

"Yeah," I said, laughing, tears in my eyes with every step.

"That's gonna hurt."

"Yeah." I looked down to examine my shin, where the lump was already growing. "It was awesome."

CHAPTER 33

Mom and Melinda Oates declare it's a sign from the universe that there is a night where Ben Oates is in town and there are no sporting events, music lessons, board meetings, or other events on either family's calendar. This is not strictly true, because Tyler is supposed to be at a hockey scrimmage, but Mom decides to ignore it because Melinda Oates has asked us all to dinner and maybe the universe didn't have the updated hockey schedule.

"Whose house are we going to again?" Tyler asks. He's on his third shirt in ten minutes. Mom wasn't satisfied when she told him to wear something other than a dirty old Chicago Blackhawks T-shirt and he came back in a clean old Chicago Blackhawks T-shirt, so he's returned in a blue pullover that doesn't say a team but has a big Under Armour logo on the front. Mom looks at it crossly, but knows it is not going to get better than this unless she trades in Tyler for a kid who will wear something with buttons.

Luckily for me, it's gotten cold enough to wear my gray sweater with the giant floppy cowl neck, one of two non-sweatshirts I have in case Mom needs us presentable.

"My clients, the Oateses. The older boy goes to school with Greer."

"You've met them," I remind Ty. "Except for the dad." None of us have met the dad. People spot yetis more often than they spot Jackson's dad, who travels twenty-nine days out of every month, including February.

Tyler's cramming on his shoe without untying it. I realize that I never see him tie or untie his shoes. I wonder if he even knows how. Maybe he can't button or tie. He's wearing a pair of drawstring joggers; maybe he can't zip, either. But once he's dressed, he looks perfectly fine, like he was born wearing this ensemble, which fits exactly as it's supposed to. It's how Ty always looks. I bet he's never spent five seconds wondering if his pants are too tight or his boobs look too big. "Why are we going there?" he demands.

"Melinda wants to have us over to thank me for all the help resettling." She says it with a pleased smile, like she can't help that she's so wonderful.

"She does know that you get paid for that, right?" I ask.

"People appreciate when you go the extra mile," Mom says. I know that Mom gets reimbursed sixty cents for every mile she drives for a client, so driving extra miles translates directly to income for her, but I don't mention this. She won't think it's funny, someone will have to explain the phrase "go the extra mile" to Tyler, and Dad has just popped in from work. "We were about to leave without you," she says.

"Where're we going?"

Mom gives him a giant eye roll because she has told all of us thirty times that we are going to the Oateses' house for dinner. She and I are the only ones who are properly obsessing about it.

Mom is excited, because she loves people in general, and new people in particular, especially when she can check out their houses and furniture.

I am lukewarm on people in general, even if I'm rather enthusiastic about one in particular. I am also nervous for several reasons:

1. I've never been to Jackson's house before and that would make any reasonable person nervous. I talk to him for six minutes before math class on school days, and the bell rings before we run out of things to say. I am not convinced I can be interesting for more than seven or eight minutes. I am fairly certain he can be.

2. I'm not visiting Jackson's house with reasonable people. I'm coming with these weirdos. I might be able to avoid horrible and embarrassing things on my own, but throw Ty and my mom in the mix and who knows?

3. I need to find and rescue Grumpy Dwarf. I have no idea how I'm going to do this.

CHAPTER 34

Ben Oates swings open the door before we even knock. He is wearing an apron over a striped button-down shirt and a pair of jeans that hang loose on his hips. He's got brown wavy hair that's started to recede in twin paths on either side of his forehead. He and my dad look like they could be standing next to each other in the same Nordstrom ad, like my mom shops for both of them.

"Welcome! Come on in!" Mr. Oates leans out to hold the storm door open for us, so I have to pass really close to enter. He looks like Middle-Aged Jackson, but he smells like a delicious Indian restaurant. "Ben Oates," he says, shaking my dad's hand. "You're Eric."

"I am," Dad confirms.

"And you're Greer and . . . Tyler?" He squints up one side of his face like he's worried he's gotten Ty's name wrong. Tyler grunts a "yeah" and Mr. Oates grins. "And *you* are my wife's saving grace." He leans in to kiss Mom's cheek, and she beams.

Jackson is nowhere to be seen. I have a tiny panic that he won't be joining us, even though at school this morning he said, "Make sure you have a camera, because you will get a rare sighting of my dad." (I said, "In his natural habitat?" Jackson replied, "His natural habitat is a Hilton.")

But for someone who is making a guest appearance, he seems entirely in his element charming strangers. That must be where Jackson gets it.

"Let me get everyone a drink." Mr. Oates strides through the house and we follow, like he's a magnet and we are little bits of iron. "Jack and Mel just ran out to find some kokum." We all look blank. "It's a spice. I doubt they're going to find it. I just got back from Bangalore and one of our partners sent me home with all her mother's recipes. We can find most of the stuff, but there are a couple that I'm going to have to bring home with me next time."

He leads us into the kitchen, where there is a spread of dips, breads, spreads, and fruits that looks like it is from a magazine. There are pots steaming on every burner and it smells unbelievable, like we've just walked into Padma Lakshmi's kitchen. My mother is rapturously soaking it all in. Jackson's dad hands each of my parents a glass of red wine. "Melinda said, 'Let's just have filets or something we know how to make,' but where's the fun in that? Anybody can grill a filet. Go big or go home, right?"

I steal a glance at Tyler, the conversational void, who is looking at the spread of food like it's made of toxins and dog poop. If this is "go big," Tyler would choose go home and eat a chicken nugget.

"Either of you want to try a banana lassi?" Mr. Oates pulls the pitcher off the blender and holds it up.

"I'll try it."

He smiles at me and pours some white frothy stuff in a glass. It tastes like a banana smoothie.

"None for you?" Ty shakes his head. He can't even muster a "No, thank you." This is Ty's worst nightmare. So much food and none of it Flamin' Hot Cheetos.

"I almost went to India once," Mom says, and I realize this is kind of her nightmare, too. We've been here ten minutes and someone else has been talking the whole time.

"You should! Everyone should—"

"DAD!" Quinlan appears out of nowhere. She fidgets, pulling at the ends of her sleeves, which keep riding back up above her wrists.

"Don't interrupt, sweetie." He introduces Quinlan, who declares she already knows us.

"Is there anything *else* to eat? Crackers or something?"

Mr. Oates breathes loudly out of his nose. "I don't know where your mother keeps that stuff."

Quinlan makes a show of getting a box of Triscuits. She stands next to the magazine display of appetizers and eats them straight out of the box. She's shuffling those long legs together like a grasshopper, and I think I know the feeling. It's what happens when your body doesn't feel quite like it belongs to you anymore. Tyler is drooling, but she doesn't offer any crackers.

Every time a car makes a noise outside or Quinlan kicks her foot into a cabinet door, the butterfly stands up, thinking Jackson is about to walk in. I tell her to stop acting like an idiot, but then Tyler drops his phone going for a Triscuit Quin dropped, and she pops up again. The butterfly and Tyler are both idiots.

Mr. Oates and my dad start talking about the wine, which is another stroke of bad luck for Mom, because even though she drinks it, she leaves the fancy wine talk to my dad. She is smiling and nodding along with them, but there isn't much for her to say since by now they are deep in conversation about varietals and soil pH.

I wander back out to the living room with my banana lassi and Tyler follows. I look at the books—a lot of Reese Witherspoon's book club picks, a bunch of Malcolm Gladwell. Ty's found the shelf of Xbox games and is grunting in a way that makes me think he's unimpressed.

"Wanna see my room?" Even eating a box of crackers, Quinlan can sneak up like Spider-Man.

Tyler and I follow her upstairs to a palace of fluff. She's past that little girl pink princess phase and has moved into the jewel-colored fake fur and disco-ball phase. Her comforter looks like the skin of an aquamarine Muppet, and there are a dozen pillows shaped like lips, hearts, high-heeled shoes, birds, and the letters *O*, *M*, and *G*. She's got shelves with full collections of Japanese vinyl figurines, pop culture bobbleheads, some kind of fruit characters, and one of every tiny stuffed animal that was ever sewed together. There is something on every surface.

It's impressive that she has managed to acquire this much junk in only nine years, but also disappointing, because some-where in this chaos of tweendom is Grumpy Dwarf. Scared and alone, probably getting grumpier by the minute. If I could find him, she'd never notice that he was missing, but I'd need a week to look for him in here.

"Let's go to Jackson's room," she says.

I'm about to say "I think we should wait for Jackson," but it doesn't matter what I think, because she's pushing me through the door. We hear Jackson bound up the stairs, and Quin blurts, "Greer wanted to go in your room!" The butterfly, who has been pacing back and forth since we got here, panics and points her wing at Quin.

"Yeah, I'm sure Greer really cares what's in my room." Jackson gives his sister a look that says he understands exactly who's idea this was. He says, "It's not that interesting, but come in." His dad smelled delicious like dinner, but Jackson smells delicious like shampoo and apples and leaves.

Jackson's room is like a tastefully decorated monastery. There's a bed, dresser, desk, and bookcase that look like they were made from the kind of trees money grows on. The bed is covered in a gray-and-blue-striped wool blanket. There are two big photographs hanging, one of a colorful market and the other of a misty lake. The scrawled pencil signatures on the mats say they were taken by Jackson's father. There are a lot more of these kind of photos around the house. I wonder if Jackson's family ever thinks his dad spends a lot of time finding things to take pictures of when he's supposed to be traveling for work.

Jackson's laptop and some school books are on the desk, but there's not much that seems personal, except a single row of things on the top of the bookshelf, which don't fit the generic feel of the rest of the room.

I step closer to look up at them. There's a Lego boat made from different color bricks with a Batman driving; a Beanie Baby iguana, fairly dirty; a cup that says Monterey Bay Aquarium; one of those paper frames with a blurry picture of kids on a roller coaster; and a few other things. It's a weird collection, but it is most definitely a collection, because everything else looks like it was put here by an unimaginative interior designer. I stand on my tiptoes and read the plate on a small tennis trophy: AUSTIN FALL CLASSIC, 2ND PLACE BOYS 12U DBLS.

"Jackson has *a lot* more trophies but he doesn't put them out," says Quinlan, who has climbed on top of the desk and is reaching out toward the bookcase to grab the iguana. She has to lean on the bookcase with one hand to reach far enough and everything rocks a little. Jackson reaches up without effort, shoves it an inch out of her grasp, then lifts her down. I wonder if the iguana was what she wanted on the morning she hit him with the can opener. I wonder why he won't just let her have a Beanie Baby iguana.

"Go ask Dad when dinner's going to be," he says.

"DAD, WHEN'S DINNER?" she screams from the doorway.

"Just *go*, Quin." She puts one hand on her hip and stares at him. He says, "Mom brought you an Izze."

"What kind?"

"It's a surprise."

Quin stands there, biting her lip. It must be hard to choose between torturing us and a soda.

"If it's blackberry, save me some," I whisper. Her eyes get big and she nods. "Blackberry is the best one." We're in this thing together now. She skitters off to investigate.

For a brief second I wonder what's happened to Ty, but I don't want to wreck this moment worrying about my brother. He has probably gone back downstairs to see if Quinlan dropped any more Triscuits.

Now it's just me and Jackson. No hallway full of people rushing to class or table of flirty friends or moms comparing birth stories. I notice how horizontal that bed looks. I notice how big his hands look. I notice how lovely his mouth looks and how his lips aren't even a little chapped. They're probably so smooth. The butterfly starts to do a pole dance, and I tell her to calm herself down. This is an obligatory family dinner.

"Probably not exactly what you want to be doing on a Friday night," Jackson says.

Jackson Oates is terrible at reading minds. It is *exactly* what I want to be doing on a Friday night.

"Your dad must be a good cook," I say instead.

"My mom would say he's an *elaborate* cook. He cooks about twice a year, like this—a whole day and a million ingredients. But I'm not sure if he could make a hamburger or pancakes or whatever."

"That's too bad, because Tyler only eats hamburgers or pancakes or whatever."

"There's always white bread and Cocoa Puffs"—he shrugs— "for when Quinlan goes on hunger strike." He sits down on the bed, all the way to one end so there is room for me, but I sit on the edge of his desk instead, and take a sip of my banana lassi.

"Do you like that?"

"It's good. Like a banana smoothie."

We talk about the weirdest foods we've tried and not tried, which leads to a discussion of places we've been (me = New York, Tuscany, Florida. Jackson = everywhere). The conversation gets easier, more like when we are standing in the hall before math and less like I am in his bedroom about to lose control and launch myself into him.

"So where are the rest of the trophies?" I ask, nodding up at the bookshelf.

"I don't know why Quin said that about trophies."

"Is there a special trophy case somewhere? Do they even fit in a trophy case?" Jackson smiles and sticks out his tongue at me. "Ooh, is there an Oates family hall of fame?"

"Oh yeah. There's a special wing with all the trophies. I'm surprised Quin didn't show you. There are so many trophies. I even got a trophy for having so many trophies."

"Really? What's on the top of that trophy? A trophy?"

"Actually, I got a second-place trophy for having the second most trophies, but once I got it, it made me tied for first."

"Nuh-uh, because the first-place guy would have gotten another trophy, too, so he'd still be ahead."

"You just made that an equation, didn't you?"

"$n+1$, where n is the winning number of trophies. You had $n-1$, and then when you added one, you had n but he had $n+1$."

"Well, you're wrong, anyway."

"Oh yeah? I don't think so. If there were math trophies, I'd have n squared trophies."

"You're wrong because the first-place winner got a certificate, not a trophy. So we both had n trophies. And you're doubly wrong because the first-place winner was a girl."

"Really? The person with the most trophies—"

"*Tied* for the most trophies."

"The person tied with you for the most trophies is a girl, and now she's got one more certificate than you?"

"Oh no. Don't even get me started on certificates."

I laugh and dribble lassi from the straw. It lands, as everything does, in the middle of a boob. I wipe at the lassi with my sleeve and try to arrange the cowl neck to cover it. Thank god it was banana and not mango or strawberry or something bright. I'm trying to divert attention from Maude and Mavis, not go over them with a highlighter.

Melinda calls Jackson down to set the table before I can ask more about the things he's keeping out of reach of Quinlan. I excuse myself to the bathroom.

As I'm blotting the lassi spot with a wad of toilet paper, I peek into the shower. There's a high shelf with matching bottles of Malin+Goetz shampoo and body wash, and a lower shelf with a dozen shampoos and conditioners that say "Sugar Cookie," "Watermelon Kiwi," and "Prevents Lice." I am reaching in to take one quick whiff of Jackson's shampoo when Tyler pops in beside me.

"Look!" he whispers. He shows me a pair of earbuds that look like the heads of Mario and Luigi. They were his first night of Hanukkah gift last year, which was kind of a preview, because every other gift he got was related to video games, too (including *Ready Player One*, which I correctly guessed would trick him into reading a book).

"Mom will kill you if you wear those at dinner."

"They're mine!" he hisses.

"I *know*. I helped Mom pick them out?"

"No, I mean, she stole them."

"What? Who?" I pull Ty the rest of the way into the bathroom and close the door. Now I'm whispering, too.

"The girl! Quincy or whatever."

"Quinlan?"

"When we got here, I left them in my shoe—"

"Gross."

"—by the front door. And you know how she was acting all weird when she came into the kitchen? When we went up to her room, I saw her sneak something into her drawer—"

"You went through her drawers?!"

"I just wanted to see what she was hiding."

"Ty, they're probably hers. She probably has the same ones. Did you even go check your shoe?"

"No, but I know these are mine."

"And how do you know that?"

"Because I found this in there, too."

He unfolds his left hand. There in his palm is my dwarf. I pick up Grumps by the glass hat and turn him around slowly. He looks okay. She hasn't hurt him. She hasn't smacked him in the forehead with a can opener. I stare into his shiny face. I imagine he smiles a grateful little smile before fixing his face in a frown again. I can only imagine the things that dwarf has seen.

I realize I wasn't ever 100 percent sure Quin had him; part of me was hoping that Ty had used his pointy hat to scrape something out of his ears and forgotten to return him. But now I know Quinlan Oates is a shoplifter-in-training.

I wonder if I have some moral obligation to rat out Quinlan to her family, but I'm not going to say anything before we eat. It smells unbelievable and I haven't had anything except a Lärabar since practice. Maybe I can eat Ty's, too.

There's a plastic Amazing World of Gumball cup with orange soda at my place when I get to the table, and Quinlan bouncing on the balls of her feet waiting for me.

"It wasn't blackberry. It was clementine," Quin says. She's chosen the spot right next to mine—almost on top of me. "Do you like that kind, too?" She looks like she wants me to say I like clementine Izzes even more than she wants all the toys and clothes and pillows and junk in her room.

And I decide that I won't tell anybody about Grumpy or Mario or Luigi. She looks so little and lonely leaning into my lap, trying to fold herself into an angle that fits, and Grumpy is safe now with me—no harm. She's got all the stuff in the world, but it can't be easy to be Quinlan Oates. She's in her third elementary school in her third state. Jackson slips in and out of schools and teams and friends like he's trying on shirts, but Quinlan is a weird kid. She's smart and intense, and what my dad would call an "acquired taste." I sip the clementine Izze that she has saved for me and give her a thumbs-up. She beams.

I end up sitting between Quinlan and my dad, so I don't get to talk too much more to Jackson. He raises his eyebrows at me when his dad tries to sound younger than he is, and I cringe at him when my mom says something braggy. The two of them—Mom and Ben—dominate most of the conversation. There's been some kind of treaty that means they take turns being the charming know-it-all. Mom does American versus Scandinavian education, resurgence of independent bookstores, bar and bat mitzvahs (even though Dad is the Jewish one), and tamales. Mr. Oates takes on Thai fish markets, Division I college sports funding, mileage rewards programs, and advances in hernia surgeries. They both sound like they read a lot of *New Yorker*s. Everybody else chimes in occasionally, except for Quin, who plays on Mrs. Oates's phone, except when she's whispering occasional unrelated facts to me. "Only two kids in my class have been to France, and I've been there twice." "My teacher loves how I write *Q*s, but everyone else thinks they look like twos." She's funny, though, and the food is fantastic (and since I'm next to Dad, the two of us nearly polish off the pot of butter chicken without Mom noticing). The lassi has dried without looking like a bull's-eye around my nipple. And nobody does anything more horrifying than usual.

The night is not perfect, but it's pretty good. It's like going to dinner at a neighbor you don't mind (if there was one neighbor in particular you wished would have come to dinner without a shirt on). Plus Tyler accomplished the rescue mission!

As we're leaving, I pull Quin aside and show her the dwarf.

Her snowy cheeks turn pink. She is about to cry.

"Tyler saw you take his earbuds, and he found this, too. Don't take our stuff, okay? Ask if you want to see something." She nods and brushes her eyes with the back of her hand. "I mean, don't take anybody's stuff. People don't like it when you do that."

She looks up at me, sad and grateful. For a second it looks like she wants me to hug her, to wrap her up like you'd wrap up a much younger kid, and it occurs to me that she must be awfully lonely.

Jackson is watching us curiously, but for once, he's not who I'm worried about.

I put my finger to my lips to let her know I'm not going to rat her out. Which means, unfortunately, I don't get to rat out Tyler either, but it's only a matter of time before he does something else stupid.

Like immediately. "Tyler Owen Walsh!" Mom says, yanking Luigi out of his ear. "Get those earbuds out of your ears. That is so rude to our hosts!"

If only he'd burp right now, this night would be a total victory.

CHAPTER 35

At the next game I scan the bleachers for Jackson, even though I already know he's going somewhere with Max. I have a couple of fans, though: Mom and Tyler.

I wave to them as we begin warmups. Mom smiles and waves back, then dips her head back to her laptop. Tyler is gaping at Nasrah.

In the five-minute break before the game starts, I run over to them. Mom says, "Nervous?"

"Nah. Just adrenaline."

She looks at me and frowns. "Is your uniform top different from the others?"

I look down self-consciously. "A little. Ms. Kershaw-Bend altered it so it would fit better."

"Oh," she says with an "oh" that could mean something good or bad. "Well, it's nice. You look"—there's a long pause where I swear she's staring at my chest—"thinner."

I feel my cheeks getting red. I don't know if "thinner" is what she means. I'm glad Ty isn't paying attention. "I'm not. I'm exactly the same as before." I've actually been eating like a horse, but I've also been running around a gym for two hours after school every day, so it evens out weight-wise.

She shrugs. "I guess I haven't seen you in anything so fitted in a while. It's good," she adds.

I get it. I look "thinner" because she's used to seeing me in giant shirts, and hasn't realized how much of those shirts my breasts take up. Mom assumed I had bulked up in general. I slouch about two inches shorter.

Back on the court, Jessa walks up and down the line high-fiving people. Is everyone else thinking about how much "thinner" I suddenly am? I realize I'm being paranoid and try to shake it off.

The game starts and I'm up front. Kate gets under the serve and passes it perfectly to Sylvie, who sets it up for Nasrah's hit. The ball grounds into the other court. In the next play, there is a rally back and forth, then they hit it hard to us and Khloe's pass sends the ball flying out of the court. While someone runs to retrieve it, I notice a couple of kids in the bleachers from the other school look at me and say something behind their hands. When they see me looking at them, they look away and laugh.

The ball is back in play and now 50 percent of me is in the game and 50 percent is watching the kids who were watching me. One of them holds out his hands like he might be describing something that is big and heavy, and I promptly get hit in the shoulder with a ball I didn't see coming.

"Walsh! That was yours!" yells Jessa.

I snap back to attention, and the next few plays go fine. I keep my eye on the ball and don't mess anything up, but now that I'm forcing myself to focus so hard on the ball, I don't notice Nasrah and end up smacking into her. Coach doesn't say anything but rotates me out before I get to serve.

From the bench I can watch the bleachers.

The boys are sharing a phone back and forth, laughing at something onscreen. I look over at the girls on the other team, wondering who they might be here to see. Then a girl with short blond hair comes off the bench and one kid jabs the other kid. "Yeah, Cally!"

So maybe they were never looking at me at all, and I got myself taken out for being self-conscious and paranoid. When I sub back in, it's only for a couple of rotations.

On our side of the bleachers, Mom watches with her fists clenched, jabbing with her right hand when something goes well for us. I hope she saw the parts where I made good plays, and not the parts where I ran into Nasrah or the ball ran into me. It's best of three sets and we lose the first two, so the whole thing is over fast.

Coach gives us a quick not-so-peppy pep talk in which she declares that no one played their best today. The intent is probably to make everyone feel equally bad, but some of us feel worse.

I stop by the bleachers to tell Mom I'll be up from the locker room in a minute. She says a generic, "Good effort, sweetie," and Tyler says, "Did you guys win?"

I'm on my way to the locker room when I run into the two boys from the other team. They look like they're trying to keep straight faces. The one who yelled for Cally says, "My friend likes your jersey." He busts out laughing, and the friend smacks him and goes, "Oh my god, Christian!" and starts laughing, too.

I'm caught completely off guard. They don't even know how perfect their timing is because they didn't see the way my mom looked at me before the game. I walk as fast as I can to the locker room, my shoulders rounding forward as I go. I must be down to three feet tall at this point.

People aren't chatty like they were after our last match, when we won. It's mostly quiet as players change out of their uniforms. I blow by them, slam open my locker, and jerk my bag out. I rip through it to find my sweatshirt, even though I'm sweating like crazy. I pull it over my head and I am safe inside fleece again.

I'm so mad I could chew through my kneepads. I'm mad at those stupid kids, but I'm more mad at myself for letting them get to me—and for the fact that they're long gone on their way to Dairy Queen and they are still getting to me. Not this. Don't take this from me. I just need to get up to Mom and Ty and we can go home.

"Walsh? You okay?" Jessa stops me before I get to the door.

"What? Yeah, I'm fine. My mom's waiting."

"It's just a game. Win some, lose some or whatever, right?"

"I know. I'm fine." I am obviously not fine, or Jessa wouldn't be standing in front of me trying to reassure me. There is a poster about bullying behind her head, and I can see a sliver of my reflection in the silver frame around it. My cheeks are the same color as my jersey. I am so fucking hot and tired.

"Coach is just trying to get everybody court time early in the season."

"I know, Jessa. It wasn't a great game, but it's not that big a deal."

"Okay, good then, 'cuz you're really looking good out there."

"Thanks." She's trying hard, and even though I definitely do not want to talk, I love her for it. "It's not the game. Some kid just said something to me and it kind of rattled me. But it's fine. I'm fine."

"What'd they say?"

"Something about my uniform." She looks at me blankly, like she is trying to imagine what someone might say about a person's uniform that would be upsetting. "He said he liked my uniform."

"They are really cool this year." She slides her hands over her silky sleeves with approval.

"That's not what he meant."

Jessa cracks a smile. "You think he likes you?"

"No." Do I really have to explain this? "No. I think he was making a comment about the way my uniform fit. Like about my chest."

Jessa's smile fades. "Like a mean comment?"

"Well, I don't think he was trying to flatter me. I think he just wanted to embarrass me." Jessa frowns. "It worked."

Jessa's eyebrows come together, and her shoulders rise a bit. It's the same thing that happens if we're down when she's serving, or she hears someone on Varsity badmouthing a JV player. "Do you think they're still up there? I could go up and say something to him. Or I could go with you if you want?"

"I'm sure they're gone. It's fine." It would not feel any better to slouch behind Jessa while she tells the other team's boyfriends to leave the girl with the boobs alone, but it's just like her to offer. "Don't worry about it."

"Okay, but you don't worry about it, either, okay? Those guys are assholes."

I think maybe it really is that easy for Jessa. Like if she was me, she'd decide not to worry about the assholes, and then go play a killer game of volleyball. She wouldn't shrink into herself. She wouldn't crawl inside a giant sweatshirt. She would feel the way I would feel if a teacher handed out a pop quiz, or asked us to write five pages over the weekend about how the Bill of Rights both mirrored British law and expanded protections, or accidentally included problems in the homework that shouldn't be covered till Calc II. "What an asshole." Then I'd nail it anyway.

The confidence I have in my brain is the confidence Jessa has in her body, and in what her body can do.

I don't understand her at all.

CHAPTER 36

I found Kelsey Tambor and Peevish Pru after I was walking from the ice cream place to Tahlia's and someone yelled "I like your tits" out his car window. Maggie went on a diatribe about the way young males act out against women when the patriarchy is threatened. Tahlia yelled, "I bet you do, dickface." I went home and searched for "clothes that conceal breasts" and "tops for big boobs" and "make boobs look smaller."

My search yielded a lot of useless things, a few semi-useful things (turtlenecks are bad; dark colors are good), and two You-Tubers who seemed like they knew what I was talking about.

Peevish Pru is a Brit, and probably smart not to use her real name because she pisses a lot of people off. She posts a rant once a week about things that bother her, and she'll probably go on forever because that includes a lot of things: German tourists, climate change, Americans trying to do British accents, fake hellos, long goodbyes, Crocs, men who expect her to shave, women who expect her to shave, genetic engineering, reading glasses as a fashion accessory, grammar mistakes (especially apostrophes), and her own bulbous baps.

She reminds me a little of Maggie, because she gets annoyed about so many things; and a little of me, because two of those things are her breasts.

But she's different from Maggie because she's rather a snob, which I don't think Maggie is. And she's different from me because she doesn't sound angry at her body—she sounds angry on behalf of her body. She's not mad that her boobs are so big. She's mad at the store that sells slinky camisoles for not making one that would fit her. And the constant questions on Twitter about whether they are "real." And the massage therapist who didn't have any way of positioning her when she said she couldn't lie on her stomach. ("I've got this gift card from me mum because she knows how stressed I've been, but I cahnt even use it because I cahnt lie down on that on that stupid table. And then the massage therapist suggests we try the special cushion she has for ladies who are pregnant, where there's a hole for their bump? No, thank you. I'm not preggers, thank you very much. I left that massage more stressed than before.")

The unfairness of the world toward her breasts is one of her favorite topics to rant about. She has definitely never helped anyone find a shirt that camouflages curves or suggested hacks to make boobs look smaller, and I bet if someone asked about it, she'd rant about the question itself. In the comments on a post about being squashed by a safety bar at Disney Paris, someone asked whether she'd ever have breast reduction surgery, and she replied, "Why should I want my boobs to be smaller? Why shouldn't I want the world to be bigger?"

After that, there were a whole series of comments, a lot supportive and a lot completely vile (Peevish Pru takes down the threatening ones but leaves up the merely offensive so she can rant about them). There were lots of mentions of other bloggers who had addressed this issue, including Kelsey Tambor, who made a four-part series about the breast reduction surgery she got the day after her eighteenth birthday, before she went back to posting incredibly complicated makeup tutorials.

I know for a fact that Kelsey Tambor got some of the description of the procedure wrong, because that stuff is easy to find on clinic and medformation sites. What was more interesting, though, was that she talked about why she did it (back pain, breast pain, appearance, self-consciousness); what it felt like (woozy, nauseous, like someone stomped on her chest with cleats, then just bruisy, then just achy, then just a little touchy, then eventually pretty weirdly like herself); and finally what it looked like (some graphic clips of bruising, draining, and healing; and a couple months later, a photo series of herself in strapless sundresses and bathing suits). Kelsey moderates all the comments on her page, so there are only ever inspired fans telling her how amazing she is.

Those breast-reduction posts have hundreds of thousands of views—way more than her other posts. A lot of them are probably weirdos and perverts, but I wonder how many are girls like me.

I don't watch the rest of Kelsey's stuff because it's usually about fun new shades that will make your eyes pop! but I have an alert set just in case she posts any longer-term follow-ups about the surgery. I watch Pru, though, even when she's not talk-ing about her breasts. I watch because she's funny and thinks the world should be better than it is, rather than thinking she should be better than she is.

I live in the space between my large-chested internet sisters. I want to be able to stand by Pru and demand that the world make space (and bras and seat belts and crossover purses) for my kind of body. But it hurts. They hurt. My whole body hurts in all the ways you'd think it hurts and a bunch of ways you wouldn't. And so I also want to wake up in the recovery room next to Kelsey, pop a couple Vicodin, and not have to wait for the world to be better than it is.

I am ashamed of being ashamed of being ashamed. And that is the part that no one else understands.

CHAPTER 37

Mr. Coles has rejected most of Maggie's revisions to *Seven Brides*.

MC: How about one of the brothers is gay, so it's six brides
and one groom for seven brothers?

Mr. C: No. We've already cast the play.

MC: How about the girls from the village are a team of
rural health-care workers who find the brothers living in squalor and treat them for tuberculosis and
agoraphobia?

Mr. C: No. It's a love story. People love a love story.

MC: How about we call the "girls" from the village
"women," because otherwise it suggests that they are
minors and therefore Milly's being pregnant is evi-
dence of statutory rape?

Mr. C: No. A lot of the lyrics rhyme with girl. Nothing
rhymes with woman.

MC: How about instead of cleaning up for them, Milly

MY EYES ARE UP HERE
gives the brothers a copy of *The Life-Changing Magic of
Tidying Up: The Japanese Art of Decluttering and Organizing*
and they do it themselves?

MC: Never mind. That was Greer's suggestion.

Mr. Coles does agree that instead of kidnapping the *ladies* from
the village, it would be better if they consent to go with the brothers
to their lodge, and the whole group sneaks out of town together.

Tiny victories.

I head to the auditorium to wait for her after rehearsal. Practice today was dive and dig drills. My everything is sore, and I
could really use a shower.

I slip into the back of the auditorium as a few kids filter out.
Rehearsal is over.

Maggie is onstage with Rafael Ramos-Sikes, a very quiet junior
who is in the pit orchestra. Now he's at the piano, with Maggie
standing next to him. Everybody else is gone or on their way out.

Maggie is singing from a sheet of music, finding her way
through some lines.

I am on your side
There's nowhere else
I'd rather stand
Than right beside your side

It's not from the show. I've never heard it before. When Maggie can't get the melody or the cadence quite right, Rafa sings the line for her and then she repeats it perfectly. It's sweet, both the tune itself and the way they're working on it together.

> *And if you're never right*
> *I still won't see the other side*
> *Of any of your fights*
> *'Cuz you're the only side I'll be on*

"Is it too repetitive?" Rafa says, still playing.

"No, it's good like that. Like a circle."

"I was thinking of doing it in a round!"

He comes in behind her, overlapping sounds and words. Now I know why I've never heard it: Rafa wrote it. His voice is just a little lower, and they sound really good together.

He stares up at Maggie through his big Clark Kent glasses, not even looking at the piano or the music. I think he might have written it for her.

"Wait, is this next part the bridge? You sing the bridge," Maggie says.

> *And if you start a war or two*
> *That you will never win*
> *I'm in*

The line is too high. He cracks, but I love it, because it sounds so real. I want to clap. He and Maggie start laughing, though, and the piano trails off.

"That's it so far," he says. "It needs work."

"Maybe move it down a third," she says. "But otherwise it's great. Really."

It gets dead quiet. I am nervous. Not for me but for them. I wish I was the one on the bench and at the same time I am glad I'm not the one on the bench. This will always be my problem. I can't enjoy the not knowing.

Rafa says, "Would you maybe want to . . ." They have no idea I'm here and I'm pretty sure he wouldn't want me to be. I try to slide out of the seat onto the floor but the seat bottom flips up and squeaks.

"Greer?" Maggie calls.

Rafa turns pink under the stage lights. I feel terrible for him. I have completely messed up his pitch, and he is so shy when he's not singing.

"I'm going to wait outside," I yell too loudly, and trip over my backpack. "You guys sounded really awesome," I say on my way out the door.

She is out a minute after me, so I know Rafael didn't get a chance to say whatever it was he was going to say. She immediately starts ranting: Lizzie Barnes aka Milly wants all the girls to wear braids for the show.

"*That* is what she is spending time on: telling other people how they should do their hair."

"She wants everybody in braids?"

"Not everybody. Everybody *else*. She's not wearing braids. That's how we'll know she's special. She even suggested that the rest of us wear the same color dress, and she'd wear white or red or something to stand out."

"Seriously?"

"Yeah, but Ms. K-B told her there wasn't enough of any one kind of gingham in the costume shop, so that plan is off, thank god. But she talked Mr. Coles and the assistant into her fascist hair plan."

"If you need any help, Mena Patel is a miracle braider. And not a fascist."

"I was like, 'Do you mean like those beach braids you all got on spring break last year?' Remember that? She and what's-her-butt and the other what's-her-butt went to Playa del Carmen with her mom?"

What I remember is that they all came back with strapless beach tops that definitely violated the dress code and completely fascinated me. *How are they even staying up?!*

"She's like, 'NO, MAGGIE'"—she goes on in a piercing impression—"'You know what I mean. One or two braids MAXIMUM.'" Maggie thinks a second and says, "Do you think Mena can do those beach braids?"

I can't quite see where Maggie's going with this, but I don't want to accidentally put Mena in the middle of drama-kid drama. "I take it back. Leave poor Mena out of it. New subject: Did Rafa write that song?"

"Yeah. He's writing a whole musical. He's good, right?"

"Definitely. So he likes you?"

She sighs. "Maybe. But he's so shy around girls. He's like you."

"I'm not shy!"

"You know what I mean. You get weird. No offense," she adds. I want to be offended but I can't. "He was probably relieved you tripped over the chair."

"Technically, I tripped over my bag. If he's too shy, why don't you ask him out? Throw a guy a bone."

"I don't know. He's sweet and smart and an amazing musician. And somebody told me they saw him at the Women's March. But I can't get him to *talk*."

"Perfect! You'd do all the talking."

She slaps me on the arm. "Seriously. The other day at practice we sat there doing nothing for a half hour while Mr. Coles tried to teach Aidan Neal a step-ball-change. The only thing Rafael said the whole time was 'Are you allergic to anything?' and then he offered me a peanut butter PowerBar."

"You love peanut butter PowerBars."

"Yeah, but I'm telling you, he's a mouse. I mean, can you see us together, I'm kind of . . ."

"A lot," I say. She sighs and doesn't even try to argue.

We're at the car, and we both automatically climb in the back. "Ah, I feel like an Uber driver up here?" says Max from the driver's seat.

"You climb up there," Maggie says. She's already spread herself and her stuff out like she's on a transatlantic flight.

We're in a line of cars crawling toward the exit. I thread a leg through the opening between the seats and squeeze through, kneeing Max hard in the shoulder on the way up front. "Sorry!" I'm squatting on the seat trying to get my other leg free when the line stops short and he stomps on the brakes to avoid hitting the car in front of us. I tip over into his lap. "Sorry!" we both say this time. People behind us honk and Max puts his hand out the window to flip them off while I flail myself into my seat like an octopus climbing onto an English saddle.

The seat belt fits right between my breasts, like a mountain pass. Max seems uninterested in the fact that I was just sitting in his lap, but I am completely flustered. I cross my arms in front and slouch into the seat. Max looks sideways at me.

"Buckled up? Can we go now?"

"Yep. Thanks." I will probably still be blushing when I go to bed tonight.

CHAPTER 38

"My mom wants to know where you went for the Indian spices so she can put it in her resource binder."

"Her what?"

"The big three-ring binder she keeps with all her recommendations for her clients. Like where to leave yard waste and who the good orthodontists are."

"Why doesn't she ask my mom?"

"Are you kidding? That would be admitting that your mom knows something that my mom doesn't. It would undermine her authority."

"She has you doing her dirty work?"

"No, she's driving to all the specialty shops and ethnic grocery stores in a fifty-mile radius trying to figure it out. She doesn't know I'm asking."

Jackson grins. "What is this secret worth to you?"

"I have exactly two dollars if you're trying to blackmail me."

"That'll work. You only need seventy-five cents if you have a student ID."

"What are you talking about?"

"The bus. I'll take you to the secret spice hookup after school if you want."

The butterfly puts on a bus driver's uniform and drives the express all the way through my gastrointestinal system. I remind her that we are busy.

"I have volleyball."

"Can't you miss it? It's for the binder! You're excused if it's a family emergency."

"Emergency?"

"It's the binder!"

"It's a game."

"Today?"

"Away. St. Matt's."

"Ah. Okay."

Does he look disappointed or am I imagining that?

"Klaus! Klaus! Gooooten morgen!" Red Hair fahrvergnügens right up to us. The German teacher gives everyone German names and apparently "Clow-oos! Clow-oos!" is Jackson's. Red's wedged herself in at a forty-five-degree angle to face Jackson, so it's clear that it's not *me* she's talking to.

"Our group is going to work on the video after school. I can come by your locker and we can walk up to the media center together." She casually lays a hand on his arm, a line between us, and blinks her big Disney princess eyes at him.

I can't tell if she thinks she's his boss, because she's telling him what he's going to do, or his assistant, because she's graciously offering to help him find the media center in case after six weeks he's still getting lost. Either way, I've got to give it up for her flirtatious mastery. I'd fall for it. It would be sort of fascinating if it wasn't Jackson she was talking to.

And then Jackson makes a big slide to the right, pivoting the whole conversation so that she's not in between us anymore. "Well, Greer, since you have a game, and I've got to work on mein Gruppenprojekt, maybe we can do the other thing this weekend?" My mouth falls open. "Saturday morning?"

"Yeah," I manage. "Saturday. Sure. That could work."

Red scowls, like she hasn't realized until this point that I am capable of speaking. I'm a little surprised by it myself.

"Great! Have a good game tonight," he says, and allows himself to be tugged down the hall by the envious Fräulein.

"You too," I say automatically. "I mean thanks. I mean danke." They are too far gone to hear me.

I float into math class wondering what I just agreed to and land in front of Kurtis and Omar, who are comparing homework. "Greer! Can we see what you got for fourteen?" says Kurtis.

"Huh?"

"Did you do the homework?"

These guys have known me for ten years. Kennedy doesn't have a math team, but if it did, we'd be it. Have I ever *not* done the homework?

I pass my notebook back to them, trying to imagine what Jackson might be imagining about going to the spice place this weekend. Is it politeness because there's a secret shop that's off the grid and he would feel guilty if I got lost? Is it charity because my mother told his mother that I don't get out much? Is it because he's still kind of new and he doesn't have that many friends and I am not completely vile to be with when Max Cleave and the baseball team are busy? Or is it because he actually wants to do something with me?

No, just a friend thing. I'm Re-Lo Jr.! Not threatening. Friendly like a sister. A sister who is not a klepto elf.

But remember when he brought that muffin?

Kurtis and Omar are bickering behind me. They have gotten different answers on number fourteen. Whenever this happens, they check to see who got the same thing as me. "Hey, Greer!"

The problem is that all three of us have different answers this time, so there's no majority consensus.

I pull my notebook back and walk them through it. Kurtis is off from the beginning. Omar has the right idea but one of his calculations is wrong, which messes him up for all the steps afterward. Omar's handwriting is awful, so most of what he gets wrong is because he can't read what he did before. These guys trust me, though. I'm the Jessa here.

Ms. T is giving the speech she always gives before she returns a test. She knows she is dealing with a bunch of fragile smart kids. If you have a class where 100 percent of the students have been getting As in math for 80 percent of their lives, and then you set the curve so that 70 percent of them will get a B or less, you've got 90 percent of your class freaking out all the time. She explains the weighted grading and the retake policy for the hundredth time this quarter. The longer and slower she talks, the more people did badly on the test. Judging by her eulogy today, there will probably be tears.

Even though Asher Moonpie and Anitha Das get straight As,

they look like they're going to be sick before they get their tests back. I don't freak out about these things. It's not just that I know what I'm doing. It's that I know that I know what I'm doing. In math.

I freak out about legitimately scary things. Like going to shop for Indian spices with a polite and non-maniacal fellow student.

There are sighs of relief from some and tiny embarrassed gasps from others as Ms. Tanner walks the papers around. Anitha, whose eyes were watery until the moment she grabbed the paper out of Ms. T's hand, smiles at her test. She did well, as always, and is for some reason surprised, as always. Asher looks kind of sick. He's staring at the second page and scratching one spot on his head very hard. He probably got one wrong. Kurtis and Omar are handing their papers back and forth, so I'm guessing they both did all right. I know the groaning sound that Kurtis makes if he bombs a test, and I know that if Omar bombs, Kurtis tries to cheer him up.

I get a 38 out of 35. That's not bad math; it's the bonus questions. Ms. T gives everyone a minute to come down off their high or pull themselves up from the pit of despair before she starts in on homework review.

Once we dive into the homework, I have the entire period to dwell on the spice store. Until:

"Greer!" Kyle Tuck snorts as the bell sends us packing. "Could you help me with this problem?" His goony friends are standing behind him laughing through their nostrils. Kyle hands me a scrawled equation on a half sheet of notebook paper:

$$[arctan\ (1) \times 1{,}290] - 2(4!)$$

I can guess what he's trying to do, and let my hair fall in front of my face so they won't see my cheeks turn red. I'm more mad at myself than at them for that. I've promised myself I won't let them get to me, but they always do anyway. I go from the ultra-confident A student to the ultra-awkward H cup in one second flat.

Not flat.

Never flat.

I set down my backpack to edit his scrawl. "But, um, don't you want to do it on the calculator?" Kyle is disappointed that I am doing the work with a pencil, because the joke only works if it's on a calculator.

But the joke won't work on the calculator, either, because he's done it wrong. His equation equals 58,002, or ZOO,BS.

I change the last part to 7(3!) and hand back the corrected problem. That will get them the answer they want. I can't make them understand how horrible they are, but at least I can prove that I am smarter than they are.

"I think this is what you were going for. And you have to use degrees instead of radians." On my way out, I add, "How did you guys even make it into this math class?" I don't wait for them to input the problem into their calculators so they can finally see some BOO,BS.

CHAPTER 39

"Take choir. It's easy." Kate Wood is on her knees, leaning over the back of her seat to talk to me and Jess.

"I'm not really a singer," Jessa says.

"Doesn't matter. They don't grade you on your singing. They grade you on participation."

We're trying to decide what Jessa should take next year to get her second fine arts credit. It can be performing arts or visual arts or, in a very strange loophole, robotics. I already took ceramics freshman year, and Maggie wants me to do printmaking with her second semester. Maybe I should talk her into sewing with Ms. K-B—except that that class is called Fashion and Design, and Maggie thinks the "fashion industry exists to commodify women's insecurities about themselves." She might be right, but what if I could sew a shirt that fit? Maybe I could make Quin a pair of longer pants.

"Do you think you have to be good at drawing to take studio art?"

"Seriously, Jess, you don't have to *do* anything in choir. Just show up and sing. It's the best." Kate braids her hair as she talks, using an elbow for balance when the bus bangs over a pothole. The bus magnifies every bump and dip, and I feel every one of them in my nipples like a fresh bruise.

According to the tracking app on my phone, it's T-minus one day till my period and Maude and Mavis are cranky and sore. I had to carry my backpack from the locker loop this morning because they didn't like the straps rubbing against them. I check the time and it's been three hours and thirty-nine minutes since my last dose of ibu. Close enough. I want it to kick in before we get to St. Matt's Prep, because Coach will have us doing pregame drills the second we hit the gym. I dig the little bottle of Advil from my bag and shake two into my palm, think about it a second, and add one more. Long-term liver damage cannot possibly hurt like short-term period boobs.

"What's wrong?" Jessa asks.

What's wrong? I've hung ten pounds of hot, swollen breast tissue off a skeletal system designed to carry a couple of cotton balls and have been bouncing around on what feels like an unpaved road through a Central American jungle for the last hour, all while processing a surge of undiluted estrogen. I'm a leeeeetle sore.

"Shoulder?" Jess assumes.

"Yeah," I say, and rub my right shoulder. It's not a lie. That hurts, too. We worked on hitting and serving the whole practice yesterday, and everybody's shoulders are sore. I could tell Jess what hurts worse, but Kate's right there, and nobody would have any advice for me, anyway, so I'd rather let them think I'm just hurting in the way everyone else is.

"Move up by Kate," Jess says, nudging me out of the seat. I slide in next to Kate. Jess leans forward over the back of my seat, and digs her thumbs into my shoulder, massaging the stiff muscles that run all the way from the side of my neck down to the edge of my armpit. At first it makes me tense up even more. I'm not used to people touching me. Even the little hugs and taps in the games were surprising at first. But Jess finds the tightest knots I wasn't even aware of, presses and holds hard. It takes my breath away.

"We should tape her," Kate declares. She's finished her braids, and they're totally uneven. I know she's got multiple rolls of athletic tape in at least three different colors in her bag. Kate and her sister are the Tape Queens. She will mummify your knees or web all your fingers if you let her. I've never let her, but maybe today I will. Maybe if it works on my shoulder she can tape up my breasts, too.

"Heya! I'm next over here!" calls Sylvie to Jess. "Captains can't play favorites."

"I'll get to you in a minute, Soop."

I thank Jess and send her to Sylvie, who takes one arm out of her hoodie to give Jess access to her sore spots. I think Sylvie would whip off her whole shirt if the bus wasn't so cold.

My shoulder hurts more than it did before Jess started rubbing it, but differently. It's almost like it pulses. It moves. Like that one part of me has woken up. And at least it's distracting me from my boobs.

"Did that help at all?"

"Totally," I say. And I mean it. I don't know how, but I know it has.

CHAPTER 40

Jackson is ready with a pocketful of quarters when the bus pulls up. There are only a handful of other riders so far, and when I choose a seat facing the middle of the bus, he sits directly across from me. It's no problem to talk at school, when there are a million people around and there's only a few minutes to fill, or even at his house when our families could pop in at any minute. Here on a city bus, though, when we are here together by our own volition, it makes it way harder to think of things to say.

The surly silence of the other passengers doesn't help. If only they were volleyball players filling the seats we could talk about tape or braids or D3 colleges.

"Did you do anything fun last night?" Jackson finally ventures.

"Not really. I watched some stuff and then I fell asleep reading." This is the edited version of my night, but I don't want to elaborate. Really I took an extra-long shower after volleyball, shaved my legs, tried on a few tops from the vault in case my boobs shrunk in the shower (they hadn't), put on PJs, remembered Mom had a cute scarf that might make one of the shirts work (it didn't), ate dinner, watched Food Network with Dad, went to my room and watched a video of a breast surgery, watched some Amy Schumer clips to get the surgery out of my mind, and fell asleep reading an article about Maryam Mirzakhani. "How about you?"

A woman steers a stroller down the aisle with one hand. There's a baby in the seat, and a toddler trooping alongside. Jackson gets up so she can position herself and her kids together on that side of the bus. He sits down next to me.

"Thank you," says the tired mom across the aisle. She smiles at me, like I deserve credit for Jackson being a nice guy.

The bus starts up again. There's more chatter now, plus the toddler across the way watching a video on his mom's phone, so I have to lean in to hear him. His hair smells orangey.

"I took Quin ice-skating."

"At Ice Castle?"

"If that's the one in the binder."

"Was it fun?" It seems sweet but weird that Jackson would have agreed to it. He must have been more bored than I was.

"Not really."

The bus bumps along for a minute before he speaks again.

"Actually, it was kind of a disaster."

"What happened?" I'm expecting a funny story. Quin assaulted the Zamboni driver. Disney on Ice was rehearsing. He tried a triple lutz and only made a double.

"There was a birthday party there. Some kid from her school. She knew some of them were going skating last night—turns out that's why she wanted to go—but she didn't know it was a birthday party. Once she realized they were all there together she bolted."

Not a funny story. A sad one. I feel awful for the poor kid. It's terrible to be alone; it's worse to be reminded that you're alone.

"I told her to just go up and say hi," Jackson says. "They were having cake. I'm sure they would have offered her a piece."

I look at him in disbelief. "Are you serious?"

"Yeah. Why not? What's the worst thing that could happen?"

"They could reject her? They could laugh at her? They could make her feel worse?"

He's not buying it. "She says she doesn't have any friends, and there were a bunch of girls from her school right there."

"You really have no idea, do you?" I shake my head at him. "She's not like you. Most of us aren't. Moving all the time's not easy for her."

He blinks and scrunches his forehead, totally surprised. "When did I ever say it was easy?" He searches my face, but only for a second, because the bus heaves to a stop. "Scheisse! This is our stop."

CHAPTER 41

"*Schnucks*? What the hell is Schnucks?"

"I think you mean 'what the schnuck is Schnucks.' It's a supermarket."

Obviously. The bus pulls away in a cloud of hot fumes, and the other passengers descend into an oceanic parking lot. Huge SUVs, medium-size minivans, and tiny electric cars are pulling in and out of spots with dozens of near misses every second, like fish without a school. People are going in empty handed and coming out laden with bags that say, unbelievably, Schnucks. The logo is red and slanty and looks as much like it would be printed on the side of Tyler's hockey skates as a big brick grocery store.

"I think this used to be a Family Food Mart." You can barely make out the outline of the FFM, darker on the brick storefront.

"Maybe, but it's a Schnucks now."

"Is that better than Family Food Mart?"

"Probably not. It's just a supermarket."

"Wait. There's no secret exotic spice shop?"

"If it's not in the binder, I don't think it exists."

"Does this one have something the other ones don't?"

"It has a pretty big Mexican food section."

"You were getting Indian spices."

"Yeah, you can't find that stuff around here. My dad substituted tamarind paste, which is in a lot of Mexican foods."

I don't even know what to say. I thought we were going to some cool little import shop, with big jars of good-smelling ingredients and boxes of mysterious dried foods and an ancient man behind the counter offering us Turkish delight. And a travel blogger to post an adorable candid shot of Jackson feeding it to me on Instagram. But for some reason he's led me to a giant supermarket, which is not adorable at all, and which would make a terrible photo for Instagram.

"It was still good, wasn't it? Or could you taste the tamarind and you knew that something was off?" Jackson is putting on his best embarrassed face. "Tyler could probably taste the difference." He hangs his head like a guilty dog who's been caught chewing up the tamarind. I want to punch him. Lightly. In a lingering way. As in I just really want to touch him.

"You know there are like ten supermarkets that are closer than this one? Plus several Mexican markets? I'm sure they're in the binder."

He shrugs. "My mom grew up in St. Louis. They have a million Schnuckses. Mom was excited to find one up here. You know they call their coupons Schnupons?"

"Of course they do." We stand there admiring the Schnupermarket, and I wonder if this entire outing was a joke. If it was, it's still nice that he'd spend the morning on a joke for me, I guess.

But it's weird. I sort of expected Jackson to have more of a plan than this. Finally, I say, "Did you want to go in?"

"Into Schnucks?"

"Yeah? We came all this way?"

"Oh. Right. I didn't bring you here for that. Unless you need to pick up some eggs or something. I brought you here because of this." He turns me around to look across the street at a small, low building with big windows and a mural of the solar system painted on the side.

Cupernicus Coffee. It's a coffee shop named (kinda) after an astronomer.

"I thought you'd appreciate it." He takes my hand (!) and pulls me across the street. "They have unbelievable caramel rolls, too. Come on."

Oh my schnucking god.

CHAPTER 42

We sit on opposite sides of a long booth and stretch out our legs like we're on parallel couches with a table between us. We take turns unwinding the spiral of the plate-size caramel roll and tearing off pieces. He's got a chai; I've got hot chocolate. The mugs are the extra-big round kind, almost like soup bowls, and they've got the shop's logo on them: a coffee cup with little icons (car, dog, briefcase) orbiting around it. The girl at the counter has the same picture on her tee, with the words I BELIEVE IN COFFEOCENTRISM.

The warm spiciness coming off Jackson's tea smells like Christmas. He's telling me about how baseball has no off-season for Max Cleave, and since he's captain, there's no off-season for any of the other guys, either.

I know some of this from Maggie, but it's funny to hear Jackson describe it. The baseball kids kind of adopted him. He goes to the batting cages and works out with them, but I don't think they ever do anything together that's not baseball related. It's like Jackson is playing the part of a baseball player, because that's what this school needs him to be. If he was somewhere else, maybe he'd play lacrosse. Or join debate.

But Max Cleave would be who he is even if you dropped him in the middle of the ocean—or some country that doesn't play baseball. He has built his identity around one thing. (I guess I kind of have, too, but mostly because I don't want it to be about two things.)

"Does he think he's going to get drafted by the Yankees or something?"

"You did not just say that."

"Say what?"

"Yankees."

"Why not?"

"Because my dad is from Boston." I look at him blankly. "And the Red Sox and the Yankees hate each other?"

"My dad is from New York. I don't think he hates the Red Sox."

"He's supposed to hate the Red Sox."

"I'll let him know. Is there anybody else he should hate?"

"Well, ideally he'd hate the Yankees."

"I'll work on getting him to hate more things, but he's a pretty friendly guy. What team are we supposed to like?"

"Cubs!" The "duh" is implied.

"You moved here like ten seconds ago, and you're already a Cubs fan?"

Jackson shrugs.

"Does Max want to play for the Cubs? Or some other not-hateful team? Does he think he's going to be a professional baseball player?"

"Nah. He's good but that's a whole other level. He'll probably want a job where he gets to work out a lot, though."

"Gym teacher?"

"Personal trainer?"

"Firefighter?"

"Navy Seal?"

"He could be a model."

Jackson lifts his eyebrows, curious, and I wish I hadn't said it. I figured Max being attractive was a given. A fact. I wouldn't be surprised if half the teachers had his senior portrait in their cubbies. Now it looks like I'm into Maggie's brother. "I mean, everybody likes *Max*."

"Ah." He nods.

"No, I mean, not me. He's just Maggie's brother."

"Right." He doesn't buy it.

"I mean, I've known him since third grade. When their parents took them out of Catholic school. He'd pitch pine cones to us, and we'd try to hit them with our American Girl dolls. He's like a brother to me." This is not entirely true, because if I accidentally fell into Tyler's lap on the way home from practice, I'd try to fart on him, not have a heart attack.

"He's the hot older brother. Got it."

I roll my eyes and pick up some pecans that have fallen off our roll.

"So if you're not into Max Cleave, is there anybody you are into?" Jackson says.

He's looking right at me, not blinking. Maybe not breathing. Is this Jackson nervous? Does Jackson even get nervous?

The butterfly is having a conniption. *Now!* she says. *Say something! Carpe the goddamned diem!*

What she wants me to say is:

You, obviously. Only you. I can't wait to get to school in the morning to see if you're waiting for me outside of math. I look for you in lunch, just to check you're still there. When you grabbed my hand to cross the street, I felt it in my feet. I know if I kissed you right now you'd taste like chai and caramel rolls.

But I also know that if I did, one day soon you'd hold my hips and you'd touch my hair and then you'd slide your hand up my back and feel the four steel hooks that hold my bra together. And you'd be as polite as you could be and make a joke about a fortress and I'd laugh, but Maude and Mavis— they have names, I named them—would be so sweaty already that I'd want to die instead of let you near. I would be embarrassed, and you don't think you would be but you would be too. And then we couldn't just joke around in the hallway or talk about Quinlan or trophies or wistful poetry because that moment would always be there, and I would rather have those minutes with you before math every day than anything or anyone else.

"I'm pretty focused on school right now."

"Right. Of course," he says, and looks down into his chai.

I know and I don't know and I don't want to know that it wasn't the thing I was supposed to say. Like there was a turn in the path that maybe we could have taken, but I don't know where that one goes and I don't know if there's a way back if it goes nowhere.

The butterfly can't even stand to look at me anymore.

Jackson can't either.

"So do you want to know what I was really doing last night?" I finally say. I let it sit there a minute, a tiny tease, ready to throw myself under the bus. "I watched three straight hours of baking shows with my dad."

He looks up and smiles. "Seriously?"

"Eric Walsh loves baking shows. He doesn't love baking, but he absolutely loves baking shows."

"I wouldn't have guessed that."

"He keeps it on the DL. But this is the best time of year for it—there's a Christmas cookie competition and a gingerbread house one—"

"Isn't your dad Jewish?"

"Not when it comes to Christmas bake-offs."

We find our way back from the precipice to easy conversation, the kind you can have when it's clear you're not on a date, which I've just made sure we're not.

We talk about which ages we were when we read each Harry Potter, our parents' rules for phones, some of the million different places he's lived and what's weird about each one (once he lived in Tennessee and his teacher called the Civil War the War of Northern Aggression).

He tells me that Quinlan hasn't been lashing out as much but that she seems almost too quiet. I'm about to ask if he thinks she's planning a terrorist attack, but I'm glad I don't because he says, "Do you think somebody can be depressed in third grade?" and I realize he's actually worried about her. And for the record, yes, I do think somebody can be depressed in third grade.

I'm not sure if I blew a chance at something or if there wasn't any chance anyway, but if it's ever only this, I hope I can convince myself it's enough.

CHAPTER 43

Maggie didn't show up to school this morning. I get the story from Amara and Keely, two other brides, about dress rehearsal last night.

Apparently, everything was going just fine—or as fine as it could, since five of the brothers can't dance and four of them can't sing either. But everybody was in costume for the first time, and it made it all seem better.

Until the first scene that Maggie and the other girls are in. They came out, one after another, in their gingham dresses and braids (thank you, Lizzie Barnes). Even Keely, whose mousy hair is pretty short, managed to tuck it into little French braids, glued down with a can of hairspray. Lizzie's own hair grew six inches longer and three shades lighter overnight, thanks to several hundred dollars' worth of extensions, according to the girls. And then Maggie appeared, stage left. With a ponytail straight out of the top of her head like a whale spout.

"CUT!" yelled Lizzie. "CUUUUUUUTTTTTTT!" The cast was confused and the pit orchestra went on for several measures before they realized that no one was singing anymore.

A couple of the boys thought it was funny, but the rest of the cast was mad. They were tired and just wanted to get through the rehearsal.

There was a mini-conference with Mr. Coles and the other directors, Maggie, and Lizzie. Maggie stomped off and came back a few minutes later in the middle of the next number wearing two acceptable braids. She didn't say anything to anybody after rehearsal, just left the second it was over.

Now Amara, Keely, and a few of the other girls are freaking out because Maggie hasn't shown up to school and tonight is opening night.

"Oh no. Does Lizzie have to sing all her own lines if Maggie doesn't show?" says Amara.

If Amara is legitimately worried, Keely is just pissed. "None of us like Lizzie, but come on. Maggie's being really stubborn."

I snort at this, because if they think Maggie is being really stubborn now, they don't know Maggie. Really stubborn for Maggie is taking all the ornaments off the Christmas tree every night because her parents bought a Scotch pine instead of a Douglas fir, and that was when she was only six years old. Wearing a ponytail on top of her head because everybody wants her in braids is nothing.

I text Maggie and she responds immediately.

> on the wya
> opps
> way
> oops

"She's coming," I tell them. "Probably just slept in."

Lunch is almost over when Maggie finally shows up. She is striding through a sea of students. She is carrying a pile of books. She is smirking. She is already wearing braids, as required.

Except that they are neon-green braids.

CHAPTER 44

There is not a color in the spectrum that someone at Kennedy hasn't tried in their hair, sometimes all at the same time, so the bright greenness of Maggie's head isn't what draws attention. It's more the gasping of the musical kids that the rest of the lunch period responds to.

"Is she going to wear it like that for the play?" Jackson has appeared behind me. I'm too focused on watching Maggie move through the crowd—which looks evenly split between admirers and people who think she's gone too far—to think about the fact that he is so close that if I leaned back five degrees my back would be pressed against his chest.

Okay, obviously I am still able to think about that at the same time I am watching Maggie.

"It doesn't look like the kind that washes out," I say. "To get hair that dark to turn into hair that green you have to bleach it first."

Jackson lets out a low breath. "Maggie commits."

I nod. "Yeah. She does."

I don't get a chance to talk to Maggie and tell her what I think, which is "Really, Mags? You know this is going to cause you more problems than it solves" because the bell rings and people start to drift.

"See you later," I say, but Jackson stops me.

"Are you going to the play tonight?"

"Yeah, of course."

"Are you going *with* anyone?"

Technically, the answer is yes, I am going with my mom, Tyler, and the empty seat that is where my dad would be if he didn't have to go to San Francisco at the last minute. "Well, with my family, but we've got an extra ticket. Do you want to go? I mean, if you're not already meeting people or whatever. You probably are."

I've seen the kid's smile before. A hundred times in real life, a thousand times in dream life. But this time it is so easy and happy it's like I've never seen it before. And it is beautiful. He must have had a top-notch orthodontist in Cleveland. Binder-worthy dentistry.

"I'd love to," he says.

The butterfly is beaming, giving me a proud thumbs-up, but I tell her to chill out. She wants this to mean more than it does. It's not a date—it's just the school play and we have an extra ticket. She doesn't believe me, though.

CHAPTER 45

I basically agree with Maggie on most of the things she takes a stand on, but I never think it's worth the fight. She always does. It's not that I avoid conflict—I fight with Tyler all the time—it's more like I avoid being uncomfortable when I can. Socially, physically, mentally, whatever. I take the path that keeps me (and Maude and Mavis) under the radar.

So even though everyone is coming up to me to say things like "What's going to happen now?" and "Why does your friend have to be such a bitch?" I am trying to stay out of it. It was probably overboard to dye her hair green to piss off the lead of the school musical, but it's Maggie, and I love Maggie no matter what. But I also don't want to get involved.

Right after school I'm on my way to practice when I see Mr. and Mrs. Barnes march through the front doors with Lizzie. Pat Moss, our principal, greets them with a look of solidarity and outrage. They all rush off together like they're racing up the courthouse steps in a *Law & Order* episode.

Maggie is tough, but she is outnumbered.

I find her mother's number in my cell.

"Mrs. Cleave? It's Greer."

"Hey, Greer. What's up?"

"You know about Maggie's hair, right?"

"The green? Oh yes. It was quite a process."

"Well, I think she's kind of in trouble for it."

"Why else would she do it?" She sighs.

"People are saying they might kick her out of the play."

"I'm sure Maggie can handle Mr. Coles."

"Right, but it's not just him. It's Dr. Moss. And Lizzie Barnes's parents."

"The Barneses? At school?"

"Yeah. And they look pretty mad."

"Those people are the worst." She practically growls, and it sounds a lot like Maggie, both angry and excited. She runs an organization that protects rivers and lakes from environmental damage. She has to like to fight. She yells something to someone in her office and comes back to me. "I'm on my way. Thanks, Greer."

She clicks off and Jessa speeds past me.

"Walsh! Let's get moving! Practice starts in four minutes."

I don't move. I have to go to practice, but I don't want to leave Maggie alone if the Kennedy High School PTA is coming for her.

Jessa stops. "Walsh? You coming?"

"Yeah, but something's up with Maggie."

"Like about the green-hair thing?"

"You heard?"

"Everybody heard."

"I think they're going to try to kick her out of the play." I assume that Jessa will tell me to get to practice—after all, it's not our problem; it's just a musical, not VOLLEYBALL—but I'm wrong.

"They can't do that. She's been practicing all season." I don't think they call it a "season," but she gets the point.

"Lizzie Barnes just showed up with her parents."

Jessa cringes. "They go to my church. They are nasty."

This does not make me feel better.

"Suprenant! SOOOOP!" she screams across the atrium. Sylvie bounces our way. "Tell Coach that me and Walsh will be there late. We've gotta do something." Sylvie heads off to the gym and Jessa turns to me like she's been waiting for me all day. "Well? Let's go."

"Where are we going?"

She takes off toward the auditorium, where the cast is having a final run-through. It's hard to keep up with her. "To Cleave, duh. She's your best friend, right? We can't leave her to the Barneses."

And even though it's completely corny, I can't help feeling a rush. The idea that Jessa and me and Maggie and maybe Nasrah and Amara and Sylvie Suprenant and who knows who else are maybe tied together in some way? It feels pretty good. Like even if there's not an official roster, maybe we're all some kind of team.

I stand up a tiny bit straighter and jog behind Jessa toward the auditorium. Maude and Mavis bounce along, excited. Even though they blew the tryouts, they want to be part of this team, too.

CHAPTER 46

There was a really hot day in the middle of the summer when Mom was supposed to drive us to the Art Institute to see an exhibition of photos and drawings by people living in the Lagos slums. Maggie read about it and was angry because all the credit went to the artist who organized it, and all the slum residents got were out-of-date digital cameras they couldn't even charge. I know it seems like in that case we would *not* go to the exhibit, but we'd been bored for weeks and it seemed like a good excuse to get Mom to drop us in the city while she met with some big company that sends her a lot of clients.

But Mom's meeting was cancelled, and she didn't think Maggie and me scoffing at an art exhibition was enough of a reason to drive into Chicago.

So we are bored and annoyed and hot, sitting on the front steps with drippy Popsicles, paging through Mom's re-lo binder.

"How can your mom recommend Cold Stone Creamery?!"

"Um, because it's delicious? And you can mash in candy bars?"

"Yeah, but it's a chain. She should be recommending small businesses."

"Maggie, we went to Cold Stone last Thursday. You loved it."

"That's only because it was next to the theater."

We flip through to the section on Salons and Personal Services. I recognize the names of almost everyone who has ever cut my hair. She also has lists for nails, massages, facials, waxing, and laser hair removal. For some reason, Lasik eye surgery is in this section, too.

"I would never wax," Maggie says.

"Of course not. You don't even shave them."

Maggie slurps a drip from the back of her hand. "Them?"

"Your legs?"

She bumps her leg, which is in full hairy glory, into my stubbles. "I didn't mean legs. Of course not legs. I meant my vajayjay."

We both laugh, because Maggie is constantly trying out different vocabulary since her brother complained that she used the word *vagina* thirty-one times in one day. *Vajayjay* does not sound right coming from Maggie at all. I tell her so.

"Cootch?" she tries. "Hoo-haw?"

"Can we just say 'bikini area'?"

Maggie frowns at this. "Fine. I would never let anybody do that to my 'bikini area.' Imagine this," and here she reaches over and yanks a few hairs at the back of my neck, "but down there, all at once, by a stranger, with hot wax."

"Ow!" I don't want to imagine it, but I do. "How hot is the wax?" I'm thinking if it's like a bath, that part's not so bad.

"Never mind the wax. It's the ripping. I bet there's a video." In a matter of seconds she finds a video of a full Hollywood wax. We both jump when they tear the first strip off. "See what I mean? That's why I just shave."

"Wait, you shave there?" I've never paid attention to my pubic hair. It just roams wild, like one of those curly wigs Irish dancers wear. I guess if you assume no one is ever going to see you without a gigantic sweatshirt on, you don't really think about how you present naked. "You don't even shave your legs! What about not conforming to misogynistic dogma of modern beauty or whatever?"

"Yeah, but that's leg hair. I'm talking about pube hair. I'm not going to let it just bush out around my swim bottoms." She makes an exploding motion with her hands, like if she left it unrestrained, we'd be fighting a puffy pube ball.

I have a photo on my desk of us at Oak Street Beach in about fifth grade, and now all I can picture is little Maggie in that suit—a one-piece with red, white, and blue anchors—with a big, mangy mushroom cloud of hair poking out the sides. I laugh out loud.

Maggie gasps like she's just realized something amazing. "We should call Tahlia! Her health club has huge pool!" I stop laughing and swallow hard. "Want to go swimming?"

Swimming?

No, Maggie, I don't want to swim, because if I walked out onto the pool deck, half the people would lean to their friends and make the same joke about buoyancy.

I don't want to swim, because no matter how slowly I walked, every step would make my boobs shake like Godzilla stomping through a flea market.

Because I can't flip over to tan my back like the rest of you because I can't lie on my stomach. And because I'd need to do something about all these loose pubes, now that you've got me thinking about them.

I don't want to swim because as enormous as Maude is, Mavis is a little bit bigger.

I don't want to swim. Because I can't stand people thinking my body is there for their amusement. Because they're not interested in the fact that my feet are completely average size or that standardized tests are fun for me or that I'm really not nice to Tyler or that my parents named me according to Jewish tradition even though they don't believe in anything except matzo balls or that I might be hot, bored, and sweaty and just want to get in the pool like everybody else or that under all this breast tissue, which by the way is denser than fat and therefore not particularly good for buoyancy, is an actual beating human heart.

No, Maggie, I don't want to swim because I do not own a swimsuit anymore.

"No," I say. "I have my period." It is a lie.

Maggie makes a disappointed sound. I don't know if she remembers that I always get my period right after hers. I don't know if she notices that I am biting my lip.

I don't know if she realizes that even if I had a private pool all to myself, I feel so stupid and ugly I probably wouldn't swim anyway.

But I think maybe she does. And I think maybe she knows that I'm not ready to talk about it.

We stay there for a few minutes, shifting and sweaty. Finally, Maggie says, "Oh! You know what we should do? Have you heard of *In the Mind of a Maniac*? It's about psychopaths and serial killers. Let's see if we can stream it."

She wipes the Popsicle drips off the cover of Mom's binder with her arm, and I follow her into the air-conditioning to watch three seasons in seventy-two hours. I am grateful for the millionth time in my life for Maggie Cleave.

CHAPTER 47

A dozen kids are onstage shifting awkwardly while the tech crew crawls around their legs sticking colored bits of tape on the floor. Everybody pretends not to notice the whispery conference between Maggie, Lizzie, Mr. Coles, Dr. Moss, and the Barneses in the center aisle. Maggie's hair glows like something from a Dr. Seuss book.

The assistant director, a French teacher, says, "Okay, lez try like zis. Juss a few bars. Zis should geev Aidan a little more space so he doesn't step on anybody."

It's hard to hear what's happening over the commotion on-stage, but you can tell they are not letting Maggie talk. Mrs. Barnes is tittering away, her head wagging back and forth like an angry bobblehead. Maggie's cheeks are turning red.

Jessa says, "Come on," and marches down the aisle to stand with her arms folded right behind them.

Maggie gives us a tiny grateful smile.

I think of how many times I've sat on the sidelines, waiting for Maggie to talk herself into or out of trouble. This is the first time I realize how much it means to her to have me standing there.

Dr. Moss is saying how selfish it is for one student to try to take all the attention away from the others who have worked so hard. Maggie finally blurts, "That's exactly my point!"

"You admit you're just trying to steal all the attention?" says Mr. Barnes, like he can't believe the defendant has just confessed in front of the judge.

"No! My point is that it's not the Lizzie Barnes Show, so I don't know why everyone is acting like it is."

"Right! It's a team!" pipes in Jessa. All heads turn to look at us. I was assuming we were just here as silent extras, but Jess is in it.

"Jessa, what are you doing here?" Dr. Moss puts a hand on her hip.

"We came for Cleave. It's five against one."

"Oh, oh, I'm not for or against anybody!" says Mr. Coles, waving his hands around like he wants to fan away the idea that he's on one side or the other. The seven brothers in the play would have called him yella-bellied or lily-livered. Me too.

Dance practice is falling apart because everyone is trying to listen to the trial down below. The assistant director stops them and the orchestra cuts out at *exactly* the right moment for everyone to hear Lizzie's mom say, "But Lizzie *should* get more attention. She's the *star.*"

From stage, Aidan Neal says, "Excuse me?"

Mr. Coles claps his hands and rushes in front of the stage. "That's looking good, dancers. Big night tonight. Let's see everybody back here by six thirty, on the nose!"

The cast filters out, glad to be released even if the offstage drama is heating up.

Two of Lizzie's friends walk by Jessa and me. One says, "See, all the lesbians like to stick together."

Jessa, unfazed, says, "GSA meetings are every other Thursday before school. All are welcome." I don't know if Jessa is the G or the S, but she is absolutely the A. I slide a little closer to her.

The principal is ready to rule. "Maggie, whatever concerns you have should have been brought to the directors in a mature way—"

"I did! I—"

"Don't interrupt. You are not going to ruin this production for the rest of the students who have been working so hard. Not everyone can be the lead, and most students are happy with whatever part they have. Since you can't seem to understand that, you're going to sit this one out."

"ARE YOU CRAZY?"

Everyone, including me, is surprised to hear my voice. I guess I'm in it now, too.

Pat Moss turns to me like I'm a mouse that's just challenged a bobcat to a fight.

Like a mouse that realizes that everyone else in the auditorium has just stopped what they are doing to see how this turns out. In other words, to watch the mouse get swallowed whole. So much for staying under the radar.

"They can't even do the play without Maggie." Everyone is staring at me, which is not exactly comfortable. But Maggie looks like she's just discovered her best friend is secretly Spider-Man, so I keep going. "She sings half of Lizzie's parts because Lizzie can't hit anything below a G. If you take her out of the play, it's going to look bad for everybody. Including Lizzie."

Lizzie shouts, "Shut up, Greta!" Maggie and Jessa laugh out loud, which makes Principal Moss and the Barneses even angrier.

Dr. Moss says, "This has nothing to do with you two. Out of the auditorium. NOW. Or I will have Coach Reinhold bench you both for the season." We stand there, waiting for Maggie's okay. She nods and mouths, *Love you.*

"We were just on our way to practice," says Jess, as we back up the aisle. "You should come to a game sometime, Dr. Moss."

My phone buzzes and I peek at the text. "Maggie, your mom is parking. She'll be here in a minute."

"Yeah, don't say anything without your lawyer present," adds Jess.

"Bridget Cleave is on campus?" Moss is the one who looks scared now. I wish I could stay to watch, but there are sprints to hell to do in the gym.

Rafael Ramos-Sikes is waiting and watching from the back of the auditorium, so quiet we almost don't notice him, until he high-fives us on the way out.

Jessa and I will have to do extra sets of sprints for being late, but it's worth it. I would sprint to hell and back for Maggie. Or for Jess.

CHAPTER 48

Maggie is back in the play!

There's a long video message waiting for me when practice is over. Her mom showed up right after Jessa and I left. Maggie's favorite lines from her mom:

To Mr. Coles: "How can you be a director if you can't even express an opinion about anything? Isn't that your freaking job?"

To Mrs. Barnes, when she said that green hair wasn't "period" for the 1850s: "Oh, and I suppose Lizzie's balayage is?" (Sylvie, who was watching over my shoulder in the locker room, had to explain that it's a fancy hair-highlighting technique. Jessa and I were clueless.)

To everyone: "See, this is why I never wanted to do drama in high school. Everybody's so freaking EMOTIONAL about everything."

At this point, the verdict was that Maggie would perform, but that she would wear a bonnet over her green braids. Even Maggie realizes a bonnet is the best deal she's going to get, but her mom wasn't quite done.

To Pat Moss: "And in the future, if my daughter has an issue at school, I expect that you'll include me in the conversation, not some other student's parents. Or maybe the Family Educational Rights and Privacy Act means nothing to you?" Leave it to Maggie's mom to make our principal squirm.

So, Maggie's back in the play, and once Coach heard we were arguing with Dr. Moss, Jessa and I only had to do a few extra sprints. It's turned out to be a pretty good day. Everyone told me my serve looked less pathetic; Mr. Feiler says I'm far enough ahead in APUSH I can skip the next group assignment; I found my big blue cardigan in the winter bin, which will save my mother from criticizing my sweatshirt; and what was that other thing? Hmmm, was there one other thing to be glad about today?

Oh yeah. I don't have to sit next to Tyler at the musical.

Because I am going to sit next to Jackson.

It's like my freaking birthday.

σ

On the way back to school, I say super casually, "Oh, I told Jackson Oates—you know, your client's son?—that I'd sit with him tonight. He didn't have anyone else to go with." I'm trying to make it sound like I enjoy helping new folks settle in. Just like she's raised me.

"That's nice of you," says Mom, sort of suspiciously. "He can have Dad's ticket."

I am prepared for this. "Right. That's what I was thinking. But it might be better if we don't actually sit by you. Just so he can meet more people. More kid people."

She looks at me sideways. "Mmm. Of course. Good idea." I don't care what she thinks as long as we don't have to talk about it.

"Why do I have to go to this?" In the back seat, Tyler seems to be working very hard on creating a duct-tape ball. He has informed me that it must be very even and very, very tight or it won't work right. I wonder how you know if a duct-tape ball "works right."

"We're going because we like to support the arts," Mom says. What she really means is "We're going because I like to see other parents to compare children."

σ

Turns out Melinda Oates and Quinlan have also decided they wish to support the arts. Jackson sees me see them and gives a big shrug. Mom spots seats near someone she thinks Melinda should meet. Jackson and I decide to head to the other side of the auditorium where more of the underclassmen are.

"Jackson wants to sit by his new friends," Mrs. Oates tells Quin.

"But Greer can still sit with us," she says.

We take off before there's a scene. Tyler glances back at me like I've left him to the bears, which might be true in the case of Quinlan and my mom, but Mrs. Oates seems pretty nice.

We spot an open pair of seats down in front, but on the way, we hear, "Klaus! KLAUS!" German-class girl is furiously waving. I follow Jackson like a straggling sheep. "I got you a seat!" She pats the spot next to her.

Jackson looks uncomfortable. "I was going to sit with Greer."

"But I thought we were going to meet here?"

Now Jackson looks like there is an invisible scorpion stinging him. "I thought you just said you'd *see* me here."

"Well, I have this seat for you." She talks like she's giving in-structions. She crosses her legs, which makes her short skirt ride up shorter. Her legs are smooth, not a bit of stubble showing in the house lights. There are no moles, bruises, scratches, or veins, either. Maybe they are plastic. She drapes a bangled wrist over one knee, and that's when I really notice the rest of her. She's got on a sheer black top over a lacy cami. Her hair is down and she's straightened it. She's wearing enough mascara to make her eyes look like spiders (pretty spiders), and her lips are so glossy and reflective you could use them for night biking.

To a school play.

I, on the other hand, am wearing a Hagrid-size cardigan that I now see has a hole in one elbow, the same jeans I had on at school, and some faded orange Keen sneakers I borrowed from my mom on the way out because my own shoes were sweaty. This is how it is. Girls like the Fräulein bring their A game, and I don't even real-ize there's a game on. No wonder Jackson looks like he is in pain.

There's an awkward conversation in which I offer to go sit by our moms (guess who loves that plan?) but eventually the other people in the row move down so we all fit. Me, Jackson, Her. (Turns out her real name is Elliana and her German name is Monika, but I am going to keep calling her Dummkopf because every time I repeat, "Greer," she says, "Keira?")

σ

The play, surprisingly, is really good. Not the story, which is if any-thing even more ridiculous since Maggie persuaded them to make it less kidnappy. But the performance is solid.

Maybe the lights or the makeup or the acoustics make things seem better, but even the brothers are pretty good. And however much Maggie and Lizzie hate each other, they seem like the sweetest of friends out there in nineteenth-century Oregon.

There are little curls of green snaking out from under Maggie's white bonnet, like a secret she's doing a bad job of keeping, but she sings like a finalist on a TV voice competition, and when she harmonizes with Lizzie, it makes Lizzie sound better, too.

At intermission, I talk with Anitha Das and her little sister about a girls coding clinic they went to, while Jackson and you-know-who share a bag of Gummibärs. I spy my mother looking over at us. She looks disappointed. No kidding, lady. Best case was that this was kind of a fake date. Now it doesn't even turn out to be *my* fake date. I am a third wheel on someone else's fake date. Maybe this whole thing was him making sure *I* had somebody to sit next to. He seems to have no problem making friends.

The last act finishes with barely a hitch, except for Keely jumping her cue and starting a song early, and Aidan Neal stepping on another brother once or twice.

But now things get interesting. At the end of the bows, someone hands Lizzie/Milly a bouquet of grocery-store flowers, because she's the leading lady. She crosses her hands over her chest like it is the most moving gesture ever made, even though it happens in every play. The whole cast motions to the orchestra pit, as I know they've practiced, so the lowly musicians will know that we are clapping for them, too.

Here's where things go off script. Very off script. A bunch of kids from the pit orchestra stand up on their chairs so you can actually see them—or at least their heads—for the first time. They are wearing bonnets, or if not actual bonnets, then kerchiefs or babushkas tied over their heads like bonnets. Most of the audience, which doesn't know about Braidgate, laughs. They think the musicians are being cute. They don't know that bonnets are a symbol of civil unrest.

Rafa Ramos-Sikes, in a floppy, flowered sunbonnet, pulls himself onstage from the pit. He walks straight up to Maggie, bows deeply, and lays a giant bouquet of long-stemmed roses in her arms. Like Miss America roses. Only they're for Maggie, so imagine a pageant recognizing someone for their feminist achievements, or she'll get mad. Only she's not mad. She's beaming. And so is Rafa, who turns out not to be so shy after all.

Lizzie's mouth is hanging open in a way that will not look good in the yearbook photo. Picture it like this: If Lizzie's flowers were a grungy little toy poodle, which seemed really sweet, Maggie has just been presented with a thoroughbred racehorse, with silky-shiny muscles and a wreath of laurel leaves around its neck who could step on the poodle and not even notice. Maggie throws an arm around Rafa and everybody takes another bow. Lizzie Barnes looks like she's going to beat both of them to death with her own stupid flowers.

When the lights go up, everybody is still whooping their heads off, including Elliana/Monika/the Gummi Baroness, who doesn't even know why it's the most perfect thing Rafa could have done.

CHAPTER 49

Mom and I stop at Tyler's school to pick him up. She has to run in to drop off holiday gift cards for the teachers. If she sees anyone she knows—and she knows everyone—she will be a half hour at least, and a half hour in my old middle school sounds as fun as, well, a half hour in middle school, so I tilt back my seat and roll down the window to wait.

Tyler is messing around out front with a group of kids who look like they're filming an Old Navy commercial. They're wearing a rainbow of colors, no one is sulky, and everyone's hair is flopping at just the right angles. I recognize most of them, boys from his team and girls that have been in his classes forever. Seventh graders. They're little/big people—little to their families and teachers, but big to themselves. Sometimes it's the opposite when you get older.

Was this what seventh grade was like for me? I think it was. I think I've been in this ad, too.

I think I was the Emily in this crowd. Not Maya, who keeps stealing the boys' hockey sticks, or the curly-haired girl I don't know who has fixed herself to the side of one of the Sams. Emily is finishing a bag of chips that the boys passed around, talking about a statue of Crazy Horse while everyone else is hoping for Maya to steal their gear next.

"If it ever gets done, it will be bigger than Mount Rushmore. Crazy Horse's head is actually much bigger than Lincoln's head."

Maya is after Tyler now. She manages to get his stick, the one he just taped pink, and holds it up. It's warm for December, so everyone has left their jackets in a pile. Her shirt rides halfway up and at first I'm embarrassed for her until I realize it's the kind of shirt that's supposed to do that. It's tiny and short on purpose. I'm wearing a sweatshirt meant for an extra-large human male, and she's wearing a top that would fit an extra-small squirrel. She holds the stick over her head, like no one could get to it there. I worry that she's got some kind of a cognitive disorder that makes it impossible to judge relative size, because Ty has at least four inches on her.

But Tyler knows how to play this game, too, and instead of taking the stick back, he fakes her out, reaches for her butt, and grabs her phone out of her pocket. She lunges for him but he tosses it to the next kid, and Maya fake-pouts with her hands on her hips. She is not worried about that phone, though. She is in total control.

I look back to Emily, on her own. At first I think she hasn't got a clue, but then I realize she likes it this way. She's safe sitting on the bike rack watching the rest of them like it's a Sunday at the dog park. Why jump in if it just means having someone else's greasy fingerprints on your iPhone? Plus she's got the chips. I want to tell her that soon, very soon, when she decides it's not enough to be the foremost school expert on Native American monuments—when she wants Sam, or Sam, or even Tyler to look at her like they're all looking at Maya now—it's going to be way more complicated than just jumping off the bike rack and stealing someone's gear. But I don't, because she looks happy now. And I still haven't got a clue what she should do next.

CHAPTER 50

"You didn't borrow my sunglasses, did you?"

"The giant ones with the gems on the corners? What do you think?"

"You don't have to be a snot about it, Greer."

I stare into the fridge wondering if eleven fifteen is breakfast or lunch. "They're probably in the car."

Breakfast, I decide, and take out a yogurt. Maybe a freezer waffle, too. Maybe two freezer waffles, too. It's the first morning of a long and Jackson-less winter break. Yeah, yeah, Christmas, Hanukkah, school's off, blah, blah. I need these waffles.

Mom stands at the kitchen island with her hands on her hips, like she wants to scold her sunglasses for wandering away. "I *know* I had them inside, because Melinda asked me where I got them."

Madame Butterfly wakes up from her hibernation. *You said they were gone for ten days*, she accuses. "Mrs. Oates was here?"

Mom is opening and closing cupboard doors as though her glasses might have been accidentally put away with the Tervis tumblers.

"She stopped by to pick something up."

"Was she alone?"

"Jackson was not here, if that's what you're asking." She's smirking, like it's so amusing I might care whether or not Jackson was here. I don't know why I would. It's been a week since the play and everything is exactly like it was before. Plus today they are heading to Banff. The Oateses always ski at Christmas. The butterfly goes back to sleep, but not before reminding me that there is another Oates who might be responsible for the missing shades.

"Was Quin with her?"

"Yeah. They were just here a minute. Maybe I carried them with me downstairs?"

I follow Mom down the stairs. I suspect that those sunglasses are in the hot little fists of Quinlan Oates on a plane to Canada, though I thought the two of us had an understanding. She wouldn't steal stuff anymore and I wouldn't tell anyone she was a kleptomaniac. But maybe she saw those sparkly rhinestone frames and couldn't help herself.

"What were they picking up anyway?" I doubt they swung by for more of Mom's re-lo coupons and sample-size laundry detergents.

I can tell by the space before her answer that she did not mean to mention any of this to me. "Just a few hand-me-downs. Things you don't use anymore."

"Things *I* don't use anymore? I doubt Quinlan Oates needs or wants anything of mine."

"You wouldn't even notice unless I told you."

"Mom?"

She pretends to be looking for her sunglasses in the basement, but really she is trying to escape from me.

"Mom?" I repeat. She says nothing. "Toys? Clothes?" Now she's literally moving the laundry detergent jug and looking behind it, like she might have worn her sunglasses into the basement to do laundry, then taken them off between loads. She's pretending not to hear me. "Ski boots?" Please let it be ski boots. But no. Those are not the things Mom thinks take up precious shelf space that could be used for weathered wooden signs that say things like LIVE LOVE LAUGH with no punctuation. No no no. The things she thinks take up too much space are my—

"Books? Did you give her BOOKS?"

She turns to face me now. "It's a long flight."

"You gave her my books?"

"With a layover."

"The child has two iPads: one for games, one for movies."

"Mel's been telling me that Quinlan has been so quiet lately, just moping in her room, and I said you've always been like that, too, I mean not moping but alone in your room—"

"I LIKE TO READ. That's why I'm in my room. And that's why I like my BOOKS."

"We figured Quinlan would be more willing to read something if we said it was from you."

"What did you give her?"

"I don't know. *Where the Mountain Meets the Moon, Superfudge,* the one with the mouse family and the research lab. I didn't know it was going to be such a big deal. They're children's books, Greer." I am glaring at her. "You read them ages ago."

"That isn't the point. They weren't yours to give."

"Greer, that little girl is really struggling. She needs somebody looking out for her."

"Why are you always looking out for other people? Why can't you look out for me?" I ask, even though I suspect it's because I can't leave her five stars on the re-lo agent review page.

Mom huffs. "Are you really that upset about a couple of old books?"

Yes.

No.

I'm disappointed that Jackson didn't find some excuse to come with his mom to our house, even if I was sleeping. I'm stressed out that I keep changing my mind about what I want so I can't figure out if I blew it or I saved myself, but it feels more like I blew it. I'm worried that after break we'll either start all over from the beginning—or that we won't. And that Maggie will get back from the Cleave family Christmas in Iowa and spend the rest of the break helping Rafa write a musical. And now I'm upset that Maude, Mavis, and I will be alone without my chewed-up old *Mrs. Frisby and the Rats of NIMH* and a mother whose retinas are too sun damaged to drive to the library.

"They were my books," I say, without conviction.

When I come upstairs, Tyler is taking a selfie with Mom's sunglasses and my Stabilizer on, and he is eating my waffles.

CHAPTER 51

Dad and Tyler and I always pick a movie series to watch all the way through over break. Last year we watched all the *Harry Potters*. This year we were going to do a Marvel ultramarathon, but Mom interfered and said Ty was still too young for *Deadpool,* so we switched to *Lord of the Rings* and *The Hobbit.* Dad tried to talk us into a Top Ten Classics from the Nineties list but Ty and I revolted.

We watched two Hobbits yesterday and the third tonight. It's too late to start LOTR, so we're just vegging in front of the TV, Ty perched in the giant Lovesac beanbag we got for Christmas, me and Dad on opposite ends of the couch.

Ty flips the channel to a late-night talk show. The guest is an actress from a new action movie. They show a clip, just a minute of action, in which she is wearing what looks like a shiny black wetsuit, but with the front zipped down to show several inches of bulging cleavage. Her breasts don't move a bit when she's knocking out bad guys with roundhouse kicks, which is biologically impossible. The clip ends when she smothers the last villain in her chest while she breaks his neck in her arms.

The audience goes wild. I think they think this is empowering. They think this is what it looks like to be a badass woman.

"Congratulations on the movie! I heard it was a big opening weekend," chimes the host.

There's an older comic, who must have been the first guest, on the opposite side of the actress and he pipes in, "Real big. I bet it was *huge*."

The actress fans eyelashes that are like tarantulas and laughs along, like she's flattered by the attention, even if the attention is for her boobs. Is she shrinking inside, wishing she'd worn a big sweatshirt to this interview so they'd have to talk about the movie or the hundreds of hours of training she must have done instead of her body?

"We can, ah, watch something else," says my dad.

The comic butts in. "Lemme ask you something. Did you shoot that scene in a lot of takes? Was that guy you killed, like, 'Ah, can we try that again?'"

"Put on Food Network, Ty," says Dad. Ty's nestled in the bean-bag, scrolling through his phone, oblivious.

I look for a sign that the actress has had enough. But no, it's different for her. She read the script. She knew what she was there for. She might have even paid a doctor to make sure her body would always be the center of attention. Judging by how perky and happy her breasts look peering over the top of her dress, they are not made of the same stuff as mine.

They put up some pictures of her from other films and award shows. There's not a single one where she's not wearing something low cut or tight. There's even a promo picture from a film where she's wearing a fur hat and a tank top. Where is a movie supposed to take place if it's cold enough for a fur hat but warm enough for a tank top? I can tell from the live show that her biceps are cut like a boxer's, but they don't even feature in the promo shot.

"And here you are last year with your fiancé at the MTV Awards," says the host. There's a picture of her in a dress that looks like her breasts got caught in a sparkly fishing net. Her fiancé is wearing a plain black suit.

"Are you sure that wasn't at the Golden Globes?" pipes in the comic. The host indulges him with an eye roll, as if to say "Whaddya gonna do? These old guys don't know any better."

Maybe she figured it was the only way she was going to get into movies. But this can't really be what she wants, can it? Maybe it's close enough to what she wanted? To sit there and smile while some ape makes obvious boob jokes? And what if it is? What if this is everything she's ever dreamed of? What if she was considering majoring in physics and then decided, "You know what? I could split an atom, but that seems like a lot of work"? What does that do to the rest of us? But really, why should that be her responsibility? I look over at my little brother absently letting the commentary on the TV wash into him.

"Let's see what else is on," interrupts my dad. "Ty, can you find something else?" Tyler's too zoned out, too comfortable, to notice. "Tyler! Ty! Change the channel."

My dad, on the other hand, looks like he is going to be sick. We're watching Booby McBoobface being interviewed, and he is desperate to change the channel. I can tell he's trying not to look at me, and it dawns on me: He's embarrassed. He's embarrassed to be watching a guy roast a woman because of her big breasts because I'm here. Because he is imagining some guy talking about me like that. About my big breasts.

Now I'm embarrassed, too. And suddenly so, so tired.

"I'm going to bed." I leave the boys to the TV.

CHAPTER 52

"No, no. That's not true at all."

Mom and I are at a coffee shop (not one named for an astronomer; one named for whatever a Starbuck is), having just returned everything my grandparents sent for Hanukkah. A couple of tweeny girls at a nearby table are wearing elaborate outfits, including layers of necklaces and chunky-heeled boots, like what you imagine a kid imagines a supermodel would wear on her day off. I have just claimed that I must have been born without the gene that makes you interested in clothes, and Mom is disagreeing.

"What do you mean?"

"You used to dress up just like all the other little girls we knew. Or most of them, anyway. Sometimes you'd change three times a day."

This doesn't sound like me. I'd prefer to change no times a day. If I could just sleep in a sweatshirt and yoga pants, I'd be dressed for tomorrow, too. "When was that?"

"Up until you were four. Four and a half, actually." She is fidgeting with her new sunglasses, folding and unfolding the bows.

Once Tyler told her she looked like an old lady, she ditched the bedazzled ones.

"What happened?"

"We went to the mall. You had picked out your own outfit, of course. It was like a Greer Greatest Hits day. The top was from a Disney Sleeping Beauty Halloween costume. It was this cheap, knock-off satin, bubblegum pink. It Velcroed in the back, but the Velcro was 'scratchedy' so you made me cut out the Velcro and safety pin the back."

"You let me wear that in public?"

"*Let you?* I'm telling you, you were very particular about your clothes."

"What kind of pants go with a Sleeping Beauty costume top?"

"No, no. Not pants. We were going to the mall. But not the skirt from the costume, either. You had this skirt from Hanna Andersson. Maybe my favorite thing you ever wore. It's in tons of pictures."

"The bright one with all the flowers?"

"That's it. It was orange and red and blue, with this Scandinavian floral pattern, and big balloon ruffles? I had to pretend not to like it or you wouldn't have worn it. We used to say it had good twirlability."

"Did it look pretty good with the pink satin princess costume?"

"You sure thought so. But you'd had it since you were two, so it barely covered your butt. I told you if you didn't wear something under it everyone would see your undies. You wouldn't have cared, except that it was a Friday, and your Friday undies were in the wash and you had to wear Tuesday. You thought if people saw your undies, they'd think you couldn't read."

"I was worried that people would think I couldn't read my own underwear?" That sounds exactly like me. "I guess that would be kind of embarrassing. So I wore tights?"

"Flamingo bikini bottoms."

"Of course. What kind of shoes did I wear? Stilettos? Moon boots?" I still can't believe she's not making this up, because it seems so unlike me, but now that I think of it, in all the preschool pictures I'm pretty fancy. I just assumed it was Mom's fault.

"Just tennies. You've always been very practical about shoes." I look down at my feet and laugh. I've permanently taken over Mom's Keens because they are so comfortable and worn in. She is not making this up.

"So, what happened? Why was that the last time I dressed up for the mall? Did I see myself in a mirror?"

"No, actually." Mom has been having fun with this story, especially, I think, since I have been, too. We don't do this a lot, where just the two of us talk about something that's not logistics, or one of us asking the other for something, or one of us disappointed/angry/annoyed at the other. There's been a lot of family time this break, but today is nice. She changes here, though, gets more serious. She smiles to herself, remembering, and I can't tell if it's a happy smile or a sad smile. "We went to the Lego store. They used to have these big barrels of Legos out and a ramp set up, so you could build a car and race it."

"I remember that! And then you'd shower me in Purell!"

"It was you and a bunch of little boys, building cars. The boys would make these massive things with extra wheels and windows and guns and ladders and all kinds of things sticking out of them. And then they'd crash to bits at the bottom and they'd rebuild them even dumber. Yours was streamlined. After every run, you'd make adjustments: add weight, reduce drag, bigger wheels, rebalance. I mean, you didn't use those words. You just figured it out. And pretty soon, your car—actually, I think you called it a rocket car—no wait, a rocket boat—yours was beating everything. Even when the other kids tried to cheat—they'd give theirs a shove or blow on it or try to put something in the way on your track—yours beat them all, and it stayed together."

I'm proud of little Greer.

"And then the clerk from the store came over and watched some of the races and saw that your rocket boat was beating everything else by a mile. And you know what they said?" Mom looks like she's turning something over in her mouth. Something she wishes she could spit out. This memory has gone from fun to something else.

"What?"

"'Aren't you a pretty princess? Did you pick out your outfit yourself?'"

This question sits between us for a while, and for once Kathryn Walsh resists the urge to lecture me on what exactly it means, because we both know very well what it means. It means I could have built a working space station, but all anyone else saw was pink satin and a twirly skirt.

Finally, I say, "Did you tell him off?"

"Who?"

"The guy from the store?"

She looks up at the ceiling, then down at her hands. "It was a woman, Greer." Very quietly, like it hurts her to say this, she adds, "And the only thing I said was, 'Say thank you, sweetie.'"

We are both quiet again for a long minute. "That's when I stopped dressing up?"

"You stopped dressing up."

I think about this and wonder about the choice. The choice between flamingo bikini bottoms and Lego race cars. The choice between being adored and being respected. Between being a princess and being the president. But if that's the choice, there's really no contest, is there? "Better that than stop building rocket boats."

Mom laughs and pushes a piece of hair behind my ear. She doesn't even try to take credit or tell me that all my engineering abilities come from her. "I'm sorry if it feels like you have to choose, Greer. I want you to be able to do both."

CHAPTER 53

Mom drives me to school 98 percent of the time, which is why I'm on time 98 percent of the time. It's the first day back from break and by some annoying twist of fate, Dad doesn't have an early meeting to show up late for.

So today I'm in Eric Walsh's 2 percent club: in other words, late.

I'm anxious to find out if Jackson is still going to wait for me before school, or if ten days in the Canadian Rockies brought him to his senses. I heard from him a couple times in the first two days, then Quin dropped his phone off a chairlift. I know this because Quin messaged from her iPad—that and about a thousand selfies with reindeer antler or Santa hat filters.

Dad jabbers the whole ride there, showing no sign of rushing, even though we left fifteen minutes later than Mom and I do, and he's taking the rookie route that has two extra stoplights and a crosswalk choked with elementary students. I guess when you are an executive at your company, you're never actually late. Things just start when you get there.

I am not an executive at school, and school will start with or without me. The minute-warning bell rings while I'm still getting out of the car, which means I can almost make it to math if I sprint the whole way, don't stop at my locker, and turn back time by four minutes, though if that were possible I'd go back ten and say hi to Jackson.

"Thanks for the ride." I don't mean it.

"Any big tests or anything today?" He's still trying to make conversation with me.

"They don't usually give tests when you've been out for ten days." I kick the door shut behind me.

I hear the window scrolling down as I scuffle toward school. "Have a good day, G-dub! Love you, kiddo!"

I wave behind me. Nice guy, Eric Walsh, but really needs to work on time management.

The math/German/who-cares-what-else hall is empty, like I knew it would be but hoped it wouldn't be. Ms. T eyes me sliding in front of Omar and Kurtis. I give an apologetic smile and she frowns, but she doesn't send me to the office for a late pass.

They've already started on the homework when my phone chirps. I fumble it out of my bag as Ms. T exhales loudly and glares at me. I switch off the ringer, but not before I notice that it's a message from Jackson.

Ms. T asks Asher to go over the first problem with the class. She stands over his shoulder while he reads.

Where are you? Sick today?

Just late.

You?! Late?!!!

Dad's fault. I thought your phone

had a ski accident?

Got a new one last night. Plus they

bought Q her own. [eye-rolling

emoji]

[surprise-face emoji]

Wait for me after class?

"After"? Really? We never talk after. Maybe he brought me something from Canada.

"Who can do number two?" asks Ms. Tanner.

Kyle Tuck and the others laugh. Immature, yes, but come on, Ms. Tanner. You should know better.

"Seems like we've got a volunteer. Okay, Kyle, let's see your number two."

Kyle's friends are laughing so hard they can't speak.

"Do you want to tell us all what's so funny, Kyle?"

The giggles spread out from Kyle like ripples in a pond.

"Did you do number two? You had all of break to get it done."

Everyone loses it, except Asher and Anitha, who are serious about math, serious about homework, and probably serious about their number twos.

"Excuse me," pipes up Omar. "I think Kyle is having a hard time with number two."

It sends everybody over the edge, even Kyle. I'm proud of Omar.

Just for a sec?

If Jackson brought me something, I hope it's those chocolate-covered peanuts that say Moose Poop on the package.

I send back a thumbs-up emoji. And a smiley poo for good measure.

CHAPTER 54

"Are you going to eat that egg?"

"Don't you have a lunch? Do you need a dollar for a granola bar or something?"

Maggie scares away Carlisle Patone, who has been eyeing my egg. Maggie has always intimidated people, but after the play she colored over the *Seven Brides* neon with brown, and now her hair is kind of army green. It gives her a definite take-no-prisoners vibe.

"Wait!" I reach out with the egg. Carlisle takes it gratefully before he runs away from Maggie.

She rolls her eyes. I'm not sure whether it's at Carlisle or me. "I don't understand the problem! You've got weeks to find something."

We are sitting at the counter that overlooks the track. I couldn't handle Natalie and Tahlia today. It's just the two of us, sandwiched between kids who are buried in their laptops. Except Carlisle, and now that he's got my hard-boiled egg, he's left us alone.

I had an epically great five minutes this morning. Then a

horrible, crushing slide into now, where I can't even muster the enthusiasm to eat an egg. Here's what the good five minutes looked like:

"Hey!" This is Jackson, who bounds from German class so he's basically at Ms. Tanner's door the second the bell rings. His cheeks are windburned or sunburned from skiing, and the rosy color makes him look happy and bright. I'm sure mine are rosy and happy, too, and I didn't go anywhere.

It's been ten days since I saw him and my body instinctively lurches to hug him hello, but I put up my hand for a fist bump instead. He reciprocates. He knows me. Even though I told her she was not allowed to, the butterfly invited a bunch of friends over. I think they are taking a Zumba class.

"What's up?" He's not holding a bag of Moose Poop or a maple leaf pop socket, so I guess he didn't bring me anything from Canada.

"Where you going? Spanish?"

"Sí."

"I'll walk you. I can be late to gym."

"Don't blame me if she makes you run laps." I'm not worried about Jackson having to run around the gym a few times. His legs are long. But I am worried that he seems a bit amped up for the first day back at school.

"Did you have a good break?"

"It was okay. Just a lot of family time. How was Banff?"

"Also a lot of family time."

"But skiing family time is better than TV family time."

"Depends on the family," he says.

Part of me wishes Spanish were farther away so we could keep walking and talking. Like in Spain. The other part of me wants to tuck into an open locker, because once you spend enough time studying Jackson's every expression, you can see when he's anything less than perfectly confident, and his excitement today is freaking me out.

"So, what's the deal with this winter formal?" he asks.

Oh.

That.

The posters went up this morning, GET YOU'RE TIXS NOW! with messy-markered arrows pointing to a tiny printed URL for the ticket site. I complained to Kurtis and Omar about student council having no concern for grammar. I wondered who would spend their break setting it all up. And I now realize that it is exactly the kind of event a new kid set on finding his place in this school, a kid who joins things, a kid who goes places, a kid who is perfectly comfortable in awkward paired-up situations, would be interested in.

The breakfast burrito Dad insisted we had time for unwraps in my stomach. The binder hadn't mentioned the February formal and neither had I.

"Fancier than homecoming, less fancy than prom," I answer as informatively as I can. I hesitate before I add, "And freshman and sophomores can go."

"Will it be fun?"

"No idea."

"So, are you going to go?"

"I haven't really thought about it." This is a lie. It is me stalling for time because there are two ways this conversation could go:

Either he will ask for help coming up with a fun way to ask Red Riding Hood, which would be terrible and gross and predictable and heartbreaking; or . . .

"Do you think you'd want to go together?"

. . . he's going to ask me, which is awesome and fantastic and confusing and very complicated.

"Um, what?" I say, swallowing hard. The butterfly Zumba class has swarmed up my throat and is choking me.

Jackson lets out an exasperated sigh. He stands directly in front of me and speaks slowly, like he's talking to a child. Who has a limited grasp of English. And a concussion. "Do you want to go to the winter formal with me?"

Seriously? Of course I do. Obviously. The only things I want more are rational women to be elected as leaders in countries all over the world, an effective and ethical solution to global climate and sustainability challenges, and a separate refrigerator so I don't have to eat anything Tyler has touched. But the very next thing on my list, and the thing that suddenly seems achievable in this lifetime, is to go to the formal with you.

"You can say no. I won't be offended. I'll just bring my wistful poetry journal along to keep me company."

But before I scream yes, can you clarify what you mean by "with"? You mean like when we went to Maggie's play and sat with the girl from German class? Or when I ate dinner at your house and our siblings sat between us? Or when we went to Cupernicus and I gave you that bullshit about being focused on school? That, right? Can we just do that? You don't mean with *with, do you? Or do you?*

"Greer? Did the left side of your brain just shut down? Or are you trying to think of a nice way to say no?"

You know which side of the brain controls speech?! I might actually love you.

"No. I mean yes to the formal, no to my brain shutting down." This is where I should leave it. I should trust that it will all work out, one way or another, trust that he knows me well enough to get it, trust myself to take that chance, but because I'm me, I don't. I can't. I don't want to misunderstand what he means, or for him to misunderstand, so I blurt out, "We can write a review of it for the binder! For the next family." I force a laugh because this is actually not funny.

The binder. Did I really bring up the binder? Of course I did. The binder is safe. Neutral. My olly-olly-oxen-free. That's how we started and is as far as we will ever go. *I would spend every minute I could with you, Jackson, but I need to make sure you understand I'm not really dateable. I'm not really touchable. Sooner or later you will want more than this and move on.*

But could you make it later, please?

He blinks at me for what feels like an hour and says, "Sure. Right. Your whole family is really into this relocation thing, aren't you?"

He smiles, and it's not the same rosy sunburnt one as before, but it's something.

σ

I float into Spanish on a cloud of mariposas. We can get our tixs now for the February formal. A night with Jackson, when he could be with anybody else. I promise myself I'm not going to make it weird.

And then Maestra Bonnie (whose first language is Wisconsinese) starts showing pictures of her daughter's wedding and asking us to describe them in Spanish. This is one of her favorite techniques and is why my Spanish vocabulary is excellent when it comes to anything related to Bonnie's life—dogs, Christmas cookies, office supplies—and terrible when it comes to anything related to Spanish or Latin American culture. I could say "The pug rolled in a stinky place," but I have no idea if there's a Mexican national anthem or what those little pig-shaped cookies are called.

While Nella Woster is describing the vestido hermoso in great detail, it hits me that to go to the formal, I'm going to need a vestido hermoso. And how in the world are Maude, Mavis, and I going to find ourselves a beautiful gown? Should we look for one that matches my sweatshirt?

That's when my mood went to infierno. And now Maggie's spending the lunch hour trying to convince me everything is going to be okay.

"Come on, Greer. We'll find you something fabulous."

"I doubt it."

"Fine, we'll find you something pretty good."

"It's not just the dress. I'm not sure whether I want to go anyway."

"Really." She folds her arm and arches an eyebrow.

"You don't understand, Mags."

"Then explain it to me." She leans in, and I instinctively lean back. How can I explain it to her if I can't explain it to myself? I wish I'd kept my mouth shut and silently suffered through our usual lunch.

And like that, I am saved. Nat and Tahlia emerge from the wash of people leaving the cafeteria.

"Why didn't you guys sit with us?" Tahlia asks, shaking gum out of a container.

"*Oooo!*" Natalie reaches for it.

Maggie's eyes don't leave my face, but she sighs and says, "Greer was trying to explain logarithms to me."

"Mush be nysh to have your own mash geniush," Natalie manages through a mouthful. "Wait. Ish thish grape?"

I say goodbye and bolt to class. I wish it could all be logarithms.

CHAPTER 55

If I am totally honest, there was this moment—and really, it was only a moment—when Maude and Mavis were hovering around a C when I was cool with them. More than that. I kind of liked them.

I was never a kid who cared about pop stars or famous people and what they wore or did (unless you count J. K. Rowling or Bill Nye or Stephen Hawking (RIP)). And I really never thought about breasts. We were still little when Tahlia put two stuffed animals in her shirt at a slumber party and found Katy Perry on the karaoke machine. This sent the other girls scrambling, looking for bigger stuffed animals so they'd make even better Katy Perrys. Somebody found a pack of washable markers, and they drew big red lips on each other. Then someone tripped over their sleeping bag and it turned into jumping on a big pile of couch cushions. The jumping is when I got involved. Jumping I could understand the appeal of.

The point is, some girls were waiting for it. Looking for signs of bulging, weird hairs, things they thought would make them . . . women, I guess? All my downloaded images were from the Mars rovers. I wasn't waiting to be a woman; I was waiting to be a scientist.

But then right as ninth grade started, and my body started to fold into the shape it is now, my parents got invited to this fancy fundraising gala for the League of Chicago Theatres. Mom got this dress—blue, with those cap sleeves that sit off the shoulder and aren't really sleeves at all. It was tight to the waist and then flared out at the skirt. The fabric was shimmery. Not like a mirror. More like a hologram. Sapphire blue, but also violet and black and steel gray at the same time. And there were these designs embroidered into the skirt and up the sides in black thread.

Mom talked me into trying it on, just for fun. I know she wishes I cared more about that kind of stuff. She has friends that take their daughters on wild shopping trips, who complain about how they'll only wear hundred-dollar tank tops, even though that's exactly the way the moms are, too. I just put on whatever's comfortable, especially if I've been wearing it the day before, and it takes all the fun out of it for her. Ever since the Lego debacle, apparently. Now, though, maybe she's relieved that I don't want to go shopping. There's not a section in the binder for Top-Heavy Fashion Outlets.

But that day, which seems like a hundred years ago, when I slid into the dress and zipped up the side, it was like it was made for me. The neckline dipped over the tops of my breasts and hugged my sides, with just the slightest curve at my waist. I lifted and curved just where you'd want lifts and curves. My eyes looked like they were reflecting the same shimmery blue of the dress. For the first time, I didn't look like a little girl in dress-up clothes; I looked like I was born to carry a glass of champagne around a charity gala. I scooped up my hair into a messy bun to show off the full sweep of my bare shoulders and licked my lips to a shine. I even stepped into Mom's three-inch silver heels.

"Whoa, honey! You are gorgeous in that dress!"

I was.

And I loved it.

Don't get me wrong; no part of me stopped being strong and smart and sarcastic. I wasn't imagining twirling around on the arm of a man at the charity gala; I was imagining being the guest of honor at the charity gala because I'd just donated my Nobel Prize in Physics money to build a new wing at my Museum of Equal Rights. Or something like that. But I'd look stunning up at the podium, too.

I stood in front of that full-length mirror, imagining that this was what being grown would be like. It would be easy; whatever I put on would be perfect and beautiful, and I would feel perfect and beautiful. All the parts of me—the math part and the funny part and the books part and the physical part—would match.

But that was just one day. I've never felt like that in anything again. Not in my extra-large sweatshirt. Not in my custom-tailored volleyball uniform. Not even in the Stabilizer.

That bra makes things work. It does not make them beautiful. And if I tried on that dress today, I wouldn't even be able to get the zipper started.

CHAPTER 56

I am invited to go dress shopping with Jessa and some other girls from the team. Jess is going to the dance with Kermie Walltower and a bunch of other people. Kermie's actual first name is Kobe, but he's gone by Kermie ever since he brought a Kermit the Frog lunch box to school in second grade. They've been friends since they played T-ball together. Jessa said yes and then extended the invitation to five other girls and a couple of boys. She thinks everything should be done with a team. Kermie is a good sport, though.

Suzanne's Bridal & Prom is a warehouse of evening wear. It's got high ceilings and bright lights. There are racks and racks of dresses, arranged by color and length. It feels more like going to a grocery store than some elegant excursion. There's an "Everyday Steals: $79 and Under" rack, which only has dresses that are Barbie pink or puke yellow. Petites, which is swarming with tiny teenagers, gets the only patch of carpet in the place. I'm disappointed but not surprised that "Special Sizes" means dresses size 16 and up. What would really be special is if Special Sizes included something that was a 4 on the bottom and Lumberjack on the top.

I drift among the racks, occasionally giving a thumbs-up when someone holds up a hanger for a second opinion. One by one, the Kennedy girls disappear to the fitting rooms with arms full of charmeuse and beads. This place would have been magical to me as a preschooler, before I found out my outfit was getting more attention than my engineering. Everything about this store says "You are meant to be pretty." There are girls who never grow out of that, I guess, but also those like Jessa who wear Under Armour sweat-wicking pullovers and track pants most of the time but think it's fun to pull on this other identity like a costume once in a while.

"That would look great on you." I don't even hear the saleswoman come up behind me. I'm standing next to a mannequin that is wearing a strapless caramel-colored fitted dress with a slit from the floor to mid-thigh and a swirl of rhinestones. It would look great on me if I was an emaciated fifty-year-old at a Field Museum gala instead of a fifteen-year-old volleyball player hoping for the dress equivalent of a hoodie.

"I don't think so," I say.

"Not what we're looking for? What kinds of things do we like?"

If you must know, we like things that are loose, boxy, and don't make two of us chafe together. Is there a section for that?

The saleswoman grins like she wants to eat me. She's wearing a cream skirt and matching pumps, and has a measuring tape hanging around her neck. Ms. K-B's measuring tape was worn and soft, the lines and numbers faded from years wrapping around waists and up and down legs, stretching over big bolts of fabric, checking the work for errors. The tape around this woman's neck looks bright and stiff and new. This measuring tape has never met a body like mine, and there is no way she is touching me with it.

"I'm just looking around for now."

"Do we like something a little simpler? Maybe more of an A-line?"

"I just came with friends. I don't need help."

"What size are we looking for?"

"I, ah, what?"

"It's all right. If you're used to small, medium, and large, dress sizes can be confusing. It's not the same as throwing on a sweatshirt!" She nods to my sweatshirt, like I'm too stupid to have ever heard of sizes that are numbers. "Let's head back and get some measurements so we know what we're looking for." She walks away, expecting me to follow.

I do what any rational person would do: I drop to the floor, crawl under a rack of dresses, and slink away, my head ducked low.

There's a sitting area outside the fitting rooms. I slump in a flowered chair to watch the parade of girls twist in front of a panel of mirrors.

Jessa and the others are having so much fun, it's almost contagious. Not prissy fun. Just fun. It reminds me of the day we got our uniforms, with people suiting up and transforming right in front of me, and I feel a little pang of envy.

Mena, whose mother calls her skinny as an uncooked noodle, is trying on a blue dress with one bare shoulder. It bags all over the place. Jessa, pressed tight into a long black casing, stands behind her and pinches the extra fabric. "This is perfect! We can keep our phones in here. And our keys. And our jackets." Mena swats her.

"I'm sorry. Zero is the smallest that comes in," says a saleslady, "but we can alter it."

"How much does *that* cost?" asks Jessa.

"It depends on a lot of factors."

"That means it's expensive," Jess tells Mena. "Maybe you can just pin it."

"I don't recommend that," says the lady, but Mena is already closing herself back in the fitting room.

"I'm feeling pretty good about this one," says Jessa. She's dancing in front of the mirrors, grinding her hips even though Suzanne's is piping in a string quartet. She's not trying to pull the fabric away from her sides or suck in her breath. She's not scrutinizing every angle of herself. She's just moving. She's moving like bulges and curves are supposed to be part of a human body. It's like she's found a new skin. Or a new uniform. Jessa wears that dress the way she wears everything: comfortably.

"Jess? You going to get black kneepads to go with that dress?" asks Mena through the door.

"THERE we are!" It's Tape Measure, clicking toward my chair with an armload of dresses. "I thought we lost each other."

So did I.

"Here's just a couple of different styles to start with, and once we have an idea of what we like, we can go from there." She starts hanging them along the bar in an open fitting room.

"We're going to look at accessories," says Kate, who peeks in the back with Khloe. Why can't I be in their "we" instead of this messed-up "we" with pushy pumps lady?

Jessa is stripping off the black dress in front of the mirrors.

"Do you want to try on this one? It's actually really stretchy, like yoga pants or something. You want to try it? We could both get it."

See? Uniform.

She holds the tangled dress out to me, but I shake my head.

I try to feel optimistic, though, since Jessa and Mena are trying stuff on and they don't have ideal proportions, either. I have to find *something*, and here is where they have absolutely everything. I click the door behind me and slide out of my jeans. In the mirror, my legs look long and strong; not the chiseled legs of a gymnast or a dancer—just the kind of legs that no one could think of anything bad to say about except for all the new and old bruises from crashing into things on the court. My legs don't need any Special Sizes.

But then I peel off my shirt. Me from the waist up looks like it couldn't belong to the same person as me from the waist down. If my bottom half was built out of regular Legos, my top would be made of Duplos. These Sizes don't just need to be Special. They need to be Magic Sizes or I don't see how a dress is going to work.

I think I'm going to regret this, but I start in with what Tapey brought me.

The first thing is a sheath dress, like the one Mena had on. It gets to my armpits and doesn't move. I tug at the edge, but it isn't going anywhere. I pull it off and try the other way: I step into it and pull from the bottom. This time it slides up over my hips, but it gets stuck on the way up. Like if you tried to stuff a sea lion in a boot sock, only worse, because a sock would stretch a little. I take it off and hold it in front of me. It's the same skinniness from top to bottom. My optimism is starting to fade, but it's only one dress.

I carefully hang it back on the hanger because Kathryn Walsh has trained me well.

I try a pale teal dress with a full skirt next. This time I start from the bottom, pulling it on like a pair of pants. It feels right around the middle, and the fabric is this really nice kind of silk that's got imperfections in it—dupioni, it's called. It's a good length for me, a little above the knee, and I let myself pop up on my tiptoes a few times to imagine how it might look with heels.

But then I slide into the armholes and try to pull up the bodice. It's not working because my breasts are in the way. I pull the bottom up higher to give me more room and manage to get my arms all the way in. Now the top is up, stretched very tightly across my chest. The skirt is hanging wrong, higher in front than in back, I can't move my shoulders, and the whole thing looks like I've dropped a couple of ten-pound sacks of rice down around my belly. I haven't even tried to close the zipper on the side, which is gaping open about eight inches. You'd need a whole other Mena-size dress to fill in that gap.

I can't get that dress off fast enough.

"Are we finding anything?" Tape Measure says from behind the door.

Stop saying we. "Not really," I say. I slide it onto its hanger a little less carefully than the first one.

"Do we need a different size of anything?"

I mean it, lady. "I'm not sure that would help."

"What's not working for us?"

Unless you are prepared to squish inside this too-small triple-D polyester torture chamber, there is no us. I am very alone in here. "Um, they are too tight in the top."

Long pause.

"Why don't we take some measurements?" The door handle rattles but I've got it locked.

"No, thank you." *I don't need measurements. Your dresses can't count that high anyway.*

I hear Jessa now. "She has pretty big boobs. That might be it."

I glare at the door, hoping she can feel the heat of my gaze through it. Jessa has still not learned that We Don't Talk About Greer's Breasts. Jessa still believes We Talk About Whatever Comes to Mind. Usually volleyball. Sometimes protein shakes. Occasionally breasts.

I try the other dresses, each one worse than the one before. I'm leaning out the door in a T-shirt telling Kate she looks great when TM appears holding hangers in each hand. "I thought this blue might look lovely with your . . ." And somewhere in the middle of this sentence her gaze drifts from my face, lands at my chest, and stays there. ". . . eyes," she finishes.

Those aren't my eyes, I think. *My eyes are up here,* I think. "Thanks," I say, and take the dresses into my hellhole.

Why do schools even have formal dances anymore? Don't adults complain my generation only interacts on screens? Why can't we have a VR dance? I'd make my avatar a B cup. Maybe I'd give her swords for arms, too.

More consulting through the door. More failed attempts in the fitting room. But Tape Measure won't give up. She keeps bringing things, a couple at a time, and flopping them over the top of the door. She's gone from slinky to flowy, but everything, absolutely everything, is made for someone whose upper circumference is smaller than a snow tube. Zippers ain't gonna zip, lady.

Everybody else has moved on to jewelry. I told Jess to go with them. Eventually, I stop trying on what she brings me. I just take it from her at the door and hang it in the room, because none of it is going to work. None of it even comes close. I try not to think about what this means, because it means I'm going to have to make up an excuse not to go. I should have realized this right away and told Jackson I was going to be in New Mexico at a bar mitzvah or something. Now it's going to seem like I just don't want to go with him.

I scrunch on the bench playing games on my phone while the fitting room closes in like an overflowing closet.

"Now, this is a different route we could try. Remember we can alter anything." The toes of TM's cream pumps are peeking under the door into my fitting room. A circus-tent worth of fabric comes flopping over the top of the dressing room door. I decide I'll give her one last shot and then get out of here.

The dress is long, loose, and flowy. Everything else she picked out was colorful, but this is plain white. I slide it on and manage to get the long zipper most of the way up the back. A tiny bit of help and I could make it to the top, breasts and all. It's too big around the middle though—strangely big—not to mention that it's long and white. But I did manage to get Maude and Mavis contained, so that's good. And then I see myself in the mirror.

The tag hanging from the armpit says "Suzanne's Bridal Maternity Collection."

I am dressed as a pregnant bride.

This time I don't bother rehanging the dress. I just leave it in a pool on the floor and stomp on it on my way out. I don't say a word to Tape Measure, who is waiting outside with the same placid grin she's been wearing all day, that she probably wears every day, that she has probably trained herself to sleep in.

Jessa and the others are having a ball in the accessories section. They don't even notice me as I fly through the store and out to the sidewalk. I'll text Jess an apology later. I just need to be alone.

I mean *we* just need to be alone. The three of us.

CHAPTER 57

Quinlan opens the door before I knock, like she's been waiting for me. Maybe she's been watching out the window. Maybe she saw me pause at the driveway, then walk past the house, then circle back and get halfway up the drive, then leave again, sit on the curb, fidget with my phone, then finally come up to the front door.

If she's seen all that, she doesn't say anything about it. She just says, "Hi, Greer," and steps back to let me in. Her pajama bottoms have tiny whales with lacrosse sticks on them.

She notices that I'm looking at them and says, "I wanted volleyballs, but they only had these racket things." She points to a lacrosse stick. Several inches of bony ankle are visible at the bottom of her pants, the skin so pale it's almost purple. I wonder if she has any pants that are long enough.

"Those are lacrosse sticks. Tyler plays lacrosse."

"But you play volleyball."

"Yeah. I just started. Lacrosse is fun, too, though. Tyler likes it because sometimes people hit each other with sticks." She giggles.

"Thanks for the books you gave me," she says.

LOANED you, I think, but I say, "Did you read any of them yet?"

"Almost all. I'm reading *Artemis Fowl.*" *Artemis Fowl!* That's what else is missing. "Do you have all the *Artemis Fowls?*"

"I do."

"Did you read them all?"

"Of course."

"Jackson only read the first three." I'm not surprised by this.

"I think the first few are the best anyway," I tell her.

"That's what usually happens. But then I feel like I have to read them all anyway and then I get mad at the author because it's like they're not letting me read someone else's book that I would like better." I laugh, because it's exactly how I feel, too.

"Oh, it's Greer." Melinda comes to the entry. "Is your mom with you?" She looks around me, like maybe my mother is hidden behind my boobs.

"No, I just needed to talk to Jackson for a minute."

"Sure. I think he's getting out of the shower. Hang on." She bounds up the stairs, leaving me with Quinlan and a mental picture of Jackson in the shower, lathery and drippy, his abs lined like a crustacean. The butterfly mimes a striptease, but I poke my finger hard in my side to stop her. *Knock it off. You need to let this go.*

"Is that real?" Quin is squinting at my necklace, the diamond pendant Mom saved for me when Grandma died. (Technically, she bought it from Tiffany with money from selling Grandma's jewelry to an antique shop. She figured it was still like the necklace came from my dead grandmother, but this way it was a little classier than the chunky rhinestone stuff her mother liked.)

"No," I lie, tucking the chain under my shirt. "Fake." I don't know why I say this. By now I've figured out that Quin doesn't steal things because they are worth money; she steals things because they are worth something to somebody else.

Melinda pops back downstairs. "Go ahead and run up there, Greer." She blocks Quin from following me.

I was already nervous, and now my brain is split in half trying to figure out if I want him to be wearing just a towel when I get up the stairs or not. Really, though, what would I do with towelly Jackson? Shake his hand? Tell him that my mom's binder has a Men's Apparel section? Drool?

Jeans and a washed-out T-shirt. Wet hair, bare feet, and he smells like the shower. "Hey," he says and smiles. He hasn't shaved. The sun pouring through his bedroom window lights up the tiniest bit of stubble and seems completely wrong for this moment. It is aggressively bright when it should be wallowing behind a stratus cloud. "What's up?"

"Yeah, I'm, ah, just here checking on your water pressure."

He laughs, then cocks his head toward the bathroom. "You want to check it out? Let's go."

I blush hard. Damn, he's good.

"Sir, I'm from the Greater Chicago Water Conservation Bureau. We never shower." Point Greer for deflecting the flirt. "Do you know that the water from one shower could be used to brew hundreds of lattes?"

He laughs again, and he is too bright for this moment, too. Sooner or later I'm going to have to tell him why I'm here, but I don't want to. I've practiced: I'm going to look him straight in the eye and tell him that I changed my mind about the formal, that I hope we can still be friends, but that I think it would be better if he asked someone else. That's my plan. I will be frank and matter-of-fact, and he won't ask any questions—he'll probably be relieved—and we will go our separate ways, and I won't make up fantasies about his towel falling off anymore and he can get on with his life as a normal person and go to the fancy things with Angela Merkel from German class.

"Aha! I thought I recognized you. You're from Starbucks."

My face is hot again, thinking about the day I met him, thinking about how I've been thinking about him every day since then. Thinking how it was so good, when it was just that, but I wanted more than that, and now I am stuck here. "Ja, und du are ein German business fellow." It comes out too quiet and sad.

He can hear it, too. He tips his head and says nothing.

"Willst du Kartoffelsalat?" I try. He texted that one day when I was at practice and had said I was starving. It means "Do you want potato salad?" and was one of the first phrases he learned. I liked it so we sent back and forth pictures and recipes of potato salad until the assistant coach told me to go put my phone in the locker room. Why does Kartoffelsalat make me want to cry now?

"What's up, Greer?" That obnoxious, glaring sun lights up the pink shiny line on his forehead where his stitches were, caught in a wrinkle while he waits for me to answer.

It's now or never, and since never isn't an option, it's now. "I wanted to talk—" I can't look at him, because he is bright and kind and curious and then I will not be able to pretend this isn't killing me. So, I look above his head and that's when I notice that there is something new in the line of things on top of the bookshelf. There's Batman in Lego boat, Beanie iguana, Aquarium cup, tennis trophy, all the usuals, and right on the end, a mug with a picture of a dog, a car, and a briefcase orbiting around a coffee. The one from Cupernicus. *What is that doing here?*

"About anything in particular?" he prompts.

I'm tempted to ask about the mug but I've started down this path that I don't want to be on, plus I'm not sure I want to know anyway. "Yeah. Sorry. I wanted to talk about the formal."

"Okay." He waits, and when I don't say anything he adds, "I was thinking we could Uber from your house."

"Yeah," I say, still distracted by that mug. *Why does he have that? He has like four things.* "That's not what I mean. I, um, I'm not going to go."

"You're not going to go?"

"Yeah. I'm sorry. I thought I could, but I can't." *Why isn't it in the kitchen? Why is it with an iguana and a Batman?*

"You have other plans or something?"

"No. I mean, not exactly." *What makes those things a set?*

"Oh. All right." I couldn't have imagined it was possible, but Jackson looks self-conscious. Maybe even embarrassed. He looks like I probably look every time I see one of my parents' friends who hasn't seen me in a while. ("Wow, you've really gotten . . . taller.")

"It's not that I don't want to," I rush. My practice run was for nothing. That stupid mug keeps making me think about Schnucks and Cupernicus and how I felt that day—goofy and happy and hopeful—and how I thought maybe the formal could be like that, too. But you can't wear a sweatshirt to a formal, and

I can't be goofy and happy and hopeful wearing a wedding dress made for someone eight months pregnant. I can't figure out what to say here.

"It's all right, Greer. I get it."

"No, you don't," I say. He doesn't get it at all. He thinks I don't want to go with him, but he is wrong. I would go anywhere with him—Starbucks or Cupernicus or the grocery store or Cleveland—if only I didn't have to bring the rest of myself along. I look at the tiny dog circling the tiny coffee on the mug. Copernicus was an idiot. He thought the universe revolved around the sun. Not to me. To me it revolves around my boobs. "I just," I stutter, "I just don't know what I would wear."

He looks up suddenly. "What?"

I shift between my feet. "I can't really . . . there's not really a dress . . ."

"You're saying you don't want to go because you can't find a dress?"

It's obvious that he thinks it's stupid, and I feel myself getting defensive. Like now, after all this time, he's going to think I'm some flaky, ridiculous girl who is being snobby about clothes. Give me some credit.

"You want to wear a suit and I'll wear a dress?" I can't tell if he's kidding. I don't think he is.

"You don't understand." *You couldn't understand. You can just slide into anything—into anywhere—and feel like yourself.*

This is going very, very wrong, and I don't know how to stop it. I should have stuck with the bar mitzvah excuse, but eventually it was going to come to this anyway. I feel like I'm going to cry way too much lately. I didn't used to. I never cried when life was just school and Maggie and baking shows.

"Or maybe you could just wear your favorite sweatshirt." It's a dig. Not a volleyball dig. A mean, sarcastic dig and it takes my breath away.

My favorite?

I look down at my sweatshirt, pilling under the sleeves, starting to fray at the cuffs. He's right. It is my favorite. It's my favorite because it's the most boxy one, way too big, but the sleeves still aren't too long. It's my favorite because it's so heavy, the fleece doesn't cling or lie close to my body at all. It's my favorite because the elastic at the bottom isn't too tight, which makes a top balloon. It's my favorite because it's the most plain, nondescript gray, so I can pull it on day after day and people hardly notice. It's my favorite because I can dig my hands deep in the pocket if I need to feel smaller inside it. He's right: It's my favorite.

And I hate the fucking thing.

I want to say something back, to growl, to fight, to defend myself, to plead, but Jackson's cheeks are pinker than usual. And he's blinking a lot. And there is a tiny line of water threatening to spill over his beautiful lashes. He's not mad. He's hurt. The sun is still blinding bright, but he's not. He feels, I think, like I feel.

"Why didn't you just say you didn't want to go in the first place?" he asks the window.

"I'm sorry," I whisper to him. *I did,* I say, only in my head, *I do.* And I leave.

This time when I get home and close my door, I don't take off my bra and lie flat on my back. This time I curl up in a ball. And I cry.

CHAPTER 58

The good news is that when Tyler got hit in the mouth with a hockey stick, his braces cut up his mouth so badly that he got some freaky infection.

Let me start again.

It's not good news that my brother is suffering. I am not a monster. It's pretty bad. And gross. You're not supposed to be able to get infections in your mouth unless they do oral surgery, but apparently Tyler is a human petri dish. The bacteria were happy to colonize inside his lip. It swelled up to his forehead and he spiked a fever. Urgent care sent him to the emergency room, which put him on an IV drip for a few hours. Now he's home on a massive dose of antibiotics that is also killing all the good bacteria in his intestines, so he's got diarrhea and Mom's making him eat yogurt.

I realize that doesn't sound like good news. It's just that it's had this unintended silver lining, which is that my mother has been so consumed by Tyler's maxillofacial/gastrointestinal emergency, she has left me alone. When I originally told her I was going to the formal, I told her it was as a favor to Jackson because he didn't know a lot of people. She gave me a smug "Huh, Greer, that's so generous of you" that I chose to ignore. Then this weekend I told her I had good news: He found someone else and I was off the hook.

It was possibly the least convincing lie I've ever told (and one time I told her that I had just *found* baby Ty inside her rolling suitcase with all his clothes packed and a pacifier to keep him quiet). It's the kind of thing she might have hounded me about, if it weren't for Tyler coming down all red faced and puffy and saying, "Can yoo yoock at my yip a sec?"

Monday, I dawdle outside of math, trying to strike a look that says I'm waiting for Jackson if he wants to stop and talk, and that I'm standing out here for some other reason if he does not. It turns out not to matter. When the bell rings I haven't seen him at all.

Tuesday, I wait almost as long, then creep down the hall to peek into the German room. He's in the class already, sprechen with a group of Studenten (including you-know-who).

By Wednesday I just head straight into math to judge Kurtis and Omar's daily homework argument like I used to.

Now I understand that we are officially avoiding each other.

σ

Maggie's current crusade is against the "anti-feminist behaviors, wealth-biased culture, and implied measures of self-worth embedded in the outdated, unaffordable, but still prevalent practice of high school formals." She complains about it to anyone who will listen, which is mostly just me and Rafa. You would think she would protest by not going, but Maggie likes to make her objections more visible. She and Rafa are going to the dance, but she is spending lunch searching the web for a medieval dress to demonstrate how old-fashioned the whole thing is.

I had told her that it had been obvious that Jackson felt obligated to ask about the dance, and that I didn't really want to go except that I felt obligated, and that once we both realized *that* everyone was off the hook. I didn't have to go and he could ask whoever he wanted.

"That was the conversation you had?" she had said.

"It wasn't like a whole conversation or anything."

"But did he ever actually *say* he didn't want to go? Or that there was someone else he wanted to go with?"

"I mean, not exactly word for word, but it was obvious."

"It was 'obvious'? So, it wasn't about the dr—"

Before she could finish, I shut down FaceTime on my computer, then texted that there was something wrong with my Wi-Fi. That was three days ago and she hasn't tried to bring it up since.

I lean over to look at the site she's got pulled up. There is a whole page of beautiful, flowing gowns in deep burgundy and emerald, with long, drapey sleeves and gold embroidery. Most of the models are wearing crowns of flowers around their heads and one has a pair of wings that, I'd like to point out, is not historically accurate. Prices range from eight hundred fifty dollars to more than a thousand.

"So, basically you're trying to dress like you're working at the Renaissance Faire."

She chews on the side of her pinky. "Yeah, I see that now."

"Makes sense, since you're both in theater."

"Ha-ha."

"What's Rafa going to wear? Chain mail? Is he going as a knight?"

"I get it, Greer."

"Plus it's like a thousand dollars. Oh, sorry—it's a thousand *Coin of the Realm*." I use a Ren Faire turkey-leg-seller voice.

"All right! I know! Not the right era. What should I look for? Maybe Victorian? Women were oppressed in Victorian times, right?"

"Sure."

She does an image search for "Victorian dress" and we get a page full of poofy, ruffly hoopskirts with high-necked tops.

"They definitely say 'old-fashioned.'"

"Right," she says. She scrolls through the pages, looking like she's eaten a booger-flavored jelly bean. She clicks on a purple one that buttons up to the chin, with long sleeves and layers and layers of fabric. The only skin showing is the woman's face. Black lace edging gives the whole thing a Walmart/Bride of Frankenstein feel. "That's, uh—"

"Hideous." I wonder if Maggie's convictions are strong enough to make her wear something that ugly.

"What's another time in history women weren't treated equally?"

"All of them?" I say. "Yesterday? Next Thursday?"

Maggie laughs. She tries "Biblical dress," which gives us mostly things you see Mary wear in nativity scenes. "Pioneer dress" is basically her costume for the play. I lean over her and try "1950s cocktail dress." My parents have been watching *The Marvelous Mrs. Maisel* and Mom can't stop fawning over the dresses.

"Ooh. Some of these are cute," she says.

"Definitely." I pull up a photo of a woman in a short, full dress with a wide boatneck. It's lime green, with little cap sleeves. There's another one with a wrapped sleeveless top and contrasting belt. I feel a pang in my stomach, wishing for a second we were shopping for me.

"I wonder what kind of shoes you'd wear," Maggie mumbles to herself.

We find a bunch more dresses from the fifties and sixties. The thing is, if your goal was to look ridiculous so people would know you were essentially mocking the whole dance, these dresses would not do it. They are too cute. I can see Maggie make a mental shift.

"You know, if I was going to get one of those medieval dresses just to make a point, my parents would end up spending hundreds of dollars, and that's a big part of what's so wrong about the whole thing, isn't it? The amount of money you have to spend on a thing you're going to wear once? The consumerism is just as bad as the chauvinism." While she's talking she's typing "vintage clothes shop near me."

"Uh-huh."

"I mean, if I could find a vintage dress it would be reusing. It would still be a rejection of the whole prom-industrial complex."

I tug her fading green ponytail. "You'd really be making a statement," I say.

She's chewing her lip, trying to decide if she's betraying her ideals to get excited about a dress. I don't think Maggie's wanting to make a statement *and* wear a cute dress at the same time means she is less of a feminist.

All I want is to wear a cute dress and not have it make any statement at all. To blend in with all the other people in all the other dresses. What does that mean about me?

CHAPTER 59

Thursday, there is a sub in math. Ms. Tanner is the advanced math curricular lead for the whole district, so we end up with a lot of subs while she's consulting with the administration. The subs are usually not qualified to teach calc, so they hand out a worksheet at the beginning of the hour and play on their phones the rest of the time. Some kids scratch away at the problems (the Ashers and Anithas), but for Kyle Tuck and his stupid friends, it's free time. (Remember this is an honors-level class, so they aren't stupid in a technical way, just in a who-do-you-want-around-in-a-civilized-society way.) The little pod of Orcs hovers together laughing.

They might be making memes about the sub, not that she'd care. You have to have a thick skin to be a sub, and I bet this one has worked up some good calluses playing Candy Crush while the AP Bullying students teach themselves.

One by one, they keep looking my way. If they catch my eye, they whip back around. My shoulders hunch more than usual. I cave inward, crossing my arms in front of me on the desk. I know in my head that it's stupid, that I'm better than this, that what they think is as unimportant as the spray of toast crumbs Tyler leaves behind and I sweep out of the way every morning. I try to focus on working ahead through the next week's learning targets so I won't have to do it after practice. But Kyle and company keep snorting.

I'm two steps out the door before the bell even stops ringing. I don't want to play this game with them again, the game that is only fun for them. I don't have it in me today. Not this week. But I'm not fast enough.

"Hey, Greer!" I should keep my head down and keep moving, but I turn back. Kyle is standing in the doorway holding out a sheet of paper. "Do you want to try our crossword puzzle?"

"Word find, stupid," one of the other goons corrects him.

Jackson is coming down the hall. I accidentally make eye contact and he stops short and looks at the floor. This must be his strategy, to get to class extra early and run out afterward so he doesn't have to see me. I've upset the pattern by rushing out today.

"Do you want to try our word find?" says Kyle. His tortoise-turd eyes are bright with joy, like a dog that's just found a dead rabbit to roll in. He's trying to hold in a laugh as he waves the paper. It's a big handmade grid of letters and I'm pretty sure I can guess the words without even looking. Seems like a lot of extra Os in that grid. Plenty of Bs. More than an average amount of Ts.

My part of this game is supposed to be a witty comeback that proves I'm above this but you know what? It turns out I'm not. It sucks. It hurts. It makes my shoulders wilt. Instead of my usual pretend superiority, I slap the page out of Kyle's hand. "Fuck off, Kyle." The whole hallway hears. The word find drifts to the floor in front of Jackson.

I catch his look of surprise before I'm gone but he can fuck off, too.

CHAPTER 60

After practice, a bunch of us are lined up on the stone wall waiting for rides. It's January, but we were running around the gym for two hours and the crisp air feels good. Anyone with a car or a friend with a car or who lives close enough to walk is gone. Sylvie is holding one DynaFreeze instant ice pack against her knee with her elbow and another around her middle finger while she tells Nasrah about her plan to take a gap year on an olive ranch so she can get in-state tuition in California. Mena is trying to show me how to do a fishtail braid on Khloe Vang-Ellis, but Khloe's hair is too short. At least that's the excuse Mena is making, but really, I'm just no good with hair. I'm only half paying attention to her instructions, listening to Jessa give a pep talk to Kaia Beaumont.

"You'll get it. You're really fast. You really got under some of those balls today." I know Jess is stretching here, because Kaia is the biggest disappointment on the team this year. Her serves are decent, which is good because serving is the only time she's not afraid of the ball. Once it comes back toward her, she panics. She looked good in tryouts, but after you get nailed a few times, you either accept it as part of playing—like Sylvie, who is now icing the finger and the knee together with one pack so she can drink Mena's Gatorade with the other—or you shrink. To a player like Jessa, who would not be afraid of a ball if it were made from a wasp nest and shot out of a cannon, this Kaia situation must be maddening. But Jess looks sincere. Kaia's part of the team and as long as she shows up, suits up, and sweats, Jess is on her side.

Khloe's mom pulls up. She unthreads the mess I made of her hair as she heads to the car. "I hope you weren't planning on going to cosmetology school, Greer."

"Ingrate!"

Soon the others are gone, too, except for Jessa. My dad is picking me up, which means I'll be waiting for another twelve hours. Jessa's parents are late, too.

"The only way to get my dad to show up on time is to lie to him about when he's supposed to be there," I say.

"Do you do that?"

"No," I admit. "Mom and I always say we're going to, but then we worry it will be the one time he's actually on time."

"And then he'd be mad."

"Actually, no. He'd just be early." I think about this for a minute. Maybe there is no downside to telling my dad that practice ends at five instead of five thirty.

"Too bad you can't make him run laps if he's late. That motivates people."

"I wonder what motivates people who run track? I mean, if you're going to be running laps anyway . . ."

"Ha!" Jessa likes even my dumbest jokes. For a while I thought her family must be very serious, and that's why she laughed at everything, but I've met the Timmses and I think they're just people who appreciate the effort.

Jessa hops off the wall and dribbles a volleyball a few times. She sets it up, gently, then gets under it and pops it up again, over and over. When it flails out to the side, she catches it and starts over again.

"Is everybody in your family good at sports?"

"I guess so. Maddie thinks she's the best." She tries to twirl the volleyball on one finger. It doesn't make a single revolution, but she tries again.

"The one in college?" Jess's big sister plays soccer for Ohio Northern University.

"Yeah. She probably would have been good at anything she played, but she always loved soccer." She tries to bounce the ball on her knees, like a soccer player, but she can't get more than two bounces. "I was never into soccer. I'm not that good at running. She's more like my mom. I'm more like my dad." Jess goes back to setting the ball to herself.

"How do you mean?"

"She's fast and skinny. I mean not skinny-skinny. Just on the skinnier side. Which I am not." I watch Jess carefully as she says this. She is eyeing the ball. There is nothing in her voice that sounds like envy. Nothing in her face that looks like regret. Just facts. "She and my mom are good at speed and endurance, but they don't have power, you know?" She's looking straight up at the ball, calculating, moving, getting it right, again and again. She looks happy, like she's where she's supposed to be. Like she's who she's supposed to be. "My dad and my little sister and me, we've got power." I realize that this is exactly how Jessa understands herself. She doesn't think of herself as "not skinny." She thinks of herself as strong. Powerful. And she is exactly right. "Plus, we work our asses off." The ball arcs wide and comes down eight feet from her. She lunges and dives, getting her fists under it just before it hits the ground. She lands on her knees on the concrete, but the volley is saved.

When Dad finally pulls up twenty minutes late, I offer Jess a ride, since her parents seem to be MIA. "No, thanks. My dad's here." She waves at a car at the edge of the parking lot. Mr. Timms leans his head out and waves back, all smiles. I didn't see him drive in, so he must have been here the whole time. "See you tomorrow!" She jogs to the Highlander, ball under one arm, and climbs in the passenger side.

She wasn't waiting for a ride. She was waiting with the team.

CHAPTER 61

My dad prefers painting with me.

Tyler is too sloppy. Even when you think you've covered every possible surface with a drop cloth, he'll step in paint and leave a dotted trail of Spring Fawn or Whispering Walnut or whatever other on-trend beige my mother has picked out.

Mom's an excellent painter—meticulous about taping and prep, never leaves globs, edges like a razor. But she's too bossy. She considers us her apprentices.

So Dad prefers me. I never swing the roller like a lacrosse stick, and I don't tell him that he should trim the windows in a counterclockwise direction because the sheen pattern deflects light outward that way. I'm good, but not obsessive. And I like his music.

Mom's at Pilates and Ty is still in bed, watching old *Parks and Rec* episodes on the iPad. He says his mouth still hurts too much to brush his teeth. Dad and I are just about to pop open the first gallon of paint when the doorbell rings, which usually means an environmental activist with a petition or a neighborhood kid sell-ing cookie dough.

It's neither. It's Maggie with a Vitaminwater.

"We need to talk." She's wearing her business face, which could mean she has just found out that our high school uses three hundred thousand gallons of water on the football field or that rich people pay less taxes than their chauffeurs, but I kind of doubt that. I think this one is about me. "And I'd hate for your FaceTime to crap out again."

Definitely about me.

"Sure, but we were just about to start painting the office up-stairs, so . . ."

Helpful/Not Helpful Dad pops in. "You know what? I was thinking I wanted to make a coffee run before we really dive in." The man can read a room.

"Great." I try to sound enthusiastic. I love Maggie more than just about anybody, but I've done a very good job not having a serious conversation with her for almost four months and I was hoping to keep that going for at least another several years.

Dad takes off, and Maggie and I head down to the family room. She's only seen pictures of the Lovesac.

"Oh my god. You could fit your whole family in this thing!" She plops herself in the middle and insists I climb in with her, which really means climbing all over her. It's a lot of elbows and knees before we're settled, facing each other in a beanbag the size of a dwarf planet.

She hands me her Vitaminwater, watching carefully, like she's trying to figure out where to start. I realize I'm nervous. About

Maggie. This is not how things are supposed to be. "Did I tell you that my mom is getting a client from Hong Kong who has triplets?" I try.

"Jackson Oates," she replies.

I stop the bottle an inch from my lips. I shift in my spot and the foam filler resettles. "What about Jackson Oates?"

She leans forward and puts her hands together in a steeple, like one of those TV detectives who also happens to be a psychologist. "For a long time, I thought that he liked you and you didn't even realize it."

"No, he's just always been friendly because of our moms."

"Hang on. That's what I thought at first. But then I realized that wasn't it. Then I thought, he likes her, she doesn't like him, and she thinks she's being polite by pretending not to notice. Because you totally avoid conflict."

"No, Maggie, it's just because I was the first person—"

"Patience, my friend!" She grabs the bottle back from me and finishes the rest. Maggie is on a roll. "I'm only halfway through. Because then I thought, she likes him, but she doesn't realize he likes her." I roll my eyes. "But that was wrong, too, because what I now believe is this: He likes her, she likes him, she actually knows it but pretends not to so she can fuck it all up." She says it like she's solved the case, but she doesn't look triumphant. She looks sad. I pick at the fake fur under us. After a minute she says, much more softly, "The part I can't figure out is why."

I think of a hundred sarcastic comebacks, but none of them come out. I wait for a long time for her to go on, but she doesn't. When I look up, she is holding out her arms. It's probably exactly how I looked at her when her dog got leukemia. Finally, I say, "I really fucked it up."

And the second the tears start down my cheeks, they are running down hers, too.

And, for the million and first time in my life, I am grateful for Maggie Cleave.

It's hard to hug somebody in a Lovesac. Mavis takes a sharp elbow to the nipple, and my head bangs into Maggie's chin. The thing nearly swallows us up. The crying turns to laughing and oofing and more crying. Every time I try to separate us, we either sink deeper together or one of us nearly falls out. But we cling and claw our way back and then there we are, a tangle of legs, arms, and bodies, Maggie's crossed over mine, and I am breathing normally again.

"You've really put a lot of time into this Jackson thing," I say.

"I know. It's been pretty exhausting, honestly."

"You could have just asked me."

"I tried. Like forty times."

I know this is true. I have always known this was true. "I don't know what I would have said anyway." I look up at the ceiling and try to piece it together in my own mind, what I want, what I don't want, what I wish for, what I'm scared of. "It's like the ideal thing for me would be a boyfriend that was super into me, but didn't actually want to touch me."

Maggie bursts out laughing. "No, it's not."

I pull her leg hairs. Hard. "Don't laugh at me. I'm trying to be honest."

"No, you're not." I glare at her. "You're not! Really, Greer? You never think about kissing him? You never imagine running your hand up inside his shirt or kissing his chest or him sliding off those little butt huggers you wear with your volleyball costume? You are honestly telling me that you don't want Jackson Oates to *touch* you?"

"Oh god," I say, ducking my face into both my hands. Have I mentioned that Maggie Cleave can read minds? "No. No, I can't tell you that. Ugh. I like him, Mags. Really like him. Or I did. Or I do. So, so much. I don't know what I'm doing."

I flop forward over her legs, which are over mine, and sit for a minute, Maggie playing with the back of my hair. I assume that she's going to tell me that it's simple, because I assume that it's simple for her. I assume it's simple for everybody but me.

"I think . . . " She starts and stops. "It's like you've been trying to live your whole life inside your head. I mean you were always a brainiac, but the last couple of years, it's been different. Like you know in *Futurama* how they keep all the famous people's heads in jars? I could see you being a head in a jar.

"So when you said you were auditioning for volleyball, at first I was, like, How's that going to work? but once I realized you were serious, I was really excited, especially when I saw you coming out of those rehearsals. Like you were finally going to get outside your jar. You'd be sweaty and exhausted and smell like armpits (no offense), but you were also, I don't know, kind of relaxed. Loose. Happy? This sounds crazy but the first time I saw you coming from the gym, I thought you had gotten taller. I mean your posture is still terrible (no offense), but I think you actually stand straighter after you play."

We talk forever, Maggie trying to do a Dutch braid but mostly tying knots in my hair. Not only does Dad not ask me to come paint, he shows up with a tray of drinks from the coffee shop. Hot cocoa for me, a soy mocha latte for Mags. My dad is a good guy, and a good guy knows when what you need is a good girl.

It turns out Maggie doesn't tell me it's simple. She tells me it's hard. It's hard because she knows who I am. But she also tries to tell me it will get better.

"Forget about Jackson. Think about a mystery man. Imagine that everything is going great, like for some reason you're not all worked up about your boobs. And then it turns out this guy has this mole." I glare at her. "Not like a normal mole, though. It's shaped like a swastika. And he knows you're half Jewish, so he's too embarrassed to ever let you see it. He thinks you're going to freak out. What do you do?"

"I send him to a dermatologist because that sounds like a very irregular mole."

"Come on, Greer. Do you care about him enough to get past the mole?"

"Are you comparing my boobs to a Nazi mole?"

"*I* don't think your boobs are a Nazi mole. I think *you* think your boobs are a Nazi mole. And by the way, in case you missed it, straight guys usually think big boobs are a positive."

"They don't have to play volleyball with them."

"They wish they could play volleyball with them."

I pinch her, not hard. "But what's your point? That I'd still date somebody who had a weird mole? It's not the same thing, Maggie."

"I know it's not the same thing. No one has the same thing. But everybody's got *some* thing."

"I don't think Nella Woster has any things."

"I knew you were going to say that. You're practically in love with that girl."

"Here's the problem. What if I didn't mind the mole. Maybe I'm even turned on by weird moles. But what if he didn't want me to see it or touch it but it was right in the way of everything, and every time I got close to him he freaked out that I was going to freak out?"

"Okay, let's say he's got a really crooked penis."

"MAGGIE!"

"If all that happened, you wouldn't touch the mole. Not until he was ready."

"And what if I didn't want to wait for that?"

"Then you wouldn't be the right person for him. And you'd both figure that out." She puts her hand in my hand and squeezes. "But, buddy? I think you're going to want him to touch your moles. And by moles I mean—"

"MAGGIE!"

σ

Before Maggie leaves, I get the full download on Rafa, and how not shy he turns out to be, and how he's writing a musical they both hope Kennedy will do next year. She makes me promise that the next time there's a Jackson, I won't shut her out. I make her promise she won't pressure me about it, which she acts like she would never do, but which she would absolutely do. I don't want there to be a next Jackson, though. I just want there to be this Jackson.

CHAPTER 62

"We have milk if you want." As soon as I walk in the door from school, I can hear Tyler. It's Wednesday, Mom's yoga day. He must have a friend over.

I round the corner to see Quinlan sitting behind a bowl of co-op brand Cap'n Crunch. (Kommodore Krinkles, made with certified gluten-free cornmeal and real maple sugar.) "Is it almond milk or soy milk?"

"Just, um, regular milk?" replies Ty.

"Cow milk?"

"I guess?" Is it possible that my brother isn't sure where milk comes from?

"Okay, just this once."

Tyler sets the jug next to her. He shoots me a look. Quinlan's fingers are so pale and so fine, it seems like they will break under the weight of the milk jug. She pours a thin stream that floats the Krinkles to the rim of the bowl.

"Hi, Quin."

She notices me and her face brightens. "You're home! I was waiting for you!"

I am expecting to hear Mom and Melinda, but the house is silent except for the shifting of cereal in Quin's bowl. "Is your mom here? Or your brother?" It's been weeks, and Jackson and I just give a weak "hey" in the hall if we aren't able to avoid each other entirely, so if he's here somewhere, he's probably hiding.

"No." She scoops some cereal and licks a drip of milk from the bottom of the spoon.

"Did they drop you off?" Was Tyler babysitting now? The kid can barely avoid electrocuting himself with the remote control.

"I rode the school bus." She picks a piece of cereal out of the bowl and nibbles on it, as though each Krinkle needed three or four bites. I peek out into the living room; Grumpy Dwarf is safe on the bookshelf with his six brothers by his side.

"Your bus dropped you here today?"

"Quinlan came on our old bus," Tyler pipes in. "She used the school directory app on her phone to figure out who lived close to us, and then she followed Pia Katz home." His eyes are huge, like he thinks he's telling me in code that the kid is bananas. He still hasn't forgiven her for the Mario earbuds. I want to tell Tyler that a kid who is smart enough to triangulate our location to stop four on the Giraffe Bus would have already killed him if she wanted to. He doesn't know what I know. She's not a psycho. She's lonely.

"So, you're here on your own?" I say. "Did you tell your mom where you were going?"

"I brought your book back." She slides off the stool to unzip her backpack and hands me *Mrs. Frisby and the Rats of NIMH.* There's a folded-up paper in the back, like a makeshift bookmark.

"Thanks, Quinlan. You didn't have to bring it back." I realize I mean it.

"I really liked it," she says, and then, inexplicably, begins to cry. Her face crumples, and the tears come. She goes from runaway mastermind to broken, hurting little girl in no seconds flat. Tyler and I look at each other, helpless.

"God, Greer. Let her keep it!" scolds Tyler. But whatever this is, it is not about the book.

"Quin, what's going on? Did something happen at school? Tyler, go get some tissues." Ty is happy to have a job that is not talking to a sobbing child. *And call Mom,* I mouth as I squat down next to her.

She throws her arms around me, knocking me to my butt. When Tyler returns with a box of Kleenex, I am sitting on the kitchen floor with Quinlan in my lap, crying into my neck. She's long and bony, but trying to make herself small enough to fit. "It's okay, kiddo." I have no idea what *it* is, so I don't know that *it* will be okay, but how bad could it be, right? She's in third grade. Someone was probably mean to her at lunch. Or the class guinea pig picked a different kid to partner with.

"I don't want to go," she says and sniffs. "I don't want to go." She gasps between sobs. She's squished hard into my chest, shaking. She holds impossibly tight and I let her, even if it's uncomfortable.

"You can stay," I say. "We'll call your mom. We'll ask if she can pick you up later." She cries harder. "We'll pick out some more books. I've got tons and tons of books. Have you ever read *Fable-haven*? I loved that when I was your age." She's so skinny and fragile here in my lap, and so, so sad. I'd give her all my books, Grumpy Dwarf, and one of Tyler's kidneys if it would make her happy. But I'm not having any effect. She's not hearing a thing I say.

"I don't want to go again," she says. "I like it here."

"I know, buddy, we're going to call—"

"I like you guys."

"We like you, too—"

"I don't want to go to hamster den," she wails.

"You don't want to what?"

"I don't want to move to Amsterdam. I just want to stay at our house we have now."

I get a hot, sick feeling from my belly to my forehead. "What do you mean move to Amsterdam? Quin?"

She sits up, and I can see the full effect of the crying. Her eyes and nose are rimmed red, and there are wet trails down her porcelain cheeks. Her ponytail is half out like a wispy white-blond aura. She wipes her nose with the back of her hand. "And there's a really nice girl at school named Avery, and she said she would invite me to her birthday, but her birthday's not till July, so I won't even get to go to any birthdays. I didn't go to any birthdays the whole year."

And I understand. My stomach fills with wet cement. It's seeping into all my organs and the places between my organs and already starting to harden. The butterfly watches, terrified, as it covers her ankles. The panic is changing already to a dead weight. A weight that keeps increasing.

Just like Dad said. They are moving. Again. This time to Amsterdam. I don't know when, but definitely before Nice Avery's birthday party. Before junior year. Before I have had enough time to either glue my friendship with Jackson back together again and start over or convince myself that I don't want to.

I fold myself over elf girl and hold tight for both our sakes.

CHAPTER 63

The fugitive sits on her mother's lap, with my Josefina American Girl doll in her lap and a stack of my books at her feet. Her eyes are still bloodshot, but she's not crying anymore. I called Melinda from our house, and when Mom came home she drove us here. We've already been through the reunion scene, in which Melinda scolds Quinlan for having disappeared like that, and then heaps praise on all the Walshes for keeping her safe.

Ben has been offered the position in Amsterdam, she tells us, but hasn't decided yet. It's "a very big opportunity," which I assume means he will get paid a trillion dollars, and which I assume means he's going to say yes.

"I don't think Quinlan wants him to take it," I say. The girl is focused on braiding Josefina's hair, but she nods in agreement.

"Oh, Quinny's just worried about missing a birthday party." Melinda squeezes Quin's shoulders. "I told her, though, we'll actually be able to go to Disney Paris for a weekend if we want."

"But I can't bring Avery, and that's whose birthday it is."

"I know, sweetie. But maybe you'll make friends with a Dutch girl!" Quin looks at me and scrunches up her nose. Melinda goes on. "Kids make friends so easily." She pauses a minute and adds, "Well, Jackson always makes friends easily."

The cement block in my stomach increases by ten pounds. Jackson makes friends easily; what she doesn't say is that he leaves friends just as easily. I did not understand these rules before.

I want to ask what Jackson has said about the move—like maybe that he would rather live in the dumpster behind Cupernicus than leave me and Kennedy High School—but Quinlan is in front of me, poking me in the leg with Josefina.

"Greer, will you come see something in my room?"

"Sure," I say, because I don't really want to know what Jackson told his mother about the move anyway.

As I follow Quinlan upstairs, I hear Mom say, "I always thought it would be fun to go to high school in Europe!"

Jackson's door is open, but it's quiet in there. He's working out with the baseball team, Melinda said. I wonder if he's told them he might not make it to the season.

There are two other American Girl dolls in Quin's room—Kit Kittredge, who is the most famous one, and a new one I don't recognize, who is wearing doll-sized fencing gear. Quin pulls Kit off an American Girl horse and puts Josefina in her place. Makes sense, I think, since Josefina lives on a ranch. Back at my house she only had a stuffed sea lion. She'll be happy here.

I wonder what they think of American Girl dolls in Hamster Den?

Whatever Quinlan wanted to show me she has forgotten

about, lost in redistributing Kit's things to Josi. I wander around her room. It's gotten even crazier since the last time I was here. She could be on an episode of *Tween Hoarders*.

I notice a bunch of colorful globs on her dresser. They look like Play-Doh, but when I touch one, it's more like plastic.

I know what this is. It's polymer clay. You get it at the craft store. It starts out soft, but when you bake it, it hardens. Maggie and I tried making beads one summer, but they didn't work.

Quin has made all kinds of little things, some recognizable, some not. There's a pink kitten, and what's probably a frog. A lot look like chewed gum. I'm ready to dismiss them when I notice one that looks familiar. Not exactly familiar, but recognizable. It's a little man with a pointy hat and what is probably supposed to be a long white beard. It's Grumpy Dwarf. She made herself a Grumpy Dwarf.

I pick through the pile and find more dwarfs, and a skinny figure with a blue and red dress, a white head, and black hair. It's my whole set, remade in Sculpey. What's remarkable isn't that they are especially good, it's that she's made them at all.

I pick up another blob. Now that I realize what she's done, I can figure out what it's supposed to be. This one's a tennis racket stuck on a block: Jackson's doubles trophy from his bookshelf. A little iguana. I'd never guess that this speckly melty mess was a Lego boat with a Batman if I didn't know what I was looking for, but I'm sure of it. It's Jackson's stuff, in miniature.

I line them up in even rows. I find the one I'm looking for: A tiny perfect coffee mug. I can imagine those skinny fingers rolling out the minuscule handle. For a second I understand Quin entirely, because I have to work hard not to just slip it in my pocket.

Even the things I don't recognize must have a real-life counterpart somewhere. So Quinlan's got a collection, too, only hers is a collection of other people's collections. She's made a miniature copy of other people's lives.

"Did you ever make anything with Sculpey?" she asks. She's right beside me now, leaning her elf face against my arm.

"I tried. I wasn't as good as you." I finish putting all the figures in lines.

"You weren't?"

"Nope. I only made little balls."

"For what?"

"They were supposed to be beads, but the holes closed up in the oven."

Quin reaches out to straighten my rows, evening up the space between the kitten and a volleyball. "What were you going to do with the beads?"

"Maggie and I were going to make bracelets. And then Tyler ate a couple of them." Quin gasps and giggles. "It wasn't his fault. He was little and they looked like candy. I mean if you didn't know better, wouldn't you try to eat this?" I hold up a plump purple heart, which matches a monster fur pillow on her bed. Quin takes it from me and puts it back in its row. "So my mom threw them away."

Quin thinks about this for a minute. "I don't let my mom throw things away."

I look around the chaos of her room, with its overflowing bins and shelves piled deep, its mountains of clothes and stuffed animals, and stacks and stacks of games no one plays with her. It's obvious no one has ever thrown any of her things away. This is what she does, I guess. The moving truck must get bigger and bigger. If you keep moving around the world, you try to take the world with you.

Unless you're Jackson. Then you do the opposite. You leave everything behind.

"You do have a lot of stuff," I say.

"Thanks," says Quin, like it's a compliment.

CHAPTER 64

Jackson is sitting on the floor leaning against my locker. There's virtually nobody else here this early. (Mom drove.) I was planning to be safe inside math long before the bell. He must have suspected this, because here he is, looking like he slept here.

A few weeks ago, this would have had me blushing from the inside out. Now it just makes the cement block in my belly heavier and harder.

But still, that stupid butterfly keeps beating herself against the wall 150 times a minute. She doesn't understand there's no point. There never has been.

Not a butterfly. My stupid heart.

He messaged me last night. Said he would have told me himself but Quin beat him to it. Said it wasn't final yet, so nobody was supposed to know. Said once you told people you weren't coming back the next year, they kind of stopped bothering with you.

My responses were:

No problem

Got it

[insincere sad-face emoji]

The sad-face emoji is just a sad-face emoji. There's not a special one for insincere sad face. Only I knew it was insincere.

He said other things, too, but none of them were "This sucks" or "I hate my parents" or "Let's run away to Stockholm and watch them award the Nobel Prize in Physics." None of them were the kinds of things I wished he would say.

I would be less disappointed if I thought he was more disappointed. What I felt like writing was:

> Just go away already. You are a ten-second mirage in the four years I'm going to spend in this stupid school and it was easier before you. I'm going to go back to the short list of things I am good at, and you are not one of them.

But obviously I wasn't going to send that, so I ended with a GIF of a cartoon cow shrugging its shoulders and went to bed.

And now he's sitting against my locker where I can't just cartoon cow him. He is all bent arms and legs. He looks like a lean letter M. If I sat like that, Maude and Mavis would fill all the space between my body and my knees. I'd be like a filled-in O on a standardized test.

I hover over him waiting to open my locker.

"My mom wanted me to give you these," he says. He hands me a paper bag. "To thank you for taking care of Quinlan yesterday. She's never done something like that before." The bag is warm. Inside there are fresh blueberry scones.

They smell like waking up on top of a mountain in the spring-time. I mean in a fancy lodge on a mountain, not actually out-doors where a grizzly could maul you and eat your scone. At least I understand how his *mom* feels about me: nice girl with a big ap-petite. "Tell her thanks."

I wait patiently till he gets up and out of the way of my locker, unload my books, and wonder what I'm supposed to say next. Good luck in Amsterdam? I hope there are goede relokateun aadveusers there?

"This was supposed to be the last move until Quin gradu-ates. That's what they said when we left Cleveland. That's what I thought." I'm still waiting for him to say he's going to fight it. I keep rearranging things in my locker. "But my dad says it's a once-in-a-lifetime opportunity," he adds.

My sarcastic sniff comes out accidentally. *Come on. It's not like your dad's an ambassador.*

We're talking again, except that this talking feels worse than not talking. I need to make this casual. I need to prove that none of this bothers me. To convince myself, at least. I don't feel like eat-ing with all that dead weight in my belly, but I feel like looking like I can eat. I take a scone from the bag. "Amsterdam sounds cool. Plus you can add another souvenir to your collection."

"I don't have a souvenir collection."

"Sure you do. On your bookshelf. You can get a wooden shoe or a Van Gogh key chain. I don't know what else is there. Maybe The Hague has war criminal magnets!" I'm trying to make this better. Fun. Because now all the pressure is off. I swallow a bite of the scone, which mostly stays in my throat because of the whole insides-filled-with-cement thing.

"What are you talking about?"

"The Netherlands?"

All the pressure isn't off. I can't stand here with him and not feel disappointed and angry and embarrassed. I let that caterpillar of an idea in, the idea of Jackson and me, and she spun and emerged and grew and stretched out her wings, and then I killed her.

I start walking toward math and Jackson follows.

"So, are you ready for the formal this weekend? I heard there will be dance trophies, and you've been falling behind on trophies." Not even a smile. "You going with Elliana? Sie ist probably a sehr gut danzer." I hate saying her real name out loud.

"No." He sounds surprised, like he can't figure out where I'd get that idea. In my head, that's where. "I'm just meeting some people there."

"Cool. That's a good way to do it," I say. I bet there will be a line of girls in pretty dresses waiting for him like in an episode of *The Bachelor*. "Or maybe there's a wistful poets meet-up at the snack table," I try.

"Sure." It's not working. He's not picking up his side. The hallways are starting to fill up. Lots of people nod or wave at Jackson as we make our way toward first period. We pass by Mena and Khloe, who raise their eyebrows curiously. They have no idea.

In a break in the crowd, Jackson reaches out for my arm. "Greer, can you just stop for a second?" He turns to face me and takes a big breath. "I never know what you're—"

Griffin Townsend is walking past, and I see his eyes drop from my face to my chest, just for a second. I follow his line of sight and see that there's a piece of scone on my sweatshirt. Mavis caught it.

I pick off the crumb, and it leaves a bright purple smear right at my nipple. I wipe again and the smudge gets bigger, streaking out across my breast. I look at my hand and see that violet has bled into the pads of my fingerprints.

There is now a bull's-eye on one boob. A purple boob's-eye. Like Barney the Dinosaur tried to feel me up. I rub with my sleeve, but it makes it worse.

I start to panic. I could run to the bathroom and try to scrub it out, but blueberry stains, and then I'd have a wet purple nipple. Kyle Tuck and his friends would think I was spontaneously lactating grape juice.

Can I call Mom and tell her to pick me up? And is "boob stain" an excused or unexcused absence? Can I hold a notebook in front of my chest for the entire day? I've done it before.

No, wait! My jacket! It's going to be hot and weird to sit through class in a winter jacket, but I'll tell people I'm cold.

I hurry all the way back to my locker, threading through the crowd of students. I flip open the lock and slide into the jacket, safe undercover again. When I shut the door, I'm surprised that Jackson has followed me. He's just standing there on the other side.

"Sorry. What were you saying?"

Around us, people bang lockers open and shut, scuttle to class, and still, Jackson says nothing. There's a couple of loud minutes where it doesn't matter that we're not talking because everyone else is talking all at once. The warning bell rings, and then the noise fades as people drift into class and we don't. I am waiting for him and I don't know what he's waiting for. The jacket crinkles as I shift back and forth.

We've been standing here so long the hall is empty again.

"I'm just going to go," he finally says.

I don't know if he means he's going to class or he's going to the Netherlands, and I realize that in some way, it's the same thing. When he turns down the hall, it feels like someone takes a sledge-hammer to the concrete block in my belly. Now the construction dust and dead butterfly parts are making it hurt to swallow.

What did I think? He'd throw himself at my parka and tell me he's madly in love with me? And then when we FaceTimed over the Atlantic every night I could position the laptop so my boobs were out of the frame? And then Maggie would be wrong and I could get everything I said I wanted?

Well, I didn't *not* think that.

"You know," I say, my voice loud and shaky. He stops and turns. "Not everyone can just run from place to place till we find the one we like."

The Adam's apple in his throat pulses hard, like he's swallow-ing the same dust I am. The corners of his eyes narrow. For a sec-ond I wonder what I've done. And then his jaw goes tight, like it does when he's growling at Quinlan.

"And we can't all just hide under a sweatshirt if we don't like the life we've got."

I watch him disappear down the hallway, walking faster than most people run. Even from behind, I can tell that he is wiping his eyes. I don't understand what just happened but I understand that

I am hurt and angry, and that Jackson is hurt and angry, too, and that I don't know how to fix it for either one of us. And this makes me even angrier.

Last year, we all went to Boston during one of Dad's work trips. Mom booked us on a whale-watching boat. Sometimes you go out to sea and don't see anything at all, but when we went, it was whale Coachella. Tons of whales, breaching, fluking, spouting—all the whale greatest hits—right next to the ship. The crew made every-one under sixteen wear a life jacket, except that none of the ones they had taken out would zip over my chest. I decided I was close enough to sixteen to skip it and could probably tread water long enough for some whale watcher to spot me if I went overboard, but the first mate disagreed. He found me a skanky old jacket that might have fit an actual whale, and the captain didn't start the tour until I was strapped into it. The thing was so oversized that I would have floated right out of it and been strangled by the straps if the *Dolphinia IV* hit an iceberg.

So my boobs weren't only annoying and embarrassing; they might have actually gotten me killed. I stood at the railing pissed the whole time, not oohing and aahing over the whales. Not giggling when a spray of the Atlantic sprinkled everyone's cameras. Not feeling profoundly guilty when the guide told us about the danger global climate change poses to these most an-cient and majestic mammals. I just stood there feeling angry. Angry at the Coast Guard for making stupid rules. Angry at the captain for enforcing them. Angry at the life jackets. Angry at Tyler for wearing one that fit. Angry at the damn whales for showing off, for not giving a shit about how ridiculously big and dumb-looking they were, just jumping and splashing and having a ball.

But mostly, angry at me.

Angry at

them.

I'm not even smiling in the photo of me and Tyler that's got a whale hula-hooping in the background.

And now I feel angry like that.

I am still holding one of Melinda Oates's perfect mountain-top scones, and I chuck it as hard as I can at the locker across from mine. It explodes into a billion crumbs and leaves a violet streak down the door. And I burn inside my parka as I walk alone to math.

CHAPTER 65

We're playing Ironwood, a tough team, and we're down two of our strongest players. It's the last game of the season, and Coach asked Jessa to play with varsity, which is a great opportunity for her but not so great for us. Sylvie's got mono, but she's come to watch, sitting with the varsity girls. This leaves Nasrah, me, and Kate Wood to hold things together. We can't afford to lose any of us. There was a game two weeks ago that would have made Misty May-Treanor proud. Today we'll be lucky if we don't get destroyed.

The gym is packed. All the parents and friends who skipped the rest of the season came to this one. Plus basketball finished yesterday, and we are the only sport still going. Rafael and Maggie are sitting two rows ahead of Mom, Dad, and Tyler. Max and some of his friends are here, but no Jackson, of course. A ton of people in purple are here for Ironwood.

Warming up, I am determined to stay focused, but I keep replaying the conversation this morning with Jackson, especially the part about hiding under a sweatshirt. He has no idea. It must be easy to be Jackson.

I pull at my jersey, miss the rotation in the warmup drill, and get knocked in the head with a ball. So much for staying focused. Jessa's off the court with the varsity players, but she gives me a what-was-*that* kind of face I haven't seen in a while.

I'm glad I'm not on the other side of the net, where the Ironwood coach can't stop screaming at his players. At one point, he grabs the water bottle out of a girl's hand and squirts it in her face. "Did I say to take a water break?"

We take our places on the court. I'm going to stay focused, I remind myself, even though I'm not used to seeing the gym this full. I scan the bleachers. There are tons of people I would not expect to see at a game. It looks like the whole school. Kids from the musical. Most of the baseball team. Soccer players, with a varsity player's number written on their cheeks. Kids I've known since we were little. Kids I barely know at all. Griffin Townsend. Elliana the German class stalker. The whole Vang side and the whole Ellis side of Khloe's family. Mr. Feiler. Natalie and Tahlia with a big group. Kurtis and Omar. Nella. A part of me wishes I was the one with mono. But I am part of this team, and I am determined to play like Jessa always plays: all in. I adjust my jersey again.

The game should be starting but the coaches' meeting with the referee is taking longer than usual. Standing out here not playing gets everybody more jittery, but the coaches are disagreeing about something.

The ref steps out and says, "There is a uniform challenge against Kennedy High. There will be a five-minute courtesy delay."

Coach Reinhold steps onto the court, looking ninety shades of furious, and I assume that she's coming to tell Nasrah that she has to lose the neon-pink shoelaces, because that happened once before. But Coach passes Nasrah and grabs me by the elbow. She pulls me off the court, and now the entire gym is interested.

She's holding a binder that Ironman brought with him—about nine thousand pages of rules and regulations from the State High School Athletic Commission.

"Walsh, I'm sorry, but he's challenging the legality of your jersey." She says it softly, so no one else can hear, but even at a near whisper, I can hear how upset she is.

She shows me the page in the book that lists all the rules—how many inches the letters can be, how many contrasting colors can be where, how long the shirts have to be. There are dozens of very specific things to complain about, probably put together by a team of people with personalities as lovable as that Ironwood coach's. Most people hardly notice the changes we made to make my uniform fit, but the other coach is very concerned about my top.

The problem is the gold part in the back of my uniform— where Glinda the Good Witch's dress shows through the maroon mesh. Our libero (and if you don't know volleyball, just know that there's one player who has a different color shirt, like the goalkeeper in soccer) wears gold, and the rules say, basically, that everybody else's jersey can only have a weensy bit of gold on it or the ref might get confused about who is who.

If this ref can't tell the difference between Kate Wood, whose libero jersey is so perfectly golden it looks like she stole it from a pirate chest, and my hodgepodge of leftover fabric scraps, we've got bigger problems than uniforms. But Coach

You're-Thirsty-When-I-Say-You're-Thirsty is going to have a tantrum if I try to play in this shirt.

I glance up from the rule book and see that my teammates are all trying to figure out what's wrong. On the bleachers, my dad is half standing. He doesn't know what's going on either, but you can see him debating whether he should come to help, because he's my dad, or leave me alone, because I'm not a child. I turn away, because if he thinks I can't handle it, he will come, and that will make it worse. I don't need anybody else looking at me.

"I need you to go put Timms's jersey on."

I shake my head.

"She won't mind. You'll trade back when varsity starts."

"I can't," I manage. "It won't fit."

"Timms is a pretty big girl. I think it will work."

I squeeze my eyes and shake my head. I already know it won't. My jersey was the same size as Jessa's before Ms. K-B altered it. Even if I could get it over my chest, I wouldn't be able to move. I wish I'd taken sign language instead of Spanish because if I try to talk, no sound is going to come out anyway.

"Kid, I know this guy is just busting balls because he can, but he's not going to back down. He's a grade A whatnot. Please, Greer. We need you." It is probably the first time she's ever called me Greer instead of Walsh, and I can see that she knows she's asking a lot, so I head toward the locker room to try. She sends Jessa down after me. I don't look at the bleachers, where there are hundreds of eyes watching me go. Why did you all have to come to this game?

If I can't play, Coach will start Kaia Beaumont, which is pretty much the same as sending a tiny, blindfolded kitten wearing roller skates into the game. Not only will we lose, Kaia will probably die.

Jessa releases a long string of swears about the guy, but understands that sports come with meaningless technicalities and has whipped off her shirt before we're down the stairs. She stands there in her sports bra, sides bulging over her shorts, holding out a shirt that's already got pit stains despite the fact that varsity hasn't even warmed up.

I swallow my usual self-consciousness and peel off my jersey. She's the only person on the planet who has seen me in this bra. Maybe her jersey will have stretched out from all her dives, digs, jumps, and stretches. Maybe it will show me some mercy, because nobody else up there is going to.

I get my head through the hole and my arms in the sleeves, but the jersey basically stalls in the middle of my breasts. The fabric rolls and bunches at the limit of its stretchiness. It's pulled so tight the maroon dye fades to pink. I empty all the air from my lungs. Maybe I can play taking only tiny breaths. I inch it down. Jessa works on the back, yanking so hard she almost pulls me over. We get the shirt over the main hump(s), but it will not come down far enough to meet the waist of my shorts.

I stand in front of the mirror, looking like I've borrowed a top from one of Quin's American Girl dolls. I am humiliated and the only other person who's even seen me yet is Jessa. Virtually everyone else I know and a whole lot of people I don't are waiting for me to walk back through that door. I blink hard. I. Can. Not. Go. Out. There.

Jessa bites her lip. "Um, can you move?"

I raise one arm, slowly. I raise the other one, and all our progress pulling the shirt down is undone. It pulls right back up. Even from here, I can hear the crowd in the gym.

"What are you doing down here?" Maggie is suddenly behind me in the mirror. I've got Jessa's jersey squeezing down the top halves of my breasts, while the bottoms squeeze out over my bare belly like an upside-down push-up bra. Maggie's eyes bug out like a cartoon.

Here's the weird thing: Instead of being horrified that Maggie is seeing me like this, I laugh. What else can I do? And when I laugh, Mags and Jess know that it's okay if they do, too. And they do. We all do. Hard. So much that I have to sit down on the bench and Maggie has tears running down her face. So much that Jessa can barely catch her breath between hyena gasps.

"Oh god, Greer, get out of that thing before it strangles you." Maggie is giggling. She and Jessa each take an edge and roll the jersey off me. I'm back to square half-naked. Two of us are sitting there without shirts on, and for once I'm not trying to cover up everything I can.

"That's a sports bra?" Somehow Max must have scraped up every last bit of sports-related DNA before Maggie was even conceived.

"The finest money can buy."

"Jeez. Now what do we do?" says Jessa.

"I can't wear yours. I don't think they're going to let me play."

"What are you talking about? They can't do that. You've been rehearsing for months."

Jess is about to correct her, but I interrupt, "She knows. She does that on purpose." I explain about the uniform and the nasty coach from the other team.

"Jessa, run up and get that binder," Maggie says. Jessa is half out the door when Mags stops her. "You want to put on a shirt first?"

When Jessa comes back with the binder, she tells us that Coach offered the other guy all her time-outs for five more minutes.

"I don't know what good five minutes is going to do," I say.

Maggie is running her finger down the uniform rules page. Every line or two, she picks up my jersey and turns it over in her hands.

"It's just this gold part," she says finally.

"Too bad she didn't make it maroon like the rest of it," says Jessa.

"Too bad Glinda the Good Witch had to be so flashy."

Maggie says, "Let's just take out that part."

"We can't. The mesh is see-through. That's why she put the gold part in there in the first place," I explain.

"There's nothing in the rules about see-through," says Maggie, offering up the binder.

"There has to be," I argue, but scanning the bullet points, it seems it's all about color. Nothing about nakedness.

"If we cut out that gold part, it's all maroon."

"But it wouldn't be all maroon. It would be maroon and me." I glare at both of them. They are not understanding why this is a problem.

"It's just the back," Maggie says.

"Yeah, but everybody could see."

"See what?"

"The Stabilizer."

"The *what*?"

"My bra."

"No offense, Greer, but I think people probably figure you're wearing a bra anyway."

"Yeah, but I don't want anybody to see it." Only I don't say "it." I mean to say "it" but what comes out is "me." I say, "I don't want anybody to see me."

Jessa and Maggie look at each other. This time it's Jessa who speaks.

"Sorry, Walsh. You can't play the game just inside your own head."

Maggie's mouth drops open, and she points at Jessa. "I LOVE HER!" To Jess she says, "I tell her that exact same thing."

Jess goes on. "I mean, what are you going to do? Just hide down here? We need you."

She's got to know by now that this is a kind of suicide mission for me, that it is possibly the hardest thing she could ask me to do, but she's asking anyway. That's not what gets me, though. It's that phrase. Why does everybody think I'm hiding?

Is that what this is? The big sweatshirt, the slouching, the crossing my arms in front of myself every time I stand up to present in class? The not talking to any boy about anything but math? The letting Jackson think I don't care if he trips into a canal in his wooden shoes and drowns?

Oh my god. Of course it is.

What has happened to me? What happened to the kid who

wanted to show off her day-of-the-week undies so people would know she could read?

I want to be as proud as I was that day, every day. That confident. That sure. That comfortable. That whole.

"You can't control what people think, Greer." Maggie pulls the loose binder out of my hair and ties it up again, tighter. "Sometimes I just settle for making them afraid of me." She's joking, but not joking. This is how Maggie faces the world. She is fierce.

"Yeah. Screw them!" Jess adds. "People are like volleyballs. Sometimes you just gotta let 'em bounce."

And these might be the sweetest three little words anyone's ever said to me.

Let 'em bounce.

This is how Jessa faces the world. She lets 'em bounce.

I grab Maggie and Jessa at once and hug them hard, even though I'm shirtless and laughing. They start laughing, too, because it's hard not to laugh when someone is squeezing really big boobs into you and laughing for no apparent reason. It's comedy gold.

This is what I want on my tombstone: I WAS FIERCE. I WAS PROUD. I LET 'EM BOUNCE. Maybe not my tombstone. Maybe my senior yearbook quote. Or a T-shirt.

Yeah. A T-shirt. Size L, no X.

I find scissors in Kate's locker with all her taping supplies, hold my breath, and cut. I hand Maggie the flap of gold lining. The back of my uniform is now holey enough you could read a book through it.

But the State High School Athletic Commission does not say

you can't have a peekaboo jersey; just that it needs to be the right color. Frankenjersey is now legal.

I slip it on. It feels the same, only breezier.

I am most at home in a baggy sweatshirt or a parka from the big and tall men's section of a department store or a circus tent. I got used to wearing that jersey because I had to, and I convinced myself that I could blend in with the team. But today one man made sure I would not blend in. He made sure that every one of those people crowded impatiently in the bleachers would be paying attention when and if number 18 came back to the court. They might as well have turned a spotlight on me.

I turn in front of the mirror so I can see over my shoulder. Everything from my neck to my shorts, including a four-inch band of military-grade spandex, is easily visible through the back. I flinch a little bit but I remind myself that no other athlete cares if anyone sees the straps of her sports bra.

I just called myself an athlete. Oh hell, Ironwood. It is on.

"Ready?" says Jess.

She pushes open the locker room door just as Coach is coaxing Kaia Beaumont off the bench. No one seems happier to see me than Kaia. She points to me and practically squeals.

As she heads back to the bleachers, Maggie says, "That bra looks like something a Navy Seal would wear. Is it bulletproof?"

Every head in the gym watches as I walk to my side of the court. My family, my friends, my teachers, my math class, people who love me, people who don't. People I will see every school day for the next two years. People from the other school who will only know me from this one moment. Skinny people and short people and pimply people and people with great hair. Heavy people and bony people and sexy people and weird people. Ones that hate themselves and ones that love themselves. Kind or crazy or confused. None of them is perfect. None of them are "regular shaped," if that is even a thing.

Or maybe all of them are. And somehow I am in the middle of them, out in the very wide open. Not hiding anymore, Jackson.

Coach Reinhold yells, "Brandi Flippin' Chastain!"

Nella stands up on the bench, and because she does, everyone around her does, too. "WOOOOOO-HOOOOOO! THAT'S MY HAIRCUT TWIN!" They stamp their feet like a drumroll and it feels like the roof is going to come down.

The Ironwood coach is flipping out, ready to explode. I can't imagine what his players are thinking or our players or my parents or anyone else for that matter, and I realize that it doesn't matter.

I am here to play.

Yeah, Maggie. It's bulletproof.

I quiet the noise inside my head, the noise of all those people, and feel their energy instead. I feel it in my body. I feel it in my bones. I feel it in the faintest flutter deep in my belly, like a tiny wing emerging from the rubble. The last thing I hear before the ref's start whistle is her small, clear voice saying, "Game on, motherfuckers."

CHAPTER 66

The same phone-playing sub is already at Ms. Tanner's desk. Written in chalk behind her is FRIDAY: CONTINUED REVIEW FOR SUMMATIVE EXAM. QUIET GROUP WORK OR INDIVIDUAL STUDY.

Kurtis and Omar have already moved my desk into an island with theirs. Kurtis is bookmarking pages and Omar's making a master sheet of formulas to memorize.

"So, Greer, are you going to the formal this weekend?" Kurtis says, pressing the book open to the summary page at the end of the first unit.

"Yeah, she's going with the new guy. Right?" Omar interjects.

"Um, not anymore." They both look at me like I said I had to put my dog to sleep. Omar actually sighs.

"I'm sorry. I would go with you but I have to go to a quinceañera. It was planned before the formal."

"Thanks, Omar. I'm all right." He squinches up his forehead like he does when he's trying to figure out a sinusoidal regression. I wonder if he's thinking about how to get out of the quince.

"I'm actually her chambelan," he says to himself. He looks up at us. "Like the escort? For my cousin? It's kind of an honor. I really have to go."

"Oh, Omar. She's lucky to have you." He still looks pained, like he's letting me down, and I decide I better change the subject before Omar disgraces his family by trying to help me out. "How 'bout you, Kurtis?"

Kurtis is instantly embarrassed. "I'm sorry, Greer, I already have a date."

"No! I didn't mean with me, I was just wondering—wait. You have a date?"

"Of course. My girlfriend."

"You have a girlfriend?"

"Yeah. Paige Polasky? She's a junior?"

"I know who Paige is. She's cute." I try not to sound surprised. "I didn't realize you two were together."

"Well, Greer, you only ever talk about *math*."

The bell rings and the sub says, "Get to work, guys." Omar and Kurtis start debating which of the review questions are most important. This whole year, while I was thinking they were those nerdy math boys who didn't know anything about girls, they were thinking I was that nerdy math girl who didn't know anything about boys. (And it seems that they were right.)

It doesn't take long before the band of losers around Kyle Tuck is snorting and giggling. This morning I found a striped waffle-weave Henley that I'd retired. It's not tight, but it's not as big as anything I've worn in a while, especially the winter coat I had on in class yesterday. In other words, it fits. In other words, my boobs are having a coming-out party. I even considered wearing the plaid

Perk Up! bra and panties set today, except that as cute as it is, that bra is less supportive than a piece of Scotch tape, so I stuck with my usual on top and just wore the unders.

Kyle fake-coughs "Hooters!" into his hand, and the boys erupt.

The sub looks up and says "Quiet, please," in their general direction.

My instinct is to bend my shoulders and slide down my chair, take a hall pass and get my jacket out of my locker. Instead, I squeeze my hands tight and feel a sharp pain where my pinky jammed going for a hit last night.

It was the best we've ever played. Everybody was on their game. And that coach who didn't like my uniform ended up getting himself thrown out (and I hope mauled by his own players on the bus back home). What happened was, when Coach finally rotated Kaia in, it was like they all smelled blood. They hit everything they could at her, and the girl could not make a block. She was desperate for Reinhold to take her out again, but Coach just said, "You got this, Beaumont. Stay with it." Finally, this giant girl from Ironwood smoked the ball like a missile, the kind of shot we'd call "kill or be killed."

And somehow Kaia blocked it. She jumped up, a perfect mirror of the hitter, hands and forearms shooting high, and the thing tipped back to their side. We all went crazy. Kaia was standing there with her mouth open like she'd just burped a cloud of sparkly rainbow-colored fireflies. The other team hit it right back over the net, and we missed it because we were too busy high-fiving Kaia. Jessa ran in from the sidelines and lifted her up.

Somehow, this sent Ironcoach completely over the edge. He

stood right on the sideline and screamed, "What are you doing? Why are you cheering? You lost the point! Don't you dummies even know you lost the point?"

Nasrah, who is usually very polite, walked right up to him, eye to receding hairline, and said, "Actually, I think *you* lost the point." Everyone who heard it went crazy, and everyone who didn't assumed she'd said something awesome and went crazy, too. The guy's head burst into a ball of fire and he said some things my grandmother would call "uncharitable," and that's when the referee told him he could either take a seat on the bleachers and be quiet, or forfeit the match. He chose Door Number Three, which was to storm out of the gym.

After the game, a player from Ironwood found me to talk about the Stabilizer. She told me they had just added colored versions and pulled back the neck of her shirt to show me her purple straps. She had been thinking about surgery but wasn't sure yet. Her mom wanted her to wait until after her first year of college, in case she felt differently, but that would be waiting two more years and she'd been this big since seventh grade. We traded numbers and she said she'd let me know if she decided to do it.

The match started with me tied up Houdini-style in Jessa's jersey and ended with me talking plus-size bras and reduction surgery with a player from a rival school. I didn't even wrap up in my sweatshirt till I was home and showered.

But today's another day and this is math, not volleyball. Yesterday I was on a team. Today I am just me. I pinch my swollen finger. Hard. It's a routine volleyball injury—if the bone is not poking straight out of your skin you don't complain—but it still hurts, and I am reminding myself what I've learned from the girls on my team: You play through the hurt. You have to or you'll never play at all.

My hand clenched, I swallow hard and walk over to Kyle's table. Even Asher and Anitha look up. The boys with Kyle look stunned, like the Rock caught them making fun of the name Dwayne. "Do you need something?" the sub says from her seat.

"Just Kyle. I tutor him on Fridays. Ms. Tanner lets us go out in the hall where it's quieter." Everyone is too curious to contradict me.

The sub shrugs. Kyle's friends giggle.

"Come on."

He stays put.

"Come *on*, Kyle," I say more firmly. Kyle looks like his name's just been drawn for the Reaping. *Guess what, asshole? It has.*

He follows me out, and I shut the door to the classroom.

"What are we doing out here?"

I step toward him until he is backed up against a locker. My chest—the whole subject of this meeting—is inches from his. We're so close I can smell the Proactiv cream on his forehead. Turns out he is not very brave without his friends around. Turns out (and this is a surprise, too) I am. He stammers, "Wh-what? What do you want?"

"Your weird obsession with my breasts ends now."

He turns red. I do not.

"What are you even talking about?"

"The math problems, the calculators, the word finds, the drawings. You need to stop. It makes you seem even dumber than you actually are, and it's really, really mean."

He looks like he's going to deny it, but he knows he can't win a debate with me. "I'm not *obsessed*. Maybe *you're* obsessed."

"That's probably true. I am kind of obsessed. But they *are* mine."

"We just joke around."

"Oh, you joke around? You're just being funny?"

"Yeah," he says and squirms.

"Am I supposed to think it's funny? Have you ever seen *me* laughing?"

He swallows hard. "We don't mean anything by it. I didn't think you cared. You always play along."

"What am I supposed to do? Look, I wish I didn't care, but I do. It makes me feel like shit."

And at this, Kyle's whole face changes. It changes from defensive and mean to surprised. Because he's been such a jerk for such a long time, I'll allow myself to say that it is still quite ugly, but maybe a little bit more human. "I, ah, um, I'm sorry?"

"Is that a question?"

"No? Sorry. I mean, I am sorry. I didn't know it bothered you."

I decide not to point out how ridiculous this is, how to "not know it bothered me" is like stabbing someone in the eye and saying you didn't know it would hurt. It's a fine excuse if you throw a nonrecyclable yogurt container in the recycling bin. It's a pretty lame one if you're making jokes about somebody's body. I just say, "Now you know."

I don't know whether it will change anything, and even if it does, there are plenty of other Kyles in the world. Some won't be as easy to intimidate. Some will intimidate me. Some will try to do worse than spell out BOOBS on a calculator. But now at least this one knows where I stand. He can't pretend he doesn't, and I can't pretend I don't care. "Never again, Kyle." I turn back to class.

"Hey, Greer?" Kyle looks hopeful. "Since we're pretending you're tutoring me anyway, would you help me with the binomial theorem?" He holds up his notebook and smiles sheepishly.

I smile back at him. "Oh, hell no, Kyle. Hell no."

CHAPTER 67

"CHEESE 'N' RICE!" Theresa Kershaw-Bend spills half her latte. "I didn't know anybody was in here."

"Sorry! The building guy said it was okay to wait for you in here."

She sets her stuff down and takes a long drag on her latte. The cup has a picture of a coffee cup being orbited by a car, a dog, and a briefcase. I decide it's a good sign. "Sister Greer of the volleyball team!"

"That's me."

"Like Greer Garson—the old movie star. Is that who you're named for?"

"I'm named for my dad's aunt Gertrude. But they thought Greer sounded better than Gert."

"Me too!" she laughs. "You know who Greer Garson was, though?"

"I've heard of her."

"She was in a lot of stuff in the forties. She starred as Marie Curie."

"Really?"

"You know who that is?"

"Curie? She discovered radium. And she died from carrying radioactive materials in her pockets."

Ms. Kershaw-Bend laughs again. "Sometimes the people you think are the smartest turn out to be the dumbest." *Ain't that the truth.* She finishes the coffee and tosses the cup in the bin. "I understand you had to make some additional alterations to your uniform at last night's game."

"You heard about that?"

"Kristine—Coach Reinhold—and I ate lunch together today. Sorry I didn't know the rule about the colors. I just thought it looked cool with the gold."

"It did! And it was fine all season—till that coach yesterday. He was just, ugh." I stop myself from swearing because I'm talking to a teacher, but it turns out not to matter because she fills in for me.

"Prick."

"Totally. But up till then the jersey was perfect. And actually, without the gold part it was less hot, so it was more perfect. Thank you again."

"My pleasure. I'm glad you had something more comfortable to play in."

"It's usually kind of a one-shape-fits-all problem with me and clothes."

"Tell me about it! Why do you think I learned to sew? Look at these legs." Ms. K-B is over six feet tall. Her waist comes up to most people's necks. "When I was in high school the style was stirrup pants—you know, with a kind of stirrup strap that fits under your feet? No? Well trust me. They do not make them for people my height. I was used to my pants stopping at my shins, but with the stirrups they were too short the other way. I couldn't pull them all the way up. My butt crack showed over my pants like a sunrise."

I wonder if young Theresa Kershaw considered wearing an extra-large sweatshirt to cover her crack? Some of them are very long.

"So that was it. If I couldn't find anything that fit, I made it myself."

"You're very good at it."

"I've been doing it a long time."

"Actually, you're amazing."

"Thank you."

"You could be a professional designer. You should be on *Project Runway*."

She tilts her head to the side and smiles. "Okay, Madame Curie. Tell me what you need."

At first, the look on her face is like if you asked the builders of the Eiffel Tower to try it again with the pointy part on the bottom. When I explain what I want, though, the corners of her mouth rise, and her face lights up like she's Bob Ross and I've asked if she has time for some last-minute touch-ups of the ceiling of the Sistine Chapel.

She sketches it out on the back of somebody's Family and Consumer Science midterm.

"I know it's a huge favor. I can pay you or babysit your kids or—"

"You sure this is what you want?" she asks, tipping the drawing toward me.

"Pretty sure." I'm not sure, not at all, but it's almost like I can hear Maude and Mavis whispering to each other, *Did she say yes? Do we get to go?*

"I'll have it done tomorrow." As I'm leaving, she opens the plastic bag I've given her and says, "Jeez, Greer. You coulda washed it."

CHAPTER 68

"You sure you don't just want a ponytail and a sweatband?"

I hand her another bobby pin.

Mom is not thrilled. When she saw the dress hanging earlier, she gasped in the same way she did when Tyler showed her his infected lip. "*That's* what you're going to wear? Did Maggie talk you into this?"

Nope. She'll see when Maggie and Rafa get here to pick me up. Maggie's "protest" dress is adorable. Retro, but adorable. The statement it makes has nothing to do with gender typing or economic disparities or outmoded rituals. The statement it makes is "I am adorable." (I haven't told Maggie; she would be so disappointed.)

Mom twists another section of hair and tucks it into the bun, and then sticks a bobby pin straight into my brain.

"Ow!" She's being more aggressive than she needs to.

"I hope at least you shaved your armpits."

I did, but I'm going to leave her guessing for now. I didn't wax anything.

When the hair and makeup are done, she disappears downstairs.

I'm getting dressed in her room. I don't have a full-length mirror. I don't have any mirrors in my room. I step out of my sweats and peel off my T-shirt, being careful not to mess up my hair. I stand in front of the mirror in my bra and undies. Cute bikini bottoms, dotted all over with tiny bluebirds and trimmed with yellow edging. On top, the white version of my usual Zappos humdinger, three-quarter-inch straps digging deep grooves into my shoulders. Not cute. Knobs of extra flesh bulge between the bra and my armpit on each side and underneath each badly fitting cup.

I know with a little dedicated research, I can do better than this.

I reach back and release the hooks. The thing sighs forward, weary from trying to hold back the flood of breasts all day long. I let it fall to the floor and force myself to keep my eyes on the mirror.

I never do this. I never look.

Maude and Mavis droop toward my belly. All the weight shifts, like if you filled a sock with sand. The pink rings around my nipples aim almost straight down. In seconds, the undersides of my breasts are sweaty.

But still I look. I rub hard against the grooves in my shoulders, and the flesh starts to fill in again. I roll my head around and feel the tight spots in my neck start to give.

I cup one in each hand and lift them up, up where they are supposed to go. Up where the Stabilizer holds them. I press them together and move them apart.

If anyone walked in, I'd be traumatized for the rest of my life. If Tyler walked in, his head would explode.

I listen at the door to make sure no one is out there and come back to the mirror. I just stand there for a minute. I look nothing like the posters. I look nothing like the online ads. I look nothing like Nella Woster probably looks without clothes on.

But neither does Jessa. Or Mena. Or Nasrah. Or Maggie. Maybe Nella doesn't even look like the Nella in my head.

I look like me. I wouldn't choose it, but this is me.

I wiggle my hips back and forth, and Maude and Mavis wiggle, too, awkwardly, like if two flabby aliens showed up in an Ariana Grande video. I stop moving, and they smack into each other. I laugh out loud. I lift my arms overhead and watch as my breasts are pulled upward, too. Like they want to be a part of whatever this is. Like they don't want to be dragging me down; they just can't help it. I almost say, "Oh, you guys!"

I know this is crazy. I am sure it's because I only slept four hours last night. But looking at them—I know you want me to say that I suddenly think they are beautiful, but they're not. They're just kind of stupid and helpless-looking. Like blobfish. But even though I don't *like* them, I really can't hate them either. They are part of me, like the blue eyes and the love of books and the fear of centipedes.

"Greer?" Mom's voice from downstairs. "Maggie and Rafael are here."

The plan was to ride with Maggie and Rafa and then find Jess and everybody else once we got there, but this morning, Maggie talked me into making one little stop on the way. I am more nervous about that part than I've ever been about anything, but at least if I crash and burn, Maggie will be out in the car to throw water on me.

Mom comes in when I've got the dress on and I'm stepping into her shoes.

"Sweetie—"

She takes one look at me and her mouth falls open. For a second I think she's going to pull some kind of Cinderella's stepmother thing and say I can't go to the ball without something more appropriate.

It gets worse. She actually starts crying and puts her hands to her face. I am literally so ridiculous that my mother is weeping at the sight of me. How did I convince myself this was a good idea?

But then she says this: "Oh my god, Greer. It's perfect. It's absolutely perfect." She pulls me to her and hugs me hard, hugs me like she did when I was little. Like she hasn't done in a long time, because I haven't let her. "It's absolutely perfect because it's absolutely you."

She is not crying because she hates the dress. She is crying because she loves it.

Let's start from the bottom.

I'm borrowing Mom's black Mary Janes. They have a high (for me) heel, about two inches, but the chunky kind, not the spiky kind, so you don't tip over. She promised they'd be comfortable, and surprisingly, they are.

My bare legs look strong from practice, the squats, the burpees, and wherever those sprints have led me and back again.

The skirt part is the bottom of Mom's fancy gala dress with the shimmery blue-black fabric, the second-to-last thing I remember wearing that I felt good in. The dress hits mid-thigh, short, but not crazy short. It's got the kind of "twirlability" I used to like in an outfit, before the world tried to tell me I had to choose between twirling and building.

The bodice of the dress is my volleyball jersey, the only other thing I've felt at home in in a long time. A modified version of my modified jersey, but still just a volleyball jersey, thankfully washed by Theresa Kershaw-Bend between my last game and her sewing it onto the skirt. It fits me like it's supposed to: close, but not tight. It follows my shape like it was made for me, because it was. She's completely taken off the sleeves, cut the collar a little deeper and sewed tiny gold seed pearls around it. She's even copied some of the black floral embroidery from the skirt straight up the sides of the shirt. The back is still see-through mesh, but my brand-new Stabilizer is a near-perfect match in maroon. Pretty sure Mom will flip when she notices the charge (plus next-day shipping) on her card, but she hasn't had to spend much on my clothes in a long time.

It's a mashup because I am a mashup. It fits together because I fit together. This dress wouldn't work for anybody else because nobody else is a mix of these parts. It doesn't just fit my not-cookie-cutter body. It fits *me*, in a hundred ways. Mom's right. I feel (almost) perfect.

Mom clips the not-really-from-Grandma diamond around my neck, smiling and shaking her head.

"Do you want my anniversary earrings from Dad? The diamond drop earrings? They'd look pretty."

"Nah. I'm good with these." I've got on the gold sigma studs Maggie got me for my birthday last year. She found them on a website that sells stuff to sororities, but she got them for me because they represent a function in calculus.

"I'm sorry I doubted you."

"I'm sorry I doubted me, too." She means it about the dress. I mean it about all sorts of things.

Dad taps on the door, and I endure his compliments and photo snapping, until Maggie pops in and says, "Oh my god. Why am I not wearing that? That's so cool. So antiestablishment. But also gorgeous."

She looks utterly fantastic in her vintage dress. It's a bright-blue floral print, with a high waist and a petticoat to make it poof out, and matching blue pumps. In order not to be too conventional, she's dyed her hair pink, but it's a pretty pink, not a Hunger Games pink.

My parents fuss over her a bit and make dumb comments to Rafael about how brave he is to be heading out with the two of us. When we leave, Mom shoots me a look that suggests that my volleyball jersey dress is one thing but Maggie's gone too far with the hair. I don't think so, though. I think she's gone just the right distance.

CHAPTER 69

After I decided to ask Ms. K-B to make the dress, I mentally prepared (by which I mean stayed awake obsessing half the night) for seeing Jackson at the formal.

It was supposed to go like this:

"Greer?"

"Oh, hi, Jackson. I didn't notice you there." (I would say this casually, then not comment on the fact that his suit doesn't fit right.)

"Wow, that dress is genius. When I look around the gym and see the conventional and off-the-rack things others are wearing, I understand why you would reject them, and I, too, reject them. Also, I now see that in fact you are not a coward hiding in a sweatshirt. And I realize that in addition to being academically gifted and athletically underappreciated, you are also conventionally pretty, though that is not my priority."

"I'm sorry, I couldn't really hear you." (I'd be surrounded by the volleyball team, my math class, the cast of the musical, and all of Nella Woster's followers.)

"Do you want to dance?"

"I promised Max Cleave I'd dance with him." Insincere sad-face real-life expression.

"But he's dancing with the redheaded girl from my German class."

"Not for long," I'd say. Then I'd walk up to Max and Red, and he'd drop her like a rock and I would suddenly know how to dance. Jackson would shuffle away in his ugly suit, get on a plane, and cry all the way to the Netherlands.

Yes, that's where my mental preparation got me.

But that was before I found this. Sitting in the back seat behind Rafa, I fold and unfold the paper in my lap.

I found it when I was putting away *Mrs. Frisby*, folded up and stuck in like a bookmark. It's Kyle Tuck's word find. I don't know why Jackson ended up with it, but since Quin takes everything of Jackson's, once it was his, it was hers.

It's been filled in. The scrawly penciled letters are circled in red ink and there are some other notes on it. The second I saw it my heart shattered into sharp bits, shrapnel cutting from the inside out. It's Jackson's writing; he makes his *G*s with a little drop in front, like a goat with a beard.

Jackson saw it? Jackson played it? Jackson kept it? I almost tear it to shreds.

But then I see that they aren't the words they're supposed to be, not the words Kyle hid. Jackson has jumped from letter to letter, turning corners, making arrows, basically breaking all the rules to make it say something else. Finding something different from what everybody else would see. He's taken a *B* from what should have read B O O B S and connected it to an R I diagonally and then made an arrow to where there is a G H T. Instead of the obvious J U G S and T I T T I E S and B I G M A M A, he's found words that Kyle and the rest didn't know were there:

B R I G H T

L O V E L Y

B R A I N I E (there is a shortage of Ys)

V O L B A L E R I N A

F U N N Y

S M A R T

C O O L (except that he had to make an O into a C because there weren't any in the puzzle)

W E I R D

W I T T I E

B O O D I F U L

G R E E R

I fold the paper again and run over the creases with my nails. Up front, Maggie and Rafa are talking about a movie they saw where all the singing parts went to movie stars instead of actual singers. They think it's unfair the way "Hollywood caves in to common perceptions of what's valuable and ignores what's actually remarkable." I've never seen Maggie enjoy agreeing with anybody before now.

I have no idea what I'm going to say. I have no idea what he's going to say, either, but since I'm the one showing up at his house uninvited in a volleyball uniform/cocktail dress, I feel like maybe it's my responsibility to lead the conversation.

The ride is both way too long and way too short. I'm suddenly standing in front of the Oateses' door without having figured anything out. Jackson answers, and I realize that all my mental preparation wouldn't have done me any good anyway, because his suit does not fit badly. It fits really, really well. It's dark and slim, not like the kind that are supposed to look too small; just slim like it was made for his body. His shirt is pale blue, and his tie is an explosion of tiny flowers. And he does not look like he would ever drift away alone and cry all the way to the Netherlands. He looks like half the school would follow him to the Netherlands if any of them could identify it on a map. The boy could sell a million of those suits. I bet Ty would wear a suit if he saw how good Jackson looked.

"Do you have a minute?"

"Um, sure. Yeah. Come in," he says, and I duck under an arm, acutely aware that the back of my dress is see-through mesh. The butterfly is in full flurry. It feels like this time she may bust her way out of my stomach like the thing that comes out of the wall in *Stranger Things*. "Who's in the car?"

"Maggie and Rafa. They don't mind." I look back at them. "It gives them a few minutes to be alone. I'm kind of crashing their night."

It's painfully awkward for four seconds before Quin barrels into me.

"GREER!" She wraps her bony arms around me and squeezes like I'm both a life preserver and a lost golden retriever. It's a nice way to be greeted.

She's not happy when Jackson and I head upstairs and he closes her out of his room, but there's no way to have a conversation with her around. Or maybe there's no way to have a conversation with me around, because I just stand there in front of him with my folded paper, staring up at the row of things on his bookcase and trying to think of where to start.

He sees me staring at the stuff and sighs. "That's what you meant by souvenirs?"

I nod.

"You want to know why I keep that stuff?" he asks.

"Sure," I manage.

"It's pretty dumb," he says, lifting down the Beanie Baby iguana. "In kindergarten, we lived in this place called Sandy Springs, Georgia. I had two friends, Willem and Charlie. We used to play this game at recess called Jump Pile. You'd make a pile of sand, and then you'd jump on it. That was the whole game. Jump Pile."

It is hard not to smile at this.

"We moved before the end of the year to Maryland, but by second grade, my dad got moved back to Georgia, and I went back to the same school. I was really happy because I already knew people this time. I thought Willem and Charlie and I would go back to playing Jump Pile. But my first day there Willem and Charlie got introduced just like everybody else. I was, like, 'Remember, guys? From kindergarten? Remember Jump Pile?' They had no idea who I was."

"Ouch."

"It wasn't their fault. I was just kind of temporary to them. That's how my family is to most people."

I want to object, but he cuts me off.

"Kids were always nice. I went to sleepovers and birthday parties. But once I was gone, I was just gone. It made me feel kind of irrelevant. If you move a lot, it's not like *you* forget. It's like nobody remembers you."

I wonder if that's how it's going to be, eventually. At my ten-year high school reunion, someone will open the yearbook and say, "I don't remember this guy. Was he an exchange student or something?" and I'll say, "I feel like his name was Jacob or Justin or something like that? Moved to Australia."

I don't think so.

"So I wanted to make sure there was somebody in each place who would remember me. I started keeping track." He holds up the dirty iguana. "Stella Goodman. Arlington, Virginia. Third grade. We made an animal shelter in her garage for neglected stuffed animals. Everyone else thought it was a garage sale. Iggie was the last one to be adopted. Even if she didn't remember me, this iguana would remind her."

He picks up the Batman Lego boat. "Tanner White. San Jose, California. Fifth grade. We made a movie of *Batman Versus Sharks* and dropped his mom's iPad in the tub. We dried it off and it still worked, so we figured it was waterproof and tried to film an underwater fight scene. He will remember me. And he'll remember *Batman versus Sharks versus Mom*." He goes through the collection, piece by piece—the doubles tennis trophy was Kai Dalin's first win and Jackson's first tournament. There's an Altoids tin with a dog biscuit in it from the dog that lived next door in Cleveland. Ruffles waited at the gate for Jackson to come home from school every day.

As he explains each thing, I start to understand. These aren't like souvenirs from vacation. They're not to check off "I've been there/lived there" or to remind him of a landmark. They are not about places at all. They're about people. They are his way of proving that the relationships that mattered to him actually mattered to someone else, too. Like a guarantee that each part of his life can be verified by another source. He really was there. He really did count. Represented by knickknacks and toys and dog biscuits, it's a collection started by a little boy before he knew what he was doing or why he was doing it. I'm not sure whether he even understands it now. But he knows they are not souvenirs. And he wants me to know, too.

And then there is the Cupernicus mug. This one he doesn't say anything about for a long time. Just holds it and doesn't look at me. He closes his eyes and a line of wet squeezes through his lashes. My stomach turns over.

"You got caught stealing a mug, but the nice barista let you keep it?"

He ignores me. Stands there for another minute, takes a breath.

"Greer Walsh. Illinois. Tenth grade." Do I want him to go on? Do I want to be in this collection? Because this is a collection of people who are important to Jackson, but he leaves anyway. "The smartest, funniest, weirdest girl I ever met, with these amazingly bright eyes. Completely clueless about everything that's not schoolwork. Except volleyball. She's okay at volleyball."

"I'm better than okay at volleyball," I whisper.

"I almost didn't keep this one because I thought it was the beginning of something I wouldn't have to remember because it would just last."

I can't say anything. I just swallow.

"But I misunderstood how you felt," he adds. "I'm sorry. I didn't mean to freak you out." He lifts the cup to me. He is giving it to me. He is letting me out of his collection.

I take the cup. I take a breath. I ask.

"What did you see when you first met me?"

"What do you mean?"

"You know what I mean. What did you notice about me?"

He looks away. He bites his lip.

"A lot of things, Greer. Everything."

I wait, trying not to fidget. A few months ago, I would have done anything to avoid a conversation like this, but now I want to know. Or I think I do.

He looks at his shelf, not at me. "You want me to say I didn't notice? You want me to say that I only ever cared about how smart you are? You want me to say I wasn't, I don't know, *surprised* at that first volleyball game, when I finally saw you in something besides your dad's clothes? I can't say that, Greer. I'm sorry. I noticed your breasts."

I don't know what I was hoping for, but at least the kid is honest. "At least we know you were paying attention."

He sighs. "Look, I'm not going to tell you I haven't thought about your body. About your breasts, okay? I can't tell you that I don't think about them."

Jackson takes a step closer, and now he's looking at me instead of the bookshelf. Really looking at me. I look down, uncomfortable. Or maybe not uncomfortable.

Is there a good kind of uncomfortable?

And then he says, "I think about your breasts. A lot. And your legs. A lot. And your hips. And the back of your neck. All the time. And the front of your neck. And your thighs. And don't tell me that's the same as your legs, because the way I think of them, they're not." His voice is quiet, and it's close.

It is suddenly very, very hot inside this dress, even though the back is made of mesh. The butterfly's jaw is hanging open. And now I wish I paid more attention when Maggie talks about waxing.

"I think about Every. Part. Of. You."

I look up and he is not even blinking.

"Including my mind, right?" I say, but honestly, my mind is the last thing on my mind.

"Sometimes. Not always. Not only." His eyes are teary, and his cheeks are flushed. He doesn't look as confident as the day I met him, but somehow he still looks like he's exactly where he wants to be.

And finally, I see it. All the ways he's open, all the ways I'm not. The way I dodge and slouch and avoid and, yeah, maybe even hide. My instinct, even now, is to say something sarcastic. To cross my arms in front of my chest and sidestep out of the room. To say *toedeledoki*, which means "toodaloo" in Dutch, according to "Ten Ways the Dutch Say Goodbye," one of the trillion stupid articles I found on my phone last night.

But I'm looking at Jackson, and he is kind and honest and

possibly the best-looking boy I've ever seen in real life and staring at me. He is brave enough to start over again and again with people who probably won't remember jumping in a pile of sand with him. To choose a girl who was afraid to be chosen. If he goes to Amsterdam, it will be without anything new for his bookshelf because the one he was counting on couldn't believe he was actually counting on her.

I'm still clutching the Cupernicus mug—really, really hard. Butterfly is on her knees with her hands clasped, begging me not to mess this up.

I set the mug on the desk, and for once, I know what to say.

Nothing.

I kiss him so suddenly and so hard that he stumbles backward and sits on the iguana. He looks up, surprised, and then he is kissing me back, and he tastes like toothpaste and lips. I can't believe how soft his face is. His hands are on my waist and mine are in his hair. My breasts are pressed up against him because we'd have to be ten feet apart if they weren't going to touch him, but it doesn't feel weird. It just feels like we are squeezed tight together—all of us—and every part of me wants to be as close to him as Maude and Mavis are.

There is so much more talking to do, about the word find and the fact that he's kept a Beanie Baby for eight years and what a wimp he still is for not refusing to move and the jerk I am for blaming him and what happens after all this and whether Quinlan is going to give back the rest of my books and all sorts of things, but none of it seems as important as what we're doing right now.

This time, I am not living only inside my head. And I think I like it out here.

And then my phone vibrates for the thirty-ninth time, and I remember that Maggie and Rafael are out in the driveway waiting.

> Are you okay? Did the sister kill
> you?
>
> > Not killed. Just distracted.

I add a winking smiley.

> Should we wait for you?

"Um, Jackson? Would you go to the winter formal with me?"

"I was wondering what you were doing here in that fancy dress."

"Well?"

"Just as friends?"

"Nope."

"Then yes. Or . . ." He sits up and squinches his forehead. "I mean, we could. Or we could also just stay here and not go to the formal."

He looks sideways at his bed, which once again looks very horizontal. His hand on my leg is warm and heavy, and I am thinking that I am rather curious about whether he's got any embarrassing moles I could find. Maybe the formal is overrated. I mean, it's not even in the binder. And staying right here with Jackson talking about my body parts for the rest of the night does not actually sound like the worst idea in the world.

But then I think, Ms. Kershaw-Bend went to a lot of trouble

to make this dress for me overnight. And I went to a lot of trouble to learn how to wear it. To wear this patchwork of parts. To wear this girl that is twirly and smart and funny and strong all at the same time.

To wear this body.

I am going to this formal. I'm going to dance and spin and laugh and make a fool out of myself, right out in the middle of everybody. My boobs are going to look huge. I'm not going to know how to dance. People will know that that's all me, too. I will hold on to Jackson and he will be holding on to me, too. The only thing that would make it better is if I drove us in a rocket boat I clicked together myself.

But I can't drive, and neither can Jackson, so we really need Rafael to wait for us.

One sec! J coming too.

There's a hard kick at the door and Quinlan barges in.

"This is for you."

She dangles a string in front of me. Clay beads, threaded into a bracelet. They are bright spheres, like you'd expect beads to be, mostly hot pink and green because Quin loves hot pink and green together lately. But a few of them are rectangles, and as I look closer I see that they are meant to be books: one with an *AF* scratched into it for *Artemis Fowl*, a mouse I can tell is Despereaux, a Clarice Bean face, and of course one for *Mrs. Frisby and the Rats of NIMH*, which just has *NIM* scratched into one side because she ran out of room.

"Those are your books."

"I can tell."

"You said you wanted a bead bracelet. You tried to make one."

"I did. I wasn't any good at it."

"Well, I am. I'm really good at making things."

"You are. Thank you for making it for me. I love it."

Jackson watches this conversation curiously, like he's not sure what to think about Monster Girl and Math Girl hanging out.

"Mom says to say you don't have to wear it tonight. It's not really for fancy things."

"Here's the thing, Quin: I'm not really for fancy things either." I hold out my arm so she can tie it on me. She beams, pulling the ends of the thread so tight I'll probably lose my fingers. I don't think she's crazy anymore. She's just more obvious about her feelings than the rest of us. Maybe that makes her less crazy.

"Mom! I *told* you Greer would wear it!" She runs down to yell at Mrs. Oates for being wrong.

I dangle my arm in front of Jackson. "Since apparently you didn't get me a corsage."

"If I'd known you were coming, I'd have gotten you a whole tree."

He kisses the inside of the wrist with the bracelet, then kisses the one without. It is weird how you can feel your wrists all the way up to the back of your neck.

"Can I ask you something?" he asks. I imagine he's going to ask why I decided to come here or what happens next or something else I can't answer.

"What?"

"Did the High School Athletic Commission approve that jersey?"

I look down at the dress. "I'll probably have to get a new one for next season."

"You going to play next season?"

"Of course! And Jessa wants me to try out for softball in a couple of weeks."

"So now you're a softballerina, too?"

"We'll see. I need to learn to bat first."

"I know a hitting instructor."

"Max Cleave is not going to want to teach me to bat."

"I meant me! Why are you so obsessed with Max Cleave?!"

"Are you any good?"

"Ouch?" He puts one hand over his heart, and I fall into his chest, laughing.

"No, no, no! I just mean I need serious help if I'm going to make the team."

"Repeat after me." He lifts one of my hands up and places the other one over my heart like I'm taking a vow. I wonder where the butterfly got a Taser. "I am."

"I am."

"The greatest."

"The greatest."

"Smartest."

"Smartest."

"Most beautiful."

I snort.

"Say it: most beautiful."

"Hottest, drop-dead-gorgeousest, sexiest . . ."

He smiles. "Softballerina, honors student, friend, dress designer, relocation advisor—"

Lepidopterist, pipes in B-fly.

"Wow," I say, laughing. "I'm kind of big deal."

He wraps his arms around me, and I can feel the heat of his hands through the mesh of my dress, and the heat of his chest against mine.

"You are a very big deal."

"Huge," I whisper, and kiss him again.

In the driveway Maggie gets out of her seat to greet us, to hug Jackson, and to kiss me on the cheek. "Took you long enough," she says, and squeezes me tight. "Jeez, did you get taller?"

As I'm getting into the car, Jackson's mom calls out from the door, holding up some kind of cream-colored wrap. "Greer honey, it's freezing out. You want to bring something to cover up?"

Maggie and Jackson turn to me, waiting. They would tell me, I think, that it's okay if I do.

"No, thank you!" I call back. "I'm good."

And I am.

ACKNOWLEDGMENTS

Thank you for reading this book. I hope you liked reading it as much as I liked writing it.

If I was a re-lo advisor, I'd make a special section in the binder called Resources for Writers of Young Adult Novels Featuring Brainy/Sporty Narrators With Imaginary Pet Butterflies (Even If You Aren't Actually Re-Locating), and then I'd put these people in it:

My editor, Andrew Karre, who should be a professional question asker. Or maybe he is a professional question asker. Andrew's instincts on where a story needs more and where less, as well as his particular brand of esoteric nerdiness, made this book a hundred times better. And about 15 percent longer.

My agent, Tina Dubois, who should be a professional question answerer. Or really she is a professional question answerer. She knows all the things, including when to step back and let m figure out for myself the things she already knew.

Erin Downing, without whom I might still be waiting i tiently for responses to query letters; Gae Polisner, who is

generous and candid with advice; and Jeff Shotts, who is who I mean when I say that I've got a guy on the inside. If you haven't read all the books they've made, I don't know what you're doing reading these acknowledgments. And Danny Weinkauf, who was wonderfully kind at just the right moment, and in whose honor I bought and wear a pair of red pants.

Julie Strauss-Gabel, Melissa Faulner, Natalie Vielkind, Anna Booth, Rob Farren, Anne Heausler, Maggie Edkins, Jennifer Dee, Chloe Goodhart, and their colleagues at Dutton and Penguin Random House, who pushed for, pushed on, and simply pushed this story. Their work is why my work works. Ana Hard, who drew a braid so beautiful it makes me want to grow my hair out. And the only fitting way to thank Caitlin Whalen is for me to name *her* firstborn someday. Snapdragon? Carlsbad? Prunilda? I'll keep thinking.

Tamara Kawar, Roxane Edouard, Savanna Wicks, Lia Chan, Randie Adler, and their colleagues at ICM Partners and Curtis Brown UK, who look out for both Greer and me, even on other continents and in other languages. I wish them each zwanzig Apfelkuchens und ein BMW, at least.

Kris Causton, Mark Zukor, Jen Aspengren, Mike Smith, Tracy ̇ Smith, Heather Eisenmenger, Sharon DeMark, and Lisa ̇ek, who read the book before it was quite a book and ̇ feedback and/or pushback. Their encouragement ̇ental equivalent of an entire crate of Lärabars. ̇d Becca Smith, excellent mathematicians/ ̇vided content expertise even during AP

ACKNOWLEDGMENTS

Thank you for reading this book. I hope you liked reading it as much as I liked writing it.

If I was a re-lo advisor, I'd make a special section in the binder called Resources for Writers of Young Adult Novels Featuring Brainy/Sporty Narrators With Imaginary Pet Butterflies (Even If You Aren't Actually Re-Locating), and then I'd put these people in it:

My editor, Andrew Karre, who should be a professional question asker. Or maybe he is a professional question asker. Andrew's instincts on where a story needs more and where less, as well as his particular brand of esoteric nerdiness, made this book a hundred times better. And about 15 percent longer.

My agent, Tina Dubois, who should be a professional question answerer. Or really she is a professional question answerer. She knows all the things, including when to step back and let m figure out for myself the things she already knew.

Erin Downing, without whom I might still be waiting in tiently for responses to query letters; Gae Polisner, who is

generous and candid with advice; and Jeff Shotts, who is who I mean when I say that I've got a guy on the inside. If you haven't read all the books they've made, I don't know what you're doing reading these acknowledgments. And Danny Weinkauf, who was wonderfully kind at just the right moment, and in whose honor I bought and wear a pair of red pants.

Julie Strauss-Gabel, Melissa Faulner, Natalie Vielkind, Anna Booth, Rob Farren, Anne Heausler, Maggie Edkins, Jennifer Dee, Chloe Goodhart, and their colleagues at Dutton and Penguin Random House, who pushed for, pushed on, and simply pushed this story. Their work is why my work works. Ana Hard, who drew a braid so beautiful it makes me want to grow my hair out. And the only fitting way to thank Caitlin Whalen is for me to name *her* firstborn someday. Snapdragon? Carlsbad? Prunilda? I'll keep thinking.

Tamara Kawar, Roxane Edouard, Savanna Wicks, Lia Chan, Randie Adler, and their colleagues at ICM Partners and Curtis Brown UK, who look out for both Greer and me, even on other continents and in other languages. I wish them each zwanzig Apfelkuchens und ein BMW, at least.

Kris Causton, Mark Zukor, Jen Aspengren, Mike Smith, Tracy
⸿ Smith, Heather Eisenmenger, Sharon DeMark, and Lisa
⸿ek, who read the book before it was quite a book and
⸿ feedback and/or pushback. Their encouragement
⸿ental equivalent of an entire crate of Lärabars.
⸿d Becca Smith, excellent mathematicians/
⸿ovided content expertise even during AP

ACKNOWLEDGMENTS

Thank you for reading this book. I hope you liked reading it as much as I liked writing it.

If I was a re-lo advisor, I'd make a special section in the binder called Resources for Writers of Young Adult Novels Featuring Brainy/Sporty Narrators With Imaginary Pet Butterflies (Even If You Aren't Actually Re-Locating), and then I'd put these people in it:

My editor, Andrew Karre, who should be a professional question asker. Or maybe he is a professional question asker. Andrew's instincts on where a story needs more and where less, as well as his particular brand of esoteric nerdiness, made this book a hundred times better. And about 15 percent longer.

My agent, Tina Dubois, who should be a professional question answerer. Or really she is a professional question answerer. She knows all the things, including when to step back and let me figure out for myself the things she already knew.

Erin Downing, without whom I might still be waiting impatiently for responses to query letters; Gae Polisner, who is always

generous and candid with advice; and Jeff Shotts, who is who I mean when I say that I've got a guy on the inside. If you haven't read all the books they've made, I don't know what you're doing reading these acknowledgments. And Danny Weinkauf, who was wonderfully kind at just the right moment, and in whose honor I bought and wear a pair of red pants.

Julie Strauss-Gabel, Melissa Faulner, Natalie Vielkind, Anna Booth, Rob Farren, Anne Heausler, Maggie Edkins, Jennifer Dee, Chloe Goodhart, and their colleagues at Dutton and Penguin Random House, who pushed for, pushed on, and simply pushed this story. Their work is why my work works. Ana Hard, who drew a braid so beautiful it makes me want to grow my hair out. And the only fitting way to thank Caitlin Whalen is for me to name *her* firstborn someday. Snapdragon? Carlsbad? Prunilda? I'll keep thinking.

Tamara Kawar, Roxane Edouard, Savanna Wicks, Lia Chan, Randie Adler, and their colleagues at ICM Partners and Curtis Brown UK, who look out for both Greer and me, even on other continents and in other languages. I wish them each zwanzig Apfelkuchens und ein BMW, at least.

Kris Causton, Mark Zukor, Jen Aspengren, Mike Smith, Tracy Kollin Smith, Heather Eisenmenger, Sharon DeMark, and Lisa Von Drasek, who read the book before it was quite a book and gave excellent feedback and/or pushback. Their encouragement was and is the mental equivalent of an entire crate of Lärabars. Rose Eisenmenger and Becca Smith, excellent mathematicians/ volleyball players, who provided content expertise even during AP testing weeks.